The Remnants

C. E. Williams

To Niki

May your adventures
not turn to horror!

Cerys

The smell of the sizzling bacon though was what shook him back into reality, that with a final call from his grandmother as she got closer to the bottom of the stairs. He knew she would call him only once more before she would walk up the stairs with a cross face, telling him that his breakfast and cup of tea would be getting cold.

Abe paused his game and quickly jumped up off the floor stretching and scrunching his toes against the warm scratchy rug on the floor of his bedroom. He quickly skipped down the wooden stairs following the smell of bacon, his nose pulling him along like a hand on a rope.

As he hopped down the last of the steps landing in the living room with a thud, his grandpa was sitting there as usual reading his newspaper. He was sitting in his armchair with his feet up on the footstool and cup of coffee on the armrest. His grandpa was a tall man, and quite stocky, he had a short white beard and not much hair, though his lack of hair was hidden by a dark green fishing cap that he wore all the time, in or out of the house. *Except* for when he was at the table, then Adelyn would always make him take it off.

'Morning Grandpa,' Abe said gladly as he hopped into the kitchen.

When he got there and he was met by a wall of smells from the breakfast that had been cooking on the stove, it was pure bliss. The smell of everything together and the warmth that made the room cosy, was comforting and familiar. His grandma was standing right next to the table by where Abe sat every single day, in between his grandparents. She was holding a frying pan full of bacon and eggs next to Abe's plate on the small round dinner table.

'Morning Abe,' she said softly.

'Morning Grandma,' he replied with a smile.

Adelyn was a short, sweet woman, with long grey and white hair that was tied up into a ponytail; she wore a long flower-patterned dress that reached down to her ankles and a sky-blue kitchen apron with white daisies on it. The apron was older than Abe was, and his grandma wore it every time she cooked and baked. Throughout his life she had baked him countless pies, cookies and cakes while wearing that apron.

Abe sat down behind his place at the table while his grandma served his breakfast and brought a cup of tea over from the countertop beside the kettle. Abe always had tea with his breakfast. It was a morning ritual and he shared it with his grandma.

His grandpa followed into the kitchen shortly after and sat down at the table next to Abe and set down his paper folded in half beside him.

'So...what are your plans for today?' he asked. Abe chewed and swallowed before he answered.

'I've got work in the store until three and then at five I'm going to head over to Ash's house,' he said before he picked up another piece of bacon.

His grandma sat down with a plate of toast and a cup of tea. 'Will you be back in time for dinner?' she asked.

Abe took a sip from his cup of tea and said that he would, as always.

'Is it alright if Ash comes for dinner?' he asked. 'His dad is still out of town and his mom is working nights, so otherwise he'll be eating alone.'

'Of course he can,' she said, with a smirk. *I'll bake a pie for dessert, that will be sure to put a smile on his face*, she thought.

Abe smiled as he continued eating, listening to the radio in the background before setting off to work. He finished the last of his breakfast and his grandma picked up his empty plate to take it to the sink to wash up. 'Could you pick me up some eggs and bread from the store on your way home please Abe?' she asked.

'Of course.'

'Oh and some worms for me too Abe. You're all set for our fishing trip on Sunday, right?' asked his grandpa.

'Yep, Grandpa no problem. I can't wait.' Abe chugged down the last of his tea and rushed upstairs to get dressed before heading to work on his bike.

Abe arrived at work and locked his bike up outside the store and walked in, the doorbell chimed as he walked in and his boss Mr. Johnson peered over the counter to greet him.

'Good morning, Abe,' he said cheerfully.

'Morning Mr. Johnson. How are you today?' Abe asked.

'I'm swell, how are your grandparents?'

'They're great thanks for asking.'

Mr. Johnson walked around from the counter with a trolley of paint cans. He was a very short, chubby man with a belly bulging out like Santa Claus. He wore a full body denim suit which was covered in patches of paint and grease, and had a brown leather utility belt around his waist with screwdrivers, hammer, measuring tape, and a change dispenser. He walked over with the trolley and handed it to Abe.

'Stack these on the back shelf would you please?' he asked politely.

'No problem,' he said as he headed to the back of the store.

The hours passed quickly as they always did. Working there at Mr. Johnsons DIY store wasn't very hard, he was either stacking things on shelves, putting price tags on things or just standing at the till waiting for someone to come in and there were only a few people that ever did. It was a small store and a small town; it wasn't very busy. The doorbell chimed as the last customer left, and Mr. Johnson flipped the small rectangular sign on the door to show that they were closed for the day.

'Feel free to go when you are ready Abe,' said Mr. Johnson.

'You sure? I can help close up if you like.'

Mr Johnson removed his glasses, cleaned them in a tissue and said, 'No, you run along and head home.' Abe finished putting price stickers on the last two items and got ready to leave.

'Don't forget to grab your pay on your way out, it's on my desk.'

Abe was on his bike riding home, and he was just around the corner. It was a short ride, maybe ten minutes if you went the quickest way, but Abe always liked going through the side roads, through the park and past the river. It easily added an extra twenty minutes to the journey.

Just before he turned the corner to their road he realised, *damn, I forgot to get eggs and bread for Grandma, and Grandpa's worms.* He turned around quickly and peddled fast as he could towards the farm. Even going the fastest way, it was going to take him twenty minutes to get there if he went as fast as he could, he was probably going to be late to Ash's.

I hope he forgives me, he thought. The farm was just outside the main part of town, normally it was a nice ride, and an easy one. It was just one long dirt road through the trees until you got to the big old brown house that Mr and Mrs Heanue lived in on the edge of their farm.

Bud the dog was barking, excited to see Abe as he arrived. He was jumping up on the wire fence that ran along the side of the house to keep him from getting free. Oftentimes when Abe got there he would go straight over and give him attention. Sometimes he would be there for half an hour before remembering that he was there to get stuff for his grandma, not for Bud. Abe ran over and leant over the fence to give him a fuss.

'Hey boy,' he said.

Bud was a bullmastiff, brown all over with orange looking eyes. His tongue was hanging out the side of his mouth as he panted and drooled. He looked as if he were smiling as Abe petted him and scratched behind his ears.

'Sorry Bud, I can't play with you for long today. I'm already really late. I'll come back tomorrow I promise.'

Bud got back down on all four paws and followed Abe along the fence as far as he could to the side of the house.

Everything there was quiet, which wasn't unusual. Behind the house was where all their farmland was. It went back a long way until you reached a line of tall trees towering into the sky. Abe liked the quiet and how peaceful it was there, you could hear the birds chirping and there were rabbits in the wood, foxes, and all other kinds of wildlife. Mr. Heanue always said that he should watch out for bears, but Abe knew that they didn't get bears around there.

Mr. Heanue always used to tell him the same story about the bear his uncle fought off in the forest. *It escaped from the circus,* he said. He said his uncle was hunting for deer and rabbits one day and it attacked him and had no choice but to shoot it. *Its ghost still walks the forest to this day*, he would say.

He said on some nights you could see a bear just walking along through the wood, and that was him. The bear from the circus.

Abe was standing on the porch of the house ringing the doorbell. He waited a few seconds, but nobody came so he rang it again and again. Still no answer.

Maybe they're in the field? he thought. He walked to the side to have a look, Bud was jumping up asking for attention as he did, but he couldn't see anyone.

They could have gone out, but their car is still here. Strange...or is it? They could just have been working

8

somewhere where he couldn't see them or gone for a walk.

Just as he was about to walk back to his bike to give up and ride home, he heard something. Suddenly, there was a nerve-shaking sound of screaming that rattled his eardrums. It was a scream of terror. Abe turned towards the direction of the woods beside the house. He could see a woman running. It was Mrs Heanue.

She saw Abe and yelled for help; she was still quite far away, and Abe didn't know if she knew it was him or not. He stopped his bike to go and check if she was okay. He had never seen someone look so terrified in his life.

Before Abe could do or say anything to help her, he saw something was running up behind. It had the shape of a man, but it wasn't at all normal. It was wearing dark checked shirt and blue trousers held up by suspenders over its shoulders, but its clothes were the only thing that made it seem remotely human. Its eyes were like the deep endless blackness of space, its hair was falling from its head, its skin was turning grey and brown, and its whole body was hunched over as it waved its arms and chased her, groaning and screaming. It looked like a savage lion that hadn't fed in weeks and was now chasing down its prey.

Abe froze completely at the shock of what he was seeing, it was like every movie or computer-game he had ever seen coming to life. Mrs Heanue stared over at him directly into his eyes with desperation on her face. As she reached the end of the wood and got close to the house the man caught up with her. It was then when Abe realised that the man was Mr Heanue, or at least it *had* been.

The thing that was Mr. Heanue caught her, dragging her to the ground by her legs as it clamped his teeth down onto her cheek, biting and tearing her flesh and swallowing one chunk at a time. As it feasted on her, the screams got quieter, the life left her body, and it wasn't long before she was just a limp, pale, bloody corpse, twitching and spewing blood onto the floor. Abe stood there, staring, unable to move a muscle from the shock. He didn't know if he was going to vomit or faint.

"Mr. Heanue" was still hunched over Mrs Heanue, feasting on her, while making noises unimaginable and terrifying. What could have happened to him that made him do this to his wife?

Whatever had happened, that thing was not Mr. Heanue. Sweat started to gather on Abe's forehead, and he grew paler as he held the vomit in his throat. Suddenly, the thing looked up at him with its soulless eyes, its chin dripped with blood and bits of flesh dangled from its mouth and teeth.

It paused as it stared at Abe for a few seconds, turning its head from side to side like a dog trying to figure something out. Abe started to back away to make a break for it on his bike, but before he could that thing pounced forward hurtling towards him as it let out a demonic wail. Abe was only about ten metres away from it. Abe's heart sank, he was now sweating heavily, and his body shook with fear and panic. Abe stumbled and tried to get on his bike but before he could cock his leg over the seat to ride away it was too late, it was right in front of him.

As it reached Abe it swung its arms through the air to grip on to him so it could sink its teeth into his flesh. Its weight on Abe knocked him backwards onto the ground, the bike between them kept it from Abe and kept it from biting him, but his mouth was just inches from his face. Abe could smell the damp stench of blood as it dripped from its mouth and onto Abe's face and neck. Abe didn't know what to do, it seemed as if now everything was moving so slowly and there was nothing else in the world but him and this thing on top of him, it was *so* heavy. He couldn't hear the birds anymore and he couldn't see the trees. It was like they were in a black void. He had to escape this thing, but he was getting tired and this thing was relentless. Even if he did manage to get free, what would he do? It's not like he had a gun and even if he did, could he really shoot it?

There was almost definitely a gun in the house - every farmer had one, but even if he did make a dash for the house he could end up with the same fate as Mrs Heanue. This thing was fast, probably faster than Abe.

Abe was starting to struggle. That *thing* was still snapping away at his face trying desperately to get close enough to sink its teeth into him. It had only been a few moments, but it felt like hours.

It was no use. Abe wasn't strong enough to push it off or hold it up any longer and his arms started to give in.

Suddenly, a rumbling noise like thunder started in the distance and got louder and louder as it got closer. It was followed by a roaring bark and in a flash, it pounced like a great wolf did on its prey and ripped the thing off the top of Abe. Abe quickly looked to his side - it was *Bud!* Somehow, he had gotten free. He must have seen what was going on and come to Abe's rescue.

Bud was now on top of the creature battling with it, growling and biting at it, tearing as much of it as he could to try and kill it or send it away by fear. But this thing was clearly not alive like a human and seemed incapable of feeling fear. Abe was saved, but Bud was still attacking this thing, he had torn a massive amount out of its infected body, but it was still struggling and now trying relentlessly to bite Bud. Abe quickly went from feeling great relief to gut wrenching fear, he didn't know what to do, he couldn't bear to see this thing kill Bud.

The air was tense, and Abe was still on the ground watching this ferocious battle unfold and suddenly the wretched thing got the upper hand over bud and turned the table, so he was on top of him. Bud was on his back; he was too tired to fight back and let out a yelp that brought sudden tears to Abe's eyes and sadness to his heart. A strike of rage hit Abe's body and his face grew red, his bike was suddenly the weight of a feather, and he threw it to one side as he bolted towards the infected thing that was on top of Bud.

Abe tackled it and had no trouble throwing it to the ground. It looked at him as he towered over it, screeching and snarling like a vicious, rabid monster with a mouth full of blood and flesh. Its hands reached out but before it could even touch him, Abe grabbed a nearby branch that had fallen from one of the trees and rammed it into its head like a spear, silencing it and sending blood spurting all over the ground.

Abe's face was still scrunched with rage and his teeth were bared. He stood over the motionless corpse that now lay completely lifeless.

There were several chunks of different sizes missing from the body from where Bud had saved Abe and tried to stop it. But how was he to know how to kill it?

Abe looked up and saw Bud lying on the ground amongst the chunks of flesh and blood

Tears now flowing from his eyes in streams, he turned to look at Mrs Heanue, lying in her own pool of blood, eyes still open staring into a world with no life or soul inside of her to see through them, her body was now just an empty shell. He looked down at his own hands covered in blood having no idea whose blood it was and looking at the corpse beneath him with the spear still stuck in its head became all too much for him and his stomach. He became dizzy and his head felt too heavy for his neck to support, and it rolled around like a boat on a choppy sea. Before he could say, move or do anything he fell flat on to his back with a great thud and fell into a deep dark unconsciousness.

Chapter 2

It was many hours later and the night had crept in. The moon stood in the sky casting a great white glow over the trees and farmland. The darkness mixed with the moonlight made the world around look slightly blue. Abe awoke and felt like he was covered in a warm, but incredibly heavy blanket.

Am I dead? he thought, that was until he realised that his eyes were open, and he was staring straight up into the night sky.

Suddenly he felt a warm, damp breath on his face, panting, so he looked up and it was *Bud,* he was laying on top of him keeping him warm, staring into his face.

Abe was ecstatic, a wide smile shot across his face, he was so happy to see that Bud was alive. Bud saw that he was awake and greeted him by licking his face from his chin to the top of his head. Abe chuckled and wrapped his arms around him. 'Thanks for saving me boy,' he said, 'and thanks for keeping me warm.'

As he thanked Bud, and touched his fur, he realised that he wasn't hurt, and as he looked to where he had seen him lying, he realised that all the blood must have belonged to Mr. Heanue and that none of it was Bud's.

Abe stood up and noticed how cold it was, it was late October and Winter was creeping in.

It was getting darker by the minute and there was no one in sight. He looked around to see the corpses of Mr and Mrs Heanue still lying there. For a moment he thought that it might have all been a dream.

How is this happening? he thought.

Everything was so normal that morning when he woke up, he went to work like any other day. It was like he had gone through some kind of wormhole and entered another world.

The question was, was Mr. Heanue the only one, or were there more? How long had he been unconscious?

He suddenly realised that if there were more, then his grandparents could be in danger. The realisation made his heart thump fast in his chest. He looked from side to side in a panic looking for his bike. He needed to get home *now.*

He jumped on his bike and started to peddle, just as he did Bud followed and he realised that Bud could slow him down and he didn't have time to look after him. He needed to get home as quick as he could and without looking out for someone else along the way. If there were more of those things and Bud came with him, there was the risk that he might get attacked. There was no telling how many of them there were.

'I don't want to leave you here, what if more of them come?'

Bud sat down looking up into Abe's eyes and let out a small bark and spun in a circle like he wanted to play.

'What boy? I can't play now I gotta go.' *But I can't just leave you here either.* 'What should I do?'

Bud ran up to towards the house and turned to look at Abe before letting out another bark, 'What is it?' Abe asked, starting to get frustrated, Bud clearly didn't understand and just wanted to play games.

Bud ran back to Abe and quickly dashed back towards the house staring at it barking and then looking back at Abe.

He's trying to tell me something.

It took another few more moments until Abe noticed he wasn't looking at the house. It was Mr & Mrs Heanue's car. It was sitting right beside the house.

'That's it!' Abe exclaimed.

With the car they would get there twice as fast and Bud could stay inside the car the whole time, he wouldn't have to worry about him getting hurt. Besides it would be even harder for those things to attack Abe as well if there were more of *them.*

'But I can't drive, I don't even have my learners permit yet.'

Abe had never driven a car before, the closest thing that came to it was when he had driven dodgems at the fayre or when he had a go of the quad bike on the farm that one time in the summer.

I'm just going to have to try, he thought.

He ran over to the car, Bud was already standing there with his front paws on the passenger side door.

Abe tried the door, but the car was locked.

Why wouldn't it be?

'Damn it,' he said. 'Why can't things ever just be easy?'

Abe needed to find the keys, he had already wasted too much time, *but where were they?* They could be anywhere; their house was huge and he had to get in the house to begin with. It wasn't a surprise when he ran up to the front door of the house to find that it was locked. Abe was starting to feel hopeless.

Then he realised, if the door was locked and there was nobody home when he got there then that meant that the keys would either be with Mr or Mrs Heanue, who were still lying on the ground, whom now had flies swarming around their carcasses.

Bud was sitting on the front porch beside Abe looking up at him with an expression on his face as if he knew what Abe had to do. If he could talk, he would say,
I don't want to do it.

Abe reluctantly walked over to the corpse on the ground that was Mr. Heanue, swatting the flies out of his face. The smell was *disgusting!* Abe had never smelled anything fouler in his life. He learnt once in school that the smell of a dead body was meant to be slightly sweet, but there was nothing sweet about that stench.

He held his breath and forced his hand into the trousers ruffling around looking for the keys, but all that was in there were dirty old tissues and some chewing tobacco. Abe let out a heavy sigh and looked up at Mrs Heanue's corpse a distance away, loathing the idea of having to do it again and at the same time his stomach was pleading him not to, causing him to wretch and almost be sick. Mrs Heanue was just as bad, if not worse. At least what was left of Mr. Heanue looked less human which made it slightly easier, but Mrs Heanue hadn't turned.

She also did not have the keys either, as soon as Abe realised he hurried away from her and gasped, taking in the air he was struggling for after holding his breath so he wouldn't smell her.

Abe was starting to get angry, 'For goodness' sake, where the hell are they?'

Then it came to him. *How could I have been so stupid?*

They were under the plant pot by the door, he was standing right next to them the whole time. He ran over as quickly as he could, not even giving enough time to get annoyed at himself for not realising it sooner.

He moved the brown flowerpot holding the purple flower and there they were. He grabbed them quickly and ran over to the car.

Their car was really old, so it didn't have a little clicker on the keys that would unlock the doors. He had to stick the little metal key in the lock of the door and open it himself.

Bud followed and jumped in behind him, trampling over his lap and into the passenger seat beside him and sat down.

'Good boy,' he said.

The car was a deep dark blue colour but had started to fade a little since it was so old. It was kind of a good thing that it was dark, it would help Abe to avoid being seen.

Abe always thought that the car looked kind of like a hearse, but Mr. Heanue called it The President. Abe never knew why.

It only took one turn of the key and the car started first time.

Maybe my luck isn't that bad after all?

Riding his bike might have actually been faster with the speed Abe was driving, but at least Bud was safe.

By the time they reached the end of the dirt road it was completely dark.

All that he had to light the way was the streetlights. Abe had tried to turn the headlights of the car on, but after a few minutes of twisting things and pushing buttons, the wipers were at full speed, the windscreen washer had sprayed everywhere, and the heater was on full blast, but no lights so he gave up trying.

Luckily for him the streets were empty, at least empty of people. It was like a hurricane had swept through knocking over garbage cans, littering the street and everyone had disappeared into thin air. There were cars abandoned everywhere, bicycles on the ground left to be stolen and even people's doors to their houses were left open. You could see trails of clothes that had been dropped as people must have been rushing from their homes.

Just as he thought to himself, *maybe there aren't any more of them,* he saw it.

As the car slowly crept down the road, Abe saw piles and piles of bodies littering the ground with blood and clumps of flesh and hair all over the road, sidewalk, gardens and even some on top of car bonnets and wind shields.

Abe's face had started to get its colour back and his stomach was just starting to feel normal again until he saw all that. He went straight back to feeling like he could throw up again.

He soon noticed something though - the dead bodies weren't people that had been attacked and eaten by any of those things. There were bullet fragments all over the ground and there were holes in the cars. It was a little further down the road when he saw that there was an abandoned army truck. They must have come to evacuate people and kill anyone that was already one of *them*.

This was good news and bad news. The good news was that people were being saved and the military were helping people. The bad news was Abe's fears were true, there were more of them and a lot of them by what he saw. The worse news was that he must have missed the evacuation while he was unconscious.

The question still remained though. *Are my grandparents okay?* Had they been evacuated, or had they been attacked and killed by one of *them*? Or...had they become infected themselves and either attacked and killed people or gotten shot by the military when they came to rescue whoever had survived?

The idea that they could be like Mr Heanue haunted Abe, it was one thing to kill one of them when it was someone who was an acquaintance of the family, but if it was his own grandparents, the people who raised him?

He couldn't even imagine hitting them let alone do what he did to that one back at the farm. The first thing he had to do was get home, maybe they were okay, maybe they were evacuated too.

Maybe they're waiting for me at home.

Chapter 3

The car sat there silently in the driveway. There was a clicking sound coming from the engine as it cooled down. Abe couldn't believe how quiet it was. There were no cars going by, nobody walking on the street, no planes flying over.

He had been sitting there for over five minutes just staring at the house. It was so dark and empty looking. It was if it was frozen in time, or like it was asleep and waiting for someone to walk through the door and wake it up.

Abe was afraid. From the outside it looked like there was nobody home, but where were they? He was afraid that if he went inside to check, he could find them and they would be just like Mr Heanue, or they could be dead. Or even worse, what if one of them had become infected, turned and killed the other like Mr Heanue did to his wife.

But...if he didn't go and check then he may never know.

He felt a damp thing rub across his face; Bud licked him like he was telling him that he could do it.

'Stay,' said Abe.

He opened the car door slowly trying to make as little noise as possible. When he got out, he looked to make sure that there was nobody else around, and that there weren't any of *them* there, but it was silent. If the wind wasn't moving the trees and bushes you could even mistake it for a picture, it was so still and lifeless. Just as he placed his first foot onto the bottom of the small creaky wooden stairs that brought you up on to the front porch, there was a clunk and a squeak followed by a long creak.

Even with the door opening it was dark inside, but there was something in the doorway, something just standing there. All Abe could see was a dark silhouette and his stomach was immediately tangled in a nervous knot. The silhouette paused for a few seconds before it shot forward, straight at him. It happened so fast. Its arms and hands were flung in the air heading right for Abe as quick as they could get to him.

Suddenly, it reached out and it latched onto him. Its arms were wrapped around Abe tightly, and a gruff voice followed, 'I'm so happy to see you.'

'Grandpa?'

Abe felt a wave of relief, he hadn't realised that his entire body before now had been completely tensed and now it felt like he was half the weight he was before.

'Are you okay?' his grandpa asked.

If he had just let go and looked at him, he would be able to tell that he was fine, but his grandpa clung on like he was never going to let go again.

'I'm fine,' Abe replied, his voice weakened into a whisper by emotion. He was on the verge of crying and so was his grandpa, so much had happened. Neither of them spoke for a few moments until Abe asked the question that was still dangling in his brain, knocking against the walls like a pendulum in a clock until he got the answer.

'Is...Grandma okay?' he asked.

The grip he had on him loosened and his grandpa stood up straight, revealing teary eyes.

It didn't look good, there could have only been one reason why she wasn't there. They were always together, no matter what. Especially in times like this.

'She's not here. She went with them.' For a moment Abe thought it was some kind of metaphor and that she was gone forever, his heart immediately sank. Then he realised what he meant.

'She was evacuated? Where did they take everybody?'

'They've taken her somewhere safe. I promised her I would find you and take you there. We were both worried sick about you and they wouldn't wait for anyone. I had to stay behind and wait for you,' he explained. 'Where were you?'

Abe took a few seconds before answering, he was so happy to hear that his grandma was okay and that she was safe.

Should I tell him about Mr Heanue? he thought. If he didn't tell him then he might wonder where they are and how he managed to get their car *and* their dog if they were still alive.

'I was at the farm getting the things Grandma asked for. Mr Heanue was one of *them* and he killed Mrs Heanue. I saw it all happen.'

Hearing this John's expression became sad. 'Are you okay?' he asked. 'Where did he go?'

'He's still there...I killed him.'

Those were three words John never thought he would hear coming out of his grandson's mouth.

'It's okay, he wasn't Mr Heanue anymore. He was already gone,' he said trying to comfort Abe, before looking over his shoulder and noticing Bud in the car.

'C'mon, let's go inside and have a cup of tea. Don't forget to bring Bud.'

It didn't really seem like the time to be having tea. There was a lot going on and they had a lot to do. Most important of all, they needed to get to where Abe's grandma was taken, but it was late and dark and even if they had a car full of food and water and the map ready to tell them where to go, it was too dangerous to go anywhere at that time of night. It was also *exactly* what his grandma would have done. In her opinion a good hot cup of tea could fix anything.

The house had never felt so absent, all the lights were off when he went inside. Looking at everything in that light made it seem like a black and white painting, all the colour was gone. His grandpa barricaded the door with a wooden plank behind them when they were inside. Bud had never been in their house before and he was *curious*. He was moving around all the rooms of the downstairs of the house sniffing all the new smells. Abe watched him move around wagging his tail and it made him smile. Bud had no idea what was going on. As far as he was concerned, he was having the best time. Abe noticed a small light peering through the bottom crack of the wooden door that led to the basement. Bud was there now too sniffing through the bottom and pawing at the door.

John walked over to it, patting Bud on the head before opening the door allowing a burst of light into the living room.

Bud sat down waiting and looking at Abe until Abe walked down the creaky stairs and he followed him, just in front of his grandpa.

The basement was completely isolated from the outside, there were no windows - the perfect place to stay hidden for the night. Just to be safe, his grandpa put a few nails into the door to lock themselves in. The basement felt much more like Abe was at home, it was bright, there were posters on the walls, freshly washed clothes on top of the washing machine from where his grandma would have done the washing that day. The smell made him feel calm and relaxed. It reminded him of his grandma, and he closed his eyes and it was like nothing bad had happened at all.

John had a camping chair set up in the corner next to a pile of newspapers. Next to it were boxes of food, everything he found in the kitchen cupboards he had packed into the boxes and brought them downstairs. There was an old sofa in the corner of the room, but it was completely covered in box after box of Abe's old comics.

His grandpa was rummaging around in some boxes that contained his fishing gear and he pulled out a camping stove and kettle. He grabbed some tea bags from the supplies he had taken from the kitchen and made them both a hot cup of tea.

They sat there in silence for a bit, both on their own camping chair, and Bud lying on the ground beside Abe. Abe was blowing on his tea as it sat in its tin cup trying to cool it down.

After a while, his grandpa asked, 'What took you so long?'

Abe was a little confused, 'What do you mean?'

'I mean if you finished work and went straight to the farm, how did it take you so long to get here?' he asked.

Abe knew why, and it would easily answer his question, but he was embarrassed. 'After *it* happened at the farm...I fainted. I woke up and it was getting dark, that's when I came home.'

John didn't reply right away and then said, 'It's okay Abe, it's nothing to be embarrassed about. Not many people are brave enough to do what you did.' Abe just responded with a small smile and took a sip of his tea.

John could tell that he didn't want to talk about it anymore, but he needed to be sure and asked, 'When *it* attacked you, it didn't cut or hurt you in any way did it?'

'No,' he said. 'Bud made sure of that, he saved me.' He looked at Bud laying on the ground as he slept peacefully and dreamed, wagging his tail and paws twitching.

'Are you hungry?' John asked.

Abe's stomach answered for him with a growl, the last thing he had eaten was breakfast that morning. His grandpa put his cup of tea down on the ground, it made a dull clink sound as the tin hit the floor. He leaned over to the box of supplies again and brought out some food, a tin of stewed steak for Abe and a tin of chicken soup for himself.

When he opened them up and placed them on the small camping stove to warm up, Bud's nose started to twitch as he slept and shortly after he woke up sniffing louder and louder as he crept towards Abe's grandpa and licked his lips.

'I'm sorry boy, I don't have any dog food here for you,' he said.

'He can have some of mine' Abe offered.

Bud sat down and offered his paw to John. 'No it's fine, I'll find something in here he can have.'

John looked around for a little while rattling all of the cans as he looked through the box for something to give to Bud and he pulled out a tin of corned beef.

At least this doesn't need heating up, he thought.

He scraped half of the tin onto a small plate and placed it down in front of Bud. As soon as he gave the word, Bud pounced on the food as fast as he could, devouring every last crumb in seconds.

John looked at the half empty tin in his hand and realised that this painted a very clear problem. He had enough on his plate having to look after Abe and making sure that he had enough food for them both, but now he was going to have to look after all three of them. He would have to make sure they had food for Bud as well. It was nice for Abe to have Bud around, but it was going to make things very difficult.

There was also no guarantee that when they got to where Adelyn was that they were going to let them take a dog in with them.

'Grandpa?' Abe questioned, pulling John from his thoughts.

Oh no...has he realised the same thing?

'Do you think that Ash is okay?'

John paused for a few seconds not really knowing how to respond, he didn't really have an answer, 'I'm sure he's fine, he's probably in the same place your grandma is right now, and you'll see both of them there when we get there.' He had no idea whether that was true or not, but he said it to try and comfort Abe.

Soon after that they ate their dinner, Abe took out some sleeping bags from out of the camping gear and settled down for the night.

His grandpa decided he would stay awake a little while to keep watch, just in case. He used the sleeping bag like a blanket as he sat in his chair facing the stairs that lead up out of the basement and into the house. John sat there quietly, listening to the house and the outside, but there was nothing.

The morning came and Abe awoke lying in his sleeping bag. Bud was curled up beside him with his head resting on his chest sound asleep.

Without moving his body to avoid waking up Bud, Abe looked at his grandpa. He was still sitting in the same spot as the night before, except he was fast asleep. His hat had slipped down in front of his face and the sleeping bag he used as a blanket had fallen so it was barely covering his legs.

It was just after 8am, Abe decided that he would try and prepare some breakfast quietly and let his grandpa sleep until it was ready.

He grabbed a tin out of the box that was labelled all-day breakfast, it had sausage, beans, bacon steaks and hash browns, all in one tin. It wasn't going to be delicious, but it would be better than nothing. He heated up the breakfast and at the same time made some coffee for his grandpa. John awoke with a yawn.

'What's this?' he asked.

'Breakfast,' Abe replied showing him the tin and passing him the coffee.

'Thank you, Abe.'

Bud had already eaten the rest of the corned beef that was left over from his dinner the night before and went back to sleep in the corner nearest the stairs.

'Do we have a plan Grandpa?' Abe asked.

His grandpa was mid-sip of his coffee when he asked, and the steam was gliding up past his face. 'Uhm, yeah. After breakfast we'll leave as soon as we can. We should only take what we need and save space in the car for food and other supplies.'

The place where John had been told that Adelyn and the others were being taken to was somewhere far away from any city or big town. It was in the middle of a desert, surrounded by nothing but sand and the hot sun. The perfect place to keep away from the infected. Those *things* couldn't drive and anything that tried to walk there would surely die trying.

'How far away is this place?' Abe asked.

'It's a long drive but it shouldn't take more than a few days to get there so long as we don't run into any trouble.'

Trouble could mean many things; it wasn't just referring to *them. They* weren't the only problem; it was the living that would be a problem as well. They would be trying to survive. Some wouldn't care about hurting others to do so, some would actively go out of their way to hurt people in order to get whatever supplies they had and take it for themselves.

Trouble could also be with fuel. They had a car, but they needed fuel to drive it, and if they couldn't find any because it had all been stolen then they may never be able to get where they needed to go. Whatever was out there was the last of it, there definitely wasn't going to be anymore made any time soon.

'What if we run in to *them?*' asked Abe. His grandpa really didn't want to think about it. When the military came to evacuate people, they did a good job of killing any that were around there and then, but that didn't mean that there weren't more out there now.

'We'll do what we have to. If we come across any we'll get through it. If we can we'll avoid them. We'll be in a car anyway, so we'll be much faster and hopefully won't have to deal with any.'

After breakfast they spent an hour gathering everything up ready to take with them and put into the car. John went up into the house first and checked outside peeking through the curtains of the living room window to see if there were any of *them* outside.

The only thing that had changed from the night before was that the sun was now out, and it was light outside.

As soon as his grandpa gave it the all-clear, Abe and Bud came up out of the basement carrying the supplies with them, ready to leave.

'Are you ready?' his grandpa asked, and he was. He had everything he needed for the journey, food, water, sleeping bags and torches. But he was leaving so much behind, his room was full of things that he collected over the years. Things that were important to him and now he had to leave it all there.

'Can I just take a few things from my room?' he asked.

'I'm sorry Abe, but we don't have the room. Besides, even if I said you could take anything I don't think you would be allowed to take it in the evacuation base when we got there.'

Abe was looking down at the ground in disappointment. *He's right*, he thought.

'None of it is useful anyway, it's just toys and comics,' he said to himself.

Finally, they were on the road, it was a little tricky at first when they left the house, dodging all the cars that had been left in the street and avoiding the bodies. Really speaking they didn't have to drive around the bodies, they could have just driven over most of them, they wouldn't really do much to the car.

It wasn't long before they came across a few of *them* though. They were only driving for about five minutes until they saw a couple, just wandering the street in a daze until they saw Abe and his grandpa driving towards them. That's when they started to run at them, at the same time letting out wailing screams. Each of *them* was covered in blood, all over their chests, the fronts of their legs and all over their mouths. A few of them even had what looked like bits of other people stuck to their faces and falling from their mouths as they groaned and screeched trying to get to Abe and his grandpa.

It wasn't hard to get past them. All John had to do was speed up a little and they drove straight past. That didn't stop them chasing though, they just groaned even louder and continued to run after the car.

Abe watched them in the rear-view mirror for as long as he could see them and as they started to disappear, he asked, 'do you think that they'll keep chasing us?'

His grandpa looked in the mirror and saw nothing but little specks in the distance and said, '*Maybe, but they won't catch us, they'll try for a while and I'm sure that they will lose interest and just start wandering around aimlessly again until they see something else.*'

That made Abe think, maybe they should have done what they could to make sure they were dead. By leaving them alive they were just allowing them to find someone else and maybe they wouldn't be so lucky. Maybe they wouldn't have a car or a dog to protect them. After a few more minutes he realised that they were close to Ash's house.

'Would it be okay if we stopped at Ash's? Just to check that he's not there?'

John looked at Abe from the side of his eye. Going and looking would be a risk. A risk that he didn't want to take. Who knows what or who they would find there, and they didn't have all the time in the world. They had to set out as soon as possible. The later they left it, the less likely they were going to be able to get in. If they left it too long there might just be too many people there for them to be let in.

No, he made a promise to Adelyn, and he had to keep it. He had to get them there safely so they could see each other again.

'I'm sorry Abe, we just can't. It's out of the way and we don't know what's out there. We can't stop...I'm sorry.'

He didn't feel good saying that, he felt terrible. He had rarely told him no unless he had no other choice. But he had never really come across this problem before. Abe was always well behaved, he never asked for too much or did anything stupid. The worst thing he had ever done was when he skipped school to go see a movie.

Abe didn't respond, he just sat in his seat staring out of the window with a sulking look on his face. His grandpa was right though, they didn't have time to stop. Plus, the more journeys they made that weren't a necessity, the more fuel would be wasted, and they had to spare every single drop.

Bud was sitting on the back seat, John looked back at him. Bud's eyes were locked on his making him feel guilty. He looked back at the road and tried to ignore him and then looked at Abe again seeing his sad face reflecting in the window.

What if Ash hadn't been evacuated and he was stuck there, and when they finally got to the evacuation base, they'd find that he wasn't there and that they could have saved him just by adding a few extra minutes to their journey? If that were the case, then John would never forgive himself.

Bud was still staring and now his nose was so close that if it was any closer it would have tickled his ear. John let out a big sigh from his chest and made a sharp turn around the next corner. Abe's face perked up and Bud laid back down on the back seat.

'Where are we going? The map says we have to go that way.' Abe said pointing in the original direction that they were driving in.

'There is a gas station a short ways up here, it's only small so people might not have gone there already. We could do with checking there for extra gas and on the way, we can park outside of Ash's house and check if he is there.'

A huge smile appeared on Abe's face.

'Thanks Grandpa,' Abe said happily.

'No need, we need fuel. It's just a happy coincidence that it's on the way,' he said pretending that he wasn't purposely making the trip for Abe's sake.

'When we do get to his house, you have no more than *five* minutes, In and out, nothing more.' Abe's smile continued. 'What if he is there?' he asked.

John hadn't thought about the repercussions if he was there, he was already worried about having to look after Abe and Bud and getting them there safely *and* feeding them. *What if Ash was there?* The car was already cramped as it was.

I guess we'll just have to cross that bridge when it comes to it, he thought.

Chapter 4

Just as he expected, the gas station looked untouched. It was just sitting there in the morning sun, nobody around. Around it was more of the same, abandoned cars and garbage littering the road and the occasional dead one of *them*.

Before he parked outside John parked across the street and pulled out an old small monocular from his coat pocket and looked around with it.

'What are you doing?' Abe asked.

'Just checking.'

'For survivors?'

'Yes, but mainly to see if there are many of those things are around,' he replied. 'We don't want to get caught off guard.'

Abe looked around himself, it was a good sign that Bud was sitting there peacefully and not barking. If he had been then they might have something to worry about.

'Can you see anything?' Abe asked.

His grandpa was still looking through the monocular when he said, 'No, not really. There are a couple down the road, but I don't think we really have to worry about them.'

What he didn't tell Abe was why they didn't really have to worry about them.

There were two of *them* but one of them was missing its entire left arm and only had a stump for a right arm and there was something dangling from it with blood gushing onto the ground.

The other was in a worse state and was dragging itself along the ground leaving a trail of blood behind.

He started the car back up and headed over to the gas station, pulling up just outside the front of the store.

'Wait here while I go and check there's nothing inside,' he said to Abe.

Abe frowned; he didn't want to wait in the car. He wanted to get out and help. He had already killed one of those things before. He didn't know if his grandpa had or not, but if he hadn't then Abe was more experienced and surely had an advantage. His grandpa had some clear advantages too though, he was *much* taller than Abe, and was almost definitely stronger than him.

Abe quickly looked about and couldn't see anyone or anything around. He saw his grandpa holding a golf club in his hand as he slowly entered the store. He decided he had to help, if he didn't and his grandpa got hurt then it would be his fault for not going with him. He quickly and quietly jumped out, Bud following behind him.

He checked again left and right but still no sign of moving except for trees and trash in the wind. He hurried over to the door quietly on his tip toes in an attempt to arrive unnoticed. Just as he turned the corner and into the store, he saw a not too unfamiliar scene.

He saw his grandpa lying on the ground flat on his back struggling with one of *them* on top of him and another walking towards him from the other side of the cashier point, wearing a red and blue staffs' uniform. Abe's body was filled with sheer panic, he got an instant rush of adrenaline and bolted forward.

Bud was at his side, baring his teeth and growling as he galloped towards them and pounced at the one that had his grandpa pinned to the ground.

He hit into it with such force that he sent it tumbling away, and he went rolling after it.

Bud found his feet quicker than Abe could blink and immediately rushed to the creature and started tearing at its throat with his teeth.

Abe at this point had run towards the other as he watched Bud battle. He picked up the golf club from the ground where his grandpa had dropped it and swung it as hard as he could into the other thing's head. As soon as the club smashed in to its head it sent a spray of blood over the wall behind it and sent the thing to the ground.

Abe turned to see Bud with the other and had it pinned down as he continued to rip and tear at it. He ran over with the club in his hand and swung again, crashing down into its skull, cracking open like a watermelon. John was still on the ground but sat up and in shock.

What just happened? He had no idea that Abe could be capable of such things. He had asked Abe to stay in the car to protect him. Maybe it was him who should have stayed in the car?

Abe turned around quickly to check on his grandpa and kneeled down on one knee as he asked hysterically, '*Grandpa!* Are you okay?'

He was silent as he stared at the corpse of that *thing* that led on the ground spewing blood out of its head.

'I'm fine, thanks to you. How did you do that?' he asked.

Abe knitted his eyebrows and replied, 'I just did what you told me...I thought how they weren't people anymore and did what I had to.'

Abe helped him to his feet, 'Are you sure you're okay Grandpa?' he asked.

'I'm fine Abe, and if it wasn't for you, I wouldn't be.'

A small smile appeared on Abe's face.

Maybe next time we should just go in together?' he asked.

His grandpa waited for a few moments and before replying.

'Hopefully there won't be a next time. From now on we have to try and avoid all contact with *them*. No matter what!'

His grandpa started out of the store; Abe was frustrated. He thought he had proved that he could look after himself.

'We can't,' he said. 'If we just ignore them and leave them alone then they might kill the next people that come along.'

John stopped in his tracks closing his eyes as he sighed deeply. Abe was right, that could happen. But it was too dangerous, he couldn't risk him getting hurt or killed. What he did had proven how brave he could be, but that wasn't enough. To him Abe *was* everyone and he's the only person he cared about saving.

He turned around back to Abe, '*Abe*, you're right. But there are just the two of us. It's not our job to save everyone. Our job is to get back to your grandma.' Abe didn't look his grandpa in the eye and instead looked at the ground feeling annoyed. What his grandpa said had made perfect sense, but he didn't want to hear it.

'What if there were more of us?' he asked. John had started to walk out of the store again and had to turn around for the second time.

'What do you mean?'

'If there were more of us then we could fight them and there wouldn't much risk. We just need to find more people.'

His grandpa was starting to get cross with Abe and he started to raise his voice. 'There is no one else out here and if there is it doesn't matter, we're not staying out here. We're going to where your grandma is.'

'But we could help people and...'

His grandpa broke into a yell and interrupted him, *'No Abe!* No "buts", we are going to find your grandma and stay there where it is safe, you are still a fifteen-year-old and *I'm* the grown up. *I* make the decisions. When you are eighteen then *you* can decide.'

John swung back around towards the exit and stormed outside leaving Abe standing where he was. He was both upset and angry. He couldn't remember the last time his grandpa had shouted at him like that. He didn't understand why he was so angry and reluctant to help people.

Abe felt stuck, he didn't want to stay standing where he was. The bodies of those things were still lying there spewing blood onto the ground, and it was creeping closer and closer towards his shoes. But he didn't want to go to the car either. He was mad at his grandpa and didn't want to see him. He sighed, realising he had no choice. He went back to the car and got inside, but this time he sat in the back to make a point that he wasn't speaking to him.

Bud followed after him and jumped on the back seat beside him. When he closed the door, his grandpa looked at him in the rear-view mirror with a frown. Both of them were mad for different reasons and both them knew that they were a bit in the wrong but just wouldn't admit it. What they really needed was for Abe's grandma to be there. She would have put it straight. No matter what was happening or how strongly either of them felt about something or didn't want to do something, if she told them to do it then that's what they did.

After they left the gas station it was a few minutes before anyone said anything. Even Bud laid quiet on the seat beside Abe.

John was the first to speak. 'I'm sorry Abe.'

There was a short silence after, and Abe didn't respond.

'I didn't mean to get so angry, it's just difficult to think of you being in danger. Even if you had an army of a hundred people at your back, I would still worry, and if you got hurt or worse...I couldn't bear to tell your grandma what happened. I promised her that when I found you, I would take you straight to her and that's what I have to do.'

Abe continued to stare out of the window until Bud poked him in the leg with his nose.

'I'm sorry too, it's my fault really. You're right,' he said. 'Maybe when I'm old enough and if this is still going on I can go out and help people.'

His grandpa's smile reappeared. 'Yeah maybe, if you can convince your grandma to let you,' he said with a laugh.

Abe smirked and thought if he could win that battle then he could win any. His grandma would never willingly let him go anywhere where there was any danger, he couldn't imagine what she would say if he wanted to go out fighting those things.

They were sitting outside of Ash's house. His house sat in a circle of houses at the dead end of a street. All the houses were made of wood and alternated in colour, blue, green and white. Each of them had a tree outside at the end of the lawn. Ash's had a tyre swing attached to it, looking at it reminded Abe of all the time he had spent on that street and playing on the tyre swing.

He remembered how in the winter they would have snowball fights with the other kids on the street. The kids on their side of the street would always team up with Ash and Abe and they would go to battle with the kids on the opposite side. They did the same in summer, except it was with water balloons and water guns. They were fond memories, but they also made him feel sad. Looking at the empty houses and abandoned cars littering the street made him think that he would never get a chance to do that again.

Everything there seemed quiet and there was no sign of any living or dead walking. Abe thought he liked the quiet, but he was starting to miss the noise of things. Like cars driving by and the sound of people chatting. He was starting to miss *people*. He hoped that he would see Ash again. He was praying that he was alive.

The people there had clearly been evacuated too, the ones that hadn't turned into one of *them* anyway. The ones that *had* were all lying in the street, like the scene back home, with bullet fragments all over the ground.

'Okay, everything looks clear. You've got five minutes and that's it.'

Abe nodded and got out of the car taking Bud with him. His grandpa followed, stretching as he got out, cracking the bones in his back, neck, and fingers. It sounded painful, but he always seemed better afterwards.

Just as John finished his stretch, he saw something - something that terrified him greatly. Fear wrapped its fist around him, and his body trembled as he yelled to Abe.

It was *them,* tens of them, maybe a hundred and they were trapped. They were in a dead end of a cul-de-sac, and *they* were headed right for them like a flood. Where had they come from? The most Abe and his grandpa had seen on the way there were in small groups, and they were able to avoid all of them without any trouble. They just drove around them and sped off. They had followed, but the car was faster. Were these all the ones they had avoided, had they followed them all the way there? By ignoring them and not dealing with them, had they condemned themselves to death? Was this their punishment for only thinking of themselves?

If this was them and they had followed them there to kill and feast on them then Abe was right. If his grandpa had listened to him then *they* would already be dealt with.

Abe turned and saw what was coming, his body now too trembled with fear. He couldn't believe what he was seeing. At that moment, Abe wasn't worried where *they* had come from, they were worried about where they could go. They needed to get away fast. There was no way that they could fight this many alone. Not just the two of them. Even with Bud there it wasn't enough. They needed to get off the street *now.*

'*Abe!* Get in the house...Now!' John yelled, louder than ever.

'What about the car?' Abe answered frantically.

'No! It's too late, get to the house,' he replied, still yelling.

His grandpa, hurrying Abe along, ran at him, pulling him along by his arm violently not thinking or caring how hard he pulled him. All he cared about was getting him safely inside. As far as he was concerned nothing else existed or mattered.

Abe dropped the golf club he had in his hand as he got dragged, Bud had followed him and his grandpa but saw him drop what he saw as a stick that master carried. He ran to pick it up and saw the herd of *them* now almost in a run heading for them. Bud felt no fear and stood his ground showing his huge teeth while growling and barking, warning them off, trying to protect Abe.

Abe and his grandpa were now at the house, Abe cried out to Bud calling him back while his grandpa banged on the front door, which was locked.

Abe was still tightly locked onto his grandpa and couldn't get free, no matter how desperately he tried.

'I have to save *Bud!*' he yelled, tears streaming down his face.

His grandpa either couldn't hear him over the sound of those things screaming and wailing, as well as Bud's barking, and his own hands banging against the door, or he was ignoring him and was only concerned with getting inside and away from *them*.

Finally, Abe was able to wiggle himself free out of his grandpa's grip and run down the wooden stairs of the porch. John immediately panicked even more than he already had been, which didn't seem possible. His eyes widened as he saw Abe run towards Bud and those things as they got closer and closer to the house. Scared was not a strong enough word for the way John felt.

'*Abe, no!*' he yelled. 'He's just a dog, come back.' He ran after him as quick as he could. Bud had seen that those *things* were getting closer, and that Abe was in serious danger. Bud ran towards them and somehow making his barks louder like claps of thunder. John caught up with Abe, grabbing him by the collar on the neck of his shirt, pulling him back into his grasp. Bud was just a few metres away from those things and they were headed right for him, there was no way he could survive all of *them*. He could just about fight off one, let alone that many.

Bud had succeeded in his mission though; he distracted those things away from Abe and his grandpa. John was now trying to drag Abe back towards the house as Abe yelled and cried trying to free himself once again to go after his dog.

He saw the flood of them go around him like the pincer of a crab, hiding him from view. Maybe that was for the best, that he didn't see what was about to happen.

The cheeks of his face were drenched in tears and both his eyes and skin were red from strain. Suddenly, the sound of gun fire surrounded them. They looked up and around and saw that people had emerged from the houses and were now shooting at the sea of the creatures. From all parts of the circle of the houses were people with guns raining fire down on *them* knocking giant chunks out of them and ripping their bodies open. *They* immediately turned their attention to them and scattered, running towards the sound, falling one by one effortlessly.

It was mere minutes before they were all flattened and nothing but a pile of bloody pulp scattered on the ground. Abe and his grandpa remained where they were stood, Abe still in his grandpa's grip. Abe shook himself free and walked a few paces away and fell to his knees in tears.

Bud was nowhere to be seen. If *they* didn't get him then the bullets surely did, and even if he wasn't hit by a single bullet, then he would have been crushed by their corpses.

Abe remained on the ground but hunched over as he sobbed into his arms. John stood back wanting to console him but didn't know how.

He had completely forgotten about their saviours until a woman appeared a short distance away and called out to them.

She was beautiful, she had pale white skin and long red hair.

'Are you okay?' she asked.

John looked at her for a few seconds before answering still in shock, 'Uh...Yeah we're fine,' he said, stuttering, 'Thank you! Thank you so much! I can't thank you enough for saving us.'

She looked at Abe hunched over on the ground as he wept, 'What's wrong with him? Is he your grandson?'

'Yes uh, he is...my Grandson. He just lost his dog. He was in the crowd of those things.'

'I'm so sorry,' she said.

Her face grew sad and remorseful. Even though she didn't know them *or* the dog, you could tell she truly meant it by the look in her eyes.

John stood there quietly looking at Abe and one of the people that saved them walked up to the lady. It was a man; he was wearing all dark clothes and held a very big gun. All John knew was that it was a machine gun. The man was as tall as John and had a very short dark beard. His hair was covered by a hat that went over his head and down to his ears where a tattoo trailed down to his neck.

'*Zoe*, what shall we do with the bodies?' he asked.

'Burn them,' she replied.

The man just nodded and turned around and met with all the other people who were similarly dressed, all with guns, both men and women.

Zoe turned back to Abe's grandpa. 'What was your name sorry?' she asked.

'John,' he replied.

Zoe smiled, 'Nice to meet you, John.'

'Nice to meet you too, and thanks again for what you and your people did for us.'

'No problem.'

The man who Zoe had ordered to burn the bodies had started to gather the others and were holding jerry cans of fuel ready to pour over the bodies. Abe saw them and shot up quickly, 'No,' he yelled.
Bud could be in there.

As he was dashing forward, Zoe caught him by the shoulder. 'What's wrong,' she asked softly.

'My dog is in there,' he said.

She knitted her eyebrows and looked up at the pile of bloody corpses that led in the middle of the street.

'*Matt,*' she called, to the man she had just ordered to burn the bodies.

'What?' he replied.

She ran over to him, 'Don't burn them here,' she said.

He twisted his face in confusion and asked, 'Why not?'

'The smoke and fire could attract more or other unwanted visitors.'

'What the hell do we do with them then?'

She thought for a few seconds and then pointed to a truck down the road. It was what looked like a parcel delivery truck.

'Load them up on that truck and drive them away somewhere and dump them and then burn them.' The man looked at Abe and his grandpa and then back at

Zoe with a heavy sigh. He didn't respond and just turned around and followed her orders.

Zoe winked at Abe and said, 'I'll keep an eye out for him for you.'

Abe wiped the drying tears from his eyes with his sleeves and said, 'Thank you.'

'What were you guys out here looking for anyway?' she asked.

'My friend,' Abe answered. 'He lives in that house that we were trying to get in to. The one with the tyre swing.'

Zoe's smile dimmed slightly. John noticed but Abe was looking the other way.

Was it more bad news? She certainly didn't look like the bearer of good news.

'Have you seen him?' John asked. 'Did you people live here before all this?'

'No,' she said. 'We're not from around here. We were being evacuated and the truck got overrun. Only a few of us actually know each other. When it was attacked most of the people died.'

'What happened?' John asked.

'Similar to what happened to you guys, we got overrun by those things. There were heaps of them in the road and we couldn't get through, so we had to fight them. Sadly, not everybody made it.'

After John probed for more information, Zoe went on to explain how many of them that there were, and it was only around twelve of them left. She explained that the children, elderly and less abled people went on trucks before them and how it was kind of lucky, because if they were on the truck instead of who *was* on there, then they probably would have *all* died.

'You're more than welcome to stay. We won't be staying here long though, we plan on going where the truck was taking us-to the evacuation point,' she said. 'You can travel with us if you like?' she added with a smile.

A smile appeared on Abe's face. This was just what they needed. More people, people that could help them and have their backs. It would also mean if they came across any more of *them,* then they could easily take them down. They would be so much safer together, and they seemed really nice. *Well,* Zoe did anyway. They hadn't really met any of the others yet.

'That would be grea...' Abe started to say, just as his grandpa interrupted.

'That's very kind, but we don't really know you people. We can't thank you enough for what you did, but you can never be too careful.'

Abe was frowning at his grandpa. *Why would they save us if they weren't on our side?* he thought.
'No of course, take your time. I completely understand. If you like you can spend the night in your friend's house and think about it.'

'Thank you,' John replied.

Abe turned to Zoe and said, 'Have you been in there?'

She had a slight worried look on her face. 'No *I* haven't, but some of my people did when they were looking for supplies.'

Abe hesitated for a moment as her look worried him, 'Did you find anyone? Or any of *them*?' he asked, gulping with unease.

She bent down closer to his level and placed her hand on Abe's shoulder, 'They did... *I'm sorry*. They were dead already. But there was no one near your age there if that helps? There was just a grown woman. I hope your friend is okay.'

Abe was both sad and relieved, Ash must have been evacuated with everyone else, but his mom was definitely dead.

'Me too,' he said.

Abe searched the entirety of Ash's house, he wanted to make sure that his friend wasn't there. The entire place had been gutted for supplies. The kitchen was completely empty, not a single tin of food was left. The rest of the house was as Abe remembered it, except a lot messier than normal. They clearly hadn't been careful when searching the place.

The thought of searching Ash's room was scary though. He stood at the bottom of the stairs in the living room looking up at the hall, thinking about what he might see when he went up there.

For some reason, his bedroom door was broken, and it was only his that was. It was if someone had been hiding in there and broke their way in to either get to them or get to something in there that they wanted. But who did it, and why?

Zoe's people could have just broken in to look for supplies, by the looks of it they might have been in there and taken a lot of the stuff that was missing.

When Ash left to be evacuated if that is where he went, he might have locked the door. He too like Abe had a lot of things in there he had collected, like, statues of characters and action figures.

It was smaller than Abe's room and it looked very similar, it had a single bed in it with superhero themed bed sheets and posters all over the walls from movies and games.

What was weird was that his videogames and console were missing, everything else though like the collectables was still there, except they were not how Ash or Abe would have left them. They had been knocked over and left on the ground, and shoved around on the shelves that they were standing on.

The most worrying part was the massive pool of blood that was staining the wooden floor just below Ash's bed, but there was no body.

Where has it gone? Abe asked himself.

He was relieved to find the body had been wrapped in a small rug and left in the garden. He didn't have to unroll it to know who it was.

He could see the bright blonde hair that was sticking out of the top and the pink patterned dress that was sticking out of the bottom. It was Ash's mom.

While he was looking around, John had taken in some stuff from their car so they could sleep there for the night. They hadn't initially planned on staying there but it was getting late, and they knew that this place was safe, especially with Zoe and her people next door. They hadn't made much of a dent in their journey, at this rate it was going to take them twice as long as they had thought, and John was worried. There was no telling how many people they were going to let in after they had evacuated everybody, if anyone at all.

After John was done unpacking stuff from the car, he walked upstairs to find Abe in Ash's room. He was tidying up.

Abe hadn't noticed his grandpa had walked up there; John was just standing in the doorway watching him. He thought it strange that he was tidying someone else's bedroom. It was a miracle to get him to tidy his own.

'What are you doing?' he asked. 'I'm tidying up Ash's things. Someone had been in and knocked over all his collectables. I'm just making sure they're safe and that they don't get damaged. Just in case he comes back.'

Abe put the last thing back in its box and up on the shelf above Ash's bed, pulled the blind down on the window and left his bedroom.

Just as they were both headed back down the stairs the doorbell rang. Abe jumped, startled. He hurried to answer the door, slightly excited thinking that it could be Ash, *but why would he ring his own doorbell?*

He twisted the cold metal doorknob and the wooden door creaked open to reveal that Zoe was standing there, smiling and holding a box. It was an amazing thing to see in such dark and unsure times, *a smile*. Such a small thing, but until now it had been taken for granted and not seen how important it was. Abe looked up at her and immediately smiled back.

'I brought you some things,' she said. At first Abe thought it was just food, but it was even better, at least for him.

It was a box of Ash's things that were missing from his room. The box was full of his video games and his games console.

'Thank you,' he said.

The sight of Abe's joy made Zoe's smile continue without fading. 'You're welcome. It was taken when my people came here for supplies. They weren't happy when I made them give it up, but I told them they'll definitely find another one in one of the other houses.' Abe was looking through the titles of the games and their pictures, sparking memories of Ash and him playing them together. It wasn't that long ago but somehow it felt so far away, like it was a completely different world.

'If you want another one, there is definitely one in that blue house over there' he said pointing, 'That's where *Randy* lives...' Then correcting himself, '...*lived.*' He scrunched his face into a frown.

He had completely forgotten about Randy. He and Ash hated him. He would always bully them in school, and it made it worse that he lived right across the street from Ash. Randy was the worst, Abe specifically remembered when he was in 1st grade, and he jabbed him in the arm with a pencil. He swore that there was a bit of the lead from the pencil still stuck in his arm. Randy followed them through every year of school and tormented them the whole way. He was taller than both of them and probably heavier than both of them combined. He had curly ginger hair and freckles all over his face.

'Thanks,' Zoe replied. 'I'll make sure that the guys know to look there.'

The question was running around in the back of his head whether Randy was dead or not, but he left it sit there and didn't ask. He wanted to forget about him and hoped that he would never see him again. John walked over and thanked Zoe, the more times they saw her the more he was starting to come to the idea of maybe travelling with them. But he was still unsure.

'Have you two got plenty of food?' she asked.

'Yes, thank you, at least for now.' John replied.

Zoe noticed that he was married by looking at the ring on his finger and carefully asked if he had lost her in what had happened.

John was quick to say *no*. He explained that she too had been evacuated and gone on the trucks. He was hoping that she was safe and that they didn't run in to any trouble like Zoe and her group did. As he talked to her about it, he grew more and more anxious, his stomach started to turn, and he began sweating. He wondered if it was just him that was hot, and it must have been as every day it got colder and colder as they got closer to winter. It wouldn't be long before the snow started to fall.

Zoe was quick to notice his anxiety in his reddening face and perspiring forehead.

She placed a hand on his shoulder to comfort him and said, 'She's fine, the trucks that took her left long before ours and were better manned and far more prepared than ours, she's safe.'

Her hand was ice cold, but not in a bad way. It was somehow soothing, and John could feel it through his clothes. John felt almost immediately better, she truly had a way of making people feel calm.

'How are you so sure?' he asked.

'They took my kids and my partner first. It was some time before more came for us.'

'Why didn't you go with them?'

'There wasn't enough room on the truck, so I waited for the next one,' she said, her gaze drifting off as she clearly thought of her partner and kids.

How did she manage to keep her smile? John wondered.

'What about the two of you?' she asked. 'Why didn't you go? Did no more trucks come for you?'

'No, but there weren't any coming back in the first place. I had to stay behind to find my grandson. When everything happened, we couldn't find him, and now we're trying to get to the same place you are. I promised my wife that I would get us both there safe.' It was clear that they both had the same goal and the same destination, it only made sense to travel together. They would be stronger as a group, that was certain. But what if when they got there, only some of them were allowed in? Who would make the decision and how? John knew if it ever came to that that Abe would be one of the first to volunteer to stay outside and put the others before him. John couldn't allow that to happen. Zoe was lovely and she couldn't have done more for Abe and John, but he had to get there first, for Abe and for Adelyn.

But how was he going to do that? Was he just going to leave in the middle of the night and hope that they didn't notice? It was going to be nothing short of a challenge to convince Abe to go along with it after all they had done for them.

Chapter 5

Abe was alone walking a few streets away from Ash's cul-de-sac, the air was blue as the night started to fall. He was looking for Bud.

The streets were empty, no birds, no cats or dogs. No people. Not even any of *them*.

He hadn't even seen any bodies lying on the ground. It was so quiet, almost like he had gone deaf and he thought maybe he had until he realised, he could hear his own heart beating and the scraping of his shoes on the ground as he walked.

Bud! he called, again and again as he walked down the street, passing house after house.

How long have I been walking down this street? he thought, it felt like it wasn't ending. That's when he looked up from his feet as he dragged a baseball bat along the floor and stared straight ahead. But he couldn't see where it ended, the street just kept going and going. He looked behind him and it looked the same. House after house, going and going. Then he realised that they weren't alternating in colour anymore, they were all grey. He turned back to the way he was walking and all of them were grey as well. He could have sworn they were different colours before.

What is going on? he thought.

He started back in the direction he was headed, but faster. A fast-paced walk started to turn into a jog, and then a run. The houses kept on going and going. He stopped and looked around him in a panic. It was the same, it was if he hadn't even moved an inch. He broke out into a sprint and pushed his feet one in front of the other as long and as fast as he could running faster than he thought possible.

The grey houses were whooshing past his eyes in a blur and suddenly he crashed into something hard, and he bounced back and fell onto his butt. A great shadow was cast upon him, the sky still cast the same light as if no time had passed, but as he looked around he was sat in a massive dark area. It was when he looked up at what he had ran into he realised that it was a shadow.

It towered up into the sky like a skyscraper or giant tree, except when Abe squinted his eyes to focus on it, he noticed that it was familiar. It wasn't a building or a cliff, it was a person. It was his grandpa, standing there. Somehow, he was a giant and Abe was sitting on the ground in his shadow.

The next thing he knew he looked down at Abe and a booming voice flooded the air and said, '*Abe!* What are you doing?'

He answered right away, 'I'm looking for Bud, Grandpa.'

Abe saw the giant thing that was apparently his grandpa shake its head in disapproval and the booming voice responded, 'What did I tell you Abe? We don't have time to mess around!'

Abe stood up onto his feet but even doing that made no difference, his grandpa was still way up in the sky towering over him.

'I'm not messing around! I have to find him!' Abe yelled back petulantly.

'*No*, Abe it's time to go,' said the booming voice as he reached down with his giant hands for Abe. Abe saw the hands moving slowly towards him and yelled

'*No,*' as he tried to run away.

He headed for one of the houses, running through the front garden in attempt to get away and run behind the house to hide.

As he ran, he noticed he was wearing different clothes than he thought he was, and he was much shorter. Just about the size of the picket fences that surrounded the houses, and now the baseball bat was a toy.

His giant grandpa followed, and the floor shook and rumbled as his giant feet hit the ground one after the other. Abe still in the darkness of his shadow, trying to run away from it so he could get away and find Bud!

'He's just a dog!' the voice boomed. 'Come back *now!*'

Abe was just approaching the back of the house and leaving his shadow, as he got there and out of the shadow it was if he was his own height again. He was bent over, hands on his knees as he panted and tried to get his breath back. He was distracted by a growl. He looked up and it was Bud! Abe was ready to jump with joy, he had found his dog.

It was Bud, but...he was growling, and his teeth were showing.

'*Bud?* What's wrong boy?' Abe asked. Bud started to move forward slowly towards Abe with his head lowered like he was a lion staring at its prey as he growled and showed his gigantic teeth.

As he got closer Abe realised it wasn't Bud anymore, he was one of them! His eyes had gone black, and his fur was falling off.

Abe started to shake from both fear and grief as he felt sick, and he cried woefully. He was sobbing and stammering his speech pleading to bud and saying, 'No,' over and over.

He was no longer holding a toy and it was again a baseball bat, but what was he going to do? Bud broke into a run as he barked furiously and headed for him as fast as he could and pounced on top of him knocking him to the floor.

Bud was on top of Abe, the bat had been knocked away and there was drool dripping on to his face. He was forced to look at his once beloved dog, now one of *them* with his jaw open staring at him, feeling his damp breath on his face.

Abe looked into his lifeless deep dark eyes and called out his name again, *'Bud?'*

Bud growled and widened his jaw further showing his huge teeth and shot down at Abe's face to bite and tear.

Abe...Abe...

;Abe suddenly felt like he was being shaken around and saw nothing but black. There was a voice somewhere calling his name, 'Abe!'

It continued to call and shake him. His eyes shot open in response to the pleading voice and the violent shaking.

He was lying in a sleeping bag and his grandpa was peering over him shaking him looking gravely concerned.

'Abe, you're okay, it was just a dream,' he said.

Abe was silent and didn't respond, he was still in shock and shaken by what had happened.

'Where am I?' Abe asked in confusion, forgetting where he was or what was going on. His grandpa took a step back, 'We're in Ash's house, don't you remember?' he asked.

He took a minute and looked around before he answered, 'Yeah...I'm fine.'

While Abe had been sleeping, John was sitting on an old wooden and creaky chair at the end of the hall, just at the top of the stairs, hidden behind the corner so nobody could see him if they came in. He was keeping watch, just in case if someone decided to break in, alive or dead, he would know.

He didn't have much in the way of weaponry, just one of his old golf clubs resting between his knees. He kept an ear out listening for anything that might be moving in or outside of the house, but all he could hear was the sound of the walls and floorboards creaking. The house was quite old and no matter what room you were in, you could hear something creaking as the wind crashed against the outside walls.

It kind of reminded him of his house that he lived in when he was growing up, that was old too, probably even older and it too had all kinds of creaks inside of it. Ones he only ever seemed to notice in the night. It was if the house slept in the day and came alive at night, creaking and rattling.

Of course, now he knew it was just an old house and the creaks were just the walls moving from the wind and the rattling were the pipes. But his brother was notorious for trying to scare him growing up. He would tell him that the creaking was the skeleton man coming in the night from his grave to take John's skin so he could have it for himself and be human again. It of course worked and scared him to the bone, even though the same sounds happened every single night and no skeleton man ever came.

As he sat in Ash's cold empty house, he knew there was no skeleton man and the creaks *was* just the wind, but... it was still creepy, knowing that *they* were out there now, and they wanted more than just your skin. They wanted every last bit of flesh and meat on your body.

A sudden gust of wind crashed against the house sending a loud creak from the wall at the end of the hall, starling John and making him jump.

The sudden movement made his golf club slip from between his knees and went crashing down onto the floor.

Bang! It went as it landed on the wooden slabs beneath his feet. John jumped up from his seat in a gasp, knocking over the little lamp he had beside him. His heart was beating out of his chest and he laughed to himself quietly, thinking how silly he was.

Maybe I should take a walk around, he thought, thinking that would calm his nerves as he reassured himself that the house *was* empty and secure. It took only a few minutes and he had done a complete loop of the house, and there was nothing to be found. He even had a quick look in the kitchen again, but they truly had gutted the place. There wasn't a single grain of rice left.

As he walked through the living room though he noticed a small cabinet beside the TV that was closed and didn't look as if it had been checked, and he was right, it hadn't.

There was almost a full bottle of scotch in there. *A small glass won't hurt*, he thought.

He returned to his chair with a mug he had found in the kitchen in which he poured a small amount of scotch for himself.

It was late, but still a long time until morning. He sat there again in the quiet and his mind wandered. He pulled a handkerchief out of his pocket to blow his nose. The handkerchief was soft and made of a light pink material, it was one of Adelyn's. It made him think of her, and how much he missed her.

The time they had spent apart over those few days had been the longest they had in a long, long time. His heart felt heavy and it ached in his chest; his eyes filled with tears. He had no way in knowing for definite if she was okay and safe somewhere.

The handkerchief was clean and fresh, and the smell reminded him of her. He decided to save it and found a crumpled tissue in another pocket with which to blow his nose and wiped the tears away with his sleeve. He was so desperate to get there now and see her again, it made him think hard on what they were going to do. Zoe was expecting him to tell her in the morning if they were going to travel with them or not.

Abe clearly wanted to, and his reasoning was sound. Travelling together would be safer, much safer. If they came into contact with another herd of those things then they could take them out together and not have to worry, and the same thing applied if they came across any unfriendly humans as well. They were lucky that they hadn't come across any already.

What if when they got there, instead of Zoe and her friends, they were a bunch of thugs? They wouldn't have saved them, and even if there wasn't any of those things after them and they ran into them, they would probably have killed them and stolen everything they had.

But...Zoe and her people could also slow them down, more people could also mean more risk. The more people there were, the more people there were to get hurt and look after, and feed as well. With her and her people, including Abe and John there were at least 14 of them.

There wasn't much food around and they had to feed all of them and give them water. That same problem was going to be thought by whoever decided whether they got into the evacuation base or not. If they all turned up together, they might not let any of them in, in fear of not having enough supplies.

However, if just Abe and his grandpa turned up, they would just look like a little old helpless man with his grandson. It was a hard decision to make, but he had to make it, for Abe and for Adelyn.

It was then that John heard Abe yelling. He immediately became worried and ran as fast as he could to Ash's room. Deep in his mind he knew that nothing could have gotten him because he had checked the whole house not moments before, but all logic was out the window when he heard him.

It was only when he swung the door open after running heavy footed through the hall to the bedroom that he realised that Abe was calling out for Bud. When Abe had finally came back around into the real world and was sat up fully awake, John knew that he had to talk to him and try to get him to understand why they had to leave on their own.

If he could, then maybe now was the best time to go, so they could slip out unnoticed and get a head start.

There was a silence hanging in the air as John tried to think how to start that conversation, but before he could think of it and bring it up, it was broken.

'I heard what you said.'

Silence followed as John tried to figure out what he meant. He pushed his eyebrows together in confusion as he thought what Abe was talking about.

'When you said that he was just a dog,' Abe reminded him. 'He wasn't just a dog, he saved me back at the farm and if it wasn't for him, I would be like *them* or just dead somewhere.'

He said it quiet and monotone but the energy from him emitted that he was angry.

John opened his mouth and tried to say something but all that came out was gruff noise before Abe butted in again, '*Why* did you have to hold me back? If you had let me go, I could have saved him and he would still be alive.'

Abe was now on his feet, his face in a hard frown as he yelled in anger.

'Abe...'

'*Forget it!*' Abe yelled. 'It's too late, he's gone.' Abe stormed back to his place and sat back down in his sleeping bag with his arms crossed over his knees. John was just left standing there awkwardly near the door. He didn't know what to say now, or whether to say anything at all. Nothing like that had ever happened before.

Maybe it was his fault, he thought. Maybe if he had let Abe run after him right away, he would have been able to rescue him, and they wouldn't be stuck in this mess.

If he had then maybe it would have been easier to convince him why they had to travel alone. Now that Abe was clearly cross with him, it was going to be even harder.

'*Abe,* listen...I'm sorry what happened to Bud, I didn't mean what I said, I was just scared,' he said apologetically as he moved to sit beside Abe. 'But your grandma needs us and you're not going to like this or agree with me, but we can't go with Zoe. We have to go alone.'

Abe was facing away from John and had edged away as his grandpa sat beside him still frowning.

'*Fine,*' he said.

John was taken back by his response; he wasn't expecting that at all.

'What?' John asked, making sure he heard what he heard.

'*I said fine!*' Abe snapped, just like a normal teenager.

John stood back up and was shocked by Abe's response. Abe's response was weird, it was normal behaviour for someone of his age to say something like that in the way that he did, but Abe wasn't a normal teenager.

'Okay...I guess I'll see you in the morning then,' said John as he backed out the door.

There was no response from Abe. He just led back down in his sleeping bag as his grandpa left the room and said, 'Good night.'

Chapter 6

The sky was pink and scattered with thin clouds. The light from the sun had only just started to light up the streets, and Abe and John were driving away from Ash's house, alone.

'We could have at least said goodbye,' said Abe, leaning his face on his fist, looking out of the window. John looked at him in the review mirror on the back seat.

'I left a note,' he said.

They hadn't spoken much up until this point. Breakfast was silent except for the noise of the camping stove burning, the clinking of tin cups, and cutlery and the sound of mouths chewing.

Abe was sitting in the back seat next to where Bud had been sitting the day before. Some of his fur was still stuck into the fabric of the seats.

They had been driving for over an hour now, but the whole time they had been zigzagging through the roads as they tried to manoeuvre around all of the abandoned cars.

They had barely driven ten miles since they had left Ash's house, and John pointed out if they kept driving the way that they were then their gas wouldn't last very long at all.

When they left home, they had a full tank and they were down to the last quarter. They had some spare in the back that they got from the gas station on the way to Ash's house, but it might not be enough to last them the rest of the journey if the roads didn't clear up. They needed to find more and sooner rather than later, as the longer they left it the less likely that there would be any left.

'We need to make a stop,' said John. Abe looked at him from his seat only slightly turning his gaze from looking through the window at the outside. 'What for?'

'We're running low on gas, I need to fill up and we'll need to keep an eye out for more along the way,' said John. 'Can you have a look on the map and see if you can see a gas station on the line I've drawn? That's where we're headed.'

Abe climbed into the front and pulled the map out of the glove compartment, but instead of staying there he went back to the back seat without saying a word.

The sun had started to set, and they had only done just over fifty miles, nowhere near what they should have done. Their fuel was being guzzled down quickly.

'How much farther are we from that other gas station?' John asked.

Abe re-opened the map, rustling the paper as he unfolded it vigorously, 'Not that much farther but it is the last one for a while.'

They had been to several gas stations along the way, each one digging a big dent in their time.

Every single one they had gone to was empty, even all the shelves in the stores had been stripped clean. The next one was their last hope. If it didn't have any, then they would be walking.

The problem was, the next one wasn't in a residential area where they could walk ten minutes or even an hour and find somewhere safe to stay, it was in the middle of nowhere along a huge stretch of road, surrounded by dirt and hills.

They were both starting to feel hopeless and scared, and seeing all the gas stations and shops around completely empty made Abe more and more anxious. He had crept back into the front seat as they searched the map and thought of ideas of what to do next. They were so used to the ease of being able to go to the shop to get anything they needed. They realised now how much they had taken it for granted. Once they had run out of food what would they do?

When they set out on their journey, they didn't think that this would be a problem, they were meant to be almost at their destination by now, and they almost definitely would have all the food that they needed there.

They had to start getting serious about rationing their food now. No more eating tins to themselves, they had to share them and spread out what they had. Especially if they were going to be travelling at this speed and maybe even forced to walk if they didn't find any more fuel.

John was thinking, *Now we have to be more careful with food, it's better we don't have any more mouths to feed*. Meanwhile Abe was thinking something totally different. *I bet Zoe and her people have all the fuel they need and their big trucks would have been able to drive straight through these cars, and Bud would have been able to help us catch rabbits.*

'So, what do we do?' Abe asked.

John stared ahead as he continued driving, turning the wheel left and right. His head was aching like an over filled balloon ready to pop from all the stress. It was him that had to make the decisions, and whatever happened would be his fault.

They couldn't risk getting to the gas station, it being empty, and them getting stuck just before nightfall. They needed to get there as early as possible to make sure they had all the light they needed to get somewhere safe.

'We'll have to stop and stay somewhere and head there tomorrow.'

'Why?' Abe asked. 'It's not even that dark yet.'

'It'll just be safer.'

John was reluctant to go searching in any of the houses without being sure of what or who could be inside, but they didn't really have much of a choice. They would be far worse off if they tried staying in the car. If they went into a house, they might be even lucky enough to find some food or even some spare fuel, however unlikely.

They pulled up outside a house that looked relatively undisturbed. A lot of the other houses had broken windows, doors left open, burnt-out cars on the driveway and even bodies in the front gardens.

Earlier on when John stopped to put the last of the fuel in the car, they saw that one of the houses had one of *them* inside of it. It was clawing away at the window staring at them. It had smeared blood all over the glass. No doubt that it was the blood of a victim, lying dead and chewed up somewhere in the house.

Before that John had considered maybe even searching through a string of houses until they found more of what they needed, but seeing that had scared him off. Some of these houses were really big and had maybe six or seven bedrooms. If the house was normally full with a big family they could have all turned, meaning if John and Abe went into that house then they would be letting themselves into a nasty trap.

John made sure that the house was small, to try and ensure that if whoever had lived there was still inside but one of *them,* then it wouldn't be too hard to deal with.

It was a nice-looking house; it was a kind of greenish blue and had white wood around the windows and doors. Even the front garden had a nice little patch of flowers that made its way around the front of the house and stopped at the steps of the porch.

It was odd to see when you compared it to a lot of the other houses, it was like this house had been untouched by the whole disaster.

'Okay, we'll stop here,' John said as he switched off the engine. 'We need to be careful when we go inside. We don't know what or who could be in there.'

Abe hopped out just after his grandpa and they started up the path towards the house. From the outside it looked empty but there was no guarantee that somebody wasn't hiding somewhere inside.

Even though there were two of them and they were both wielding a weapon - Abe a baseball bat and John a golf club, there was still an uncertainty about what was waiting for them inside. Abe knew if there was anything inside that his grandpa would try and protect him no matter what, but Abe was scared that it could mean he might lose his grandpa.

Abe didn't know what he would do if the worst happened, especially since it had only been a day since he had lost Bud. Not only this, but he was also just a kid, and he knew that if he came across any actual living people on his own, he wouldn't be able to protect himself so easily as he had against those mindless *things*. *And what happens if we both die? Grandma would be all alone in a base somewhere, waiting for us, and we'd never come.*

They both approached the front door quietly as they could, tiptoeing and trying not to creak the wood as they climbed the steps.

John went first and Abe followed behind, John stood by the white front door ready with the club in his hand ready to swing if anything or anyone came out, while Abe snuck over to the window beside it to peek into the living room to see if there was anyone or anything inside.

It was still and quiet, nothing or no one could be seen. It was just like looking at a painting of somebody's living room.

'There's nobody home,' Abe whispered.

John was the first to go inside. Luckily the door had been left unlocked and he slowly and carefully twisted the doorknob before creeping inside.

The house seemed empty, just as Abe had described, nobody was home. The door opened into the hallway with the living room on the right and the dining room on the left that connected to the kitchen. The hallway was dark, the floor was wooden and made it all that much harder to walk quietly, in case someone was hiding inside. Although, at this point, if there was someone still alive in there and they hadn't jumped out and attacked then they probably weren't going to.

Just a couple of steps away there was a dark red rug that trailed off all the way up the stairs. Every step John made to get to it was slow and vigilant but each time a foot landed it let out an echoing creak through the house.

Abe had followed in behind him just as cautiously. Thankfully, because he was much lighter and smaller than him the creaks weren't nearly as loud.

When they were both safely inside in between the dining room and the living room, John could see that at least the downstairs was empty.

He turned to Abe and said, 'I'll check upstairs, you check the living room and dining room, and then meet me upstairs.'

Abe almost had a smile on his face. *Finally,* his grandpa was allowing him to help. But...before they could move an inch, a figure from behind his grandpa came launching through the air and clawed onto him, gripping onto his back.

John was unprepared for it and immediately stumbled forward as it knocked into him. He wrestled with it and tried to fling it off him, but it was strong. It snarled and growled in his ear as it snapped its jaws trying desperately to clamp down onto his neck. John could even feel the dampness of its breath on his skin.

In the shock of it all he had dropped his club on the ground when it hit him, leaving him with nothing to defend himself with.

Abe was stood in front of him and had a baseball bat in his hand, but with it so close to his grandpa he wouldn't be able to hit very hard at all.

John fought with it trying to get it off, but it was unyielding and stuck clambering closer and closer. It opened its jaws wide as it got just millimetres away from his neck and was ready to bite down onto John's flesh, when he leaned back and pushed all his weight backwards and slammed it against the wall.

It let out a wail as John squished it into the flower-patterned wallpaper. Its grip broke off and it dropped to the floor. John turned around in a frantic panic to see that Abe was gone.

Seeing that he was missing, his head was flooded with irrational thoughts- that he was dead, had been attacked, dragged away by those things, or maybe he had even run away.

While he was panicking and looking around for Abe, he had taken himself away from what was important there and then, and he had almost forgotten the creature that had just been trying to sink its teeth into him. It reminded him of its presence by jumping back off the ground and onto John knocking him to the ground. Again, this thing was clenched onto him hungry as ever.

As John held it up with his hands and stared at it, it looked angry and rabid. *Can they even feel anger?* John wondered.

John's fists were wrapped around its neck as it continued to snarl and growl, staring right back at him with its dark eyes and drooling face. It jerked itself forward over and over again trying to push down.

John thought that this was the end. *Had Abe realised it and ran away scared?* If he had, John would rather he be safe and not see what was about to happen. Suddenly, the body of the creature on top of him spasmed and its grip loosed. Blood gushed from its face down onto John like a fountain and its body became limp.

John kept his grip on it as he closed his eyes and mouth trying to get away from the blood and to be sure it was dead. He flung it to the side, and it hit the floor with a great thud.

It had a huge kitchen knife sticking out of its head, John looked up and saw Abe standing behind him. It was he who had saved him. After realising that he couldn't use the bat to hit that *thing* because it was too close, he had run into the kitchen to grab a knife. That way he could stick it right in its head without the risk of hurting his grandpa.

John jumped to his feet panting to get his breath back. His clothes were ruined – they had blood all over them.

'*Abe?* Are you alright?' he asked.

Abe thought *he* was the one who should be worried, his grandpa was the one covered in blood and who had just been attacked.

'I'm fine,' he said with a blank expression. 'Are you okay? You're covered in blood.'

Luckily none of it was his and he didn't have a scratch on him. He had been bumped around a little though and would have a bruise or two under his clothes.

'We should probably look upstairs to make sure that there aren't any more.'

John stood up straight and let out a big breath from his chest. He was tired.

'Okay, let's go.'

They searched the house together and they were happy that neither of them found anything or anyone else in the house. They checked every single room together, John in front and Abe behind him – John had insisted.

There were only four rooms on the top floor. A small bedroom that looked like it belonged to a teenage girl, and the master bedroom which obviously belonged to the parents. It was hard to say if the thing that had attacked that was downstairs was one of them, as they noticed when looking around the house, all of the family pictures had been removed by someone. Maybe whoever managed to get out took them with them.

The other two rooms comprised of a study and bathroom. The study was littered with books all over the floor, stacked high, and a bookshelf all along the left-hand side wall was full.

The bathroom was small, It had a tiny tub with a shower inside of it and John was very happy to find that the shower was working. There was even some hot water, which helped a lot when trying to get the blood off that had covered almost his entire body.

Just before he did, he helped Abe ensure that the entire house was locked down and that nothing was getting inside unless they let it, giving John the peace of mind while he was in the shower that Abe was safe.

While he showered, it gave Abe a chance to look around the house again, but in more detail this time. The first round was so nail-bitingly tense that he had barely had a chance to take any of it in.

Since he was already upstairs, he decided to start with the two bedrooms.

The bedroom that they thought belonged to a teenage girl was cosy. The room was definitely interesting the walls were a dark red while the rest of the things in there were black, apart from the several framed pictures of different dogs that were hung on the wall in a line.

There were some other things that hung on the wall as well, but they were a little different. There was a skull of some kind of bird. Even upon close inspection, Abe could not tell what kind of bird it was. When he turned around facing the door and where the bed was sat, he noticed that there was an old stick that was nailed to the top of the door.

Beside the bed was a tiny little wooden table that had a load of different candles on top, and the table was covered in a mound of melted wax. It looked like whoever the girl was, that she had just burned every candle on top of one another and now it looked like a tide of lava made of wax.

On the other side of the room, the floor was cluttered with a pile of clothes. It was hard to tell if they had been thrown there in a panic as the person who had lived in this room packed in a hurry, or if it was just normal teenager behaviour. Either was easily believable. Behind the clothes was a white wooden wardrobe that was built into the wall. Abe walked over to have a look and when he opened it. he saw that it was still half full of the girl's dresses, and as he pushed them aside inspecting the cupboard to see if there was anything useful in there, he kind of thought he had seen these dresses before.

Maybe he had just seen people wearing them in school and when passing people on the street, he thought of it just being one of those weird moments when you were having déjà vu and forgot about it and continued looking around.

The master bedroom was a lot less intriguing, it just looked like any other adult's bedroom. It had a big bed against the left wall as you entered the room, with pearl white sheets, a massive wardrobe on the right-hand side, and a nice little dressing table that sat in the window.

The study didn't have a lot to rave about, but Abe did find one really exciting thing – it was a really old first edition of his favourite book. He remembered reading the same book, of course not a first edition, to his grandpa a lot of nights before bed.

It was in pristine condition and the temptation to take it and put it in his bag was great, *but* he placed it back on the shelf where it belonged and left it there. It wasn't his to take.

The kitchen, living room and dining room weren't all that interesting. The only vaguely exciting thing was that there were some food items in the cupboards, including tins of soup, tomatoes and beans, and some old bars of chocolate that had expired a long time ago. The owner of the house had obviously not had a clean out in a long time.

His grandpa came down shortly after, fresh after a shower and not a speck of blood was on him.

Abe noticed that somehow his clothes were clean of blood too. 'How did you get the blood out of your clothes?' he asked.

John hadn't washed them though, he always wore the same clothes and had plenty of the same type of pants and shirts.

Abe prepared dinner for them using the food he had found there in the cupboard. They shared a tin of beef stew and some old crackers that he had found there as well. Although they were a little stale, they were better than nothing. Some bread would have been nice though. His grandma always gave him the nicest chunk of bread with a thick spread of butter on top whenever she made her stew or casserole.

He really missed her homemade meals, he remembered all the times he had taken them up to his room so he could eat them while playing a video game, only giving half of his attention to the food.

Now he would give anything for a bowl of her food and the chance to stay downstairs, sit at the table with his grandparents and enjoy a home cooked meal together.

It won't be long, he thought.

Just a couple more days maybe at the most and he would see his grandma again.

John told Abe that he needed to get some rest and should go to sleep in one of the bedrooms while he stayed downstairs to keep watch, but he had done it the night before and Abe told him that they should take it in turns. His grandpa, after all, must have had next to no sleep the night before.

John agreed but on the condition that Abe would stay upstairs while he was asleep, just to be safe if someone did break in.

Abe sat at the top of the stairs and read from a book he had borrowed from the study.

It was unsettlingly quiet while he sat there, though he was completely immersed into the book he was reading. He only noticed how quiet it was when the wind wailed, and it gave him flashbacks of when he had been attacked back at the farm.

His grandpa was sleeping in the master bedroom, and after a few hours he came out and switched with Abe. Instead of sitting at the top of the stairs, he sat in the living room and lit a fire in the fireplace to warm up the house, which had gotten cold due to the frost outside.

John sat there for around thirty minutes playing with the fire, poking it with a metal stick before he heard something - something that wasn't the wind, or the floorboards creaking, or the pipes rattling, or the trees rustling outside.

It was the roaring engine of a car, piercing through the silence of the night. John froze and his stomach knotted nervously. He hoped that it would pass and thought, *It's fine. All of the lights are off, and the curtains are drawn. They won't know we're in here.*

Then the smell of the smoke from the fire tickled his nose and the hot flames brushed his face, and it became clear.

The smoke coming from the chimney.

If they were looking, they would see that there was smoke rising out of the chimney and probably would be the only one around.

He rapidly jumped to the fire and threw the contents of his water bottle over it and stomped on it with his boot. It only made even more smoke as it extinguished and sent a huge cloud out of the chimney.

If they were already looking and were unsure before, then now they would know that there was someone in there, but John hoped that they had not yet noticed, and he had done it just in time for them not to see.

As he held his breath in worry, the engine grew louder as it got closer to the house before he saw the headlights of the vehicle swing in the air as it parked itself on the driveway and beamed into the house. It made the curtains glow and cast its pattern around the room.

John's heart was pounding hard in his chest, he didn't know what to do. He couldn't call for Abe, if he did, they could hear him.

If he didn't and stayed quiet and they came inside, maybe they would only think that he was there and no one else.

A few seconds later and the headlights were turned off and the rattling of the engine died with it. They were coming inside.

John crawled slowly over to hide behind a pillar to the left of the doorway from the hall that led into the living room, wielding the golf club in his hand ready. The worst thing that could happen right now would be for Abe to wake up without realising what was happening and come down the stairs just as they came in.

John could hear the clicking of their shoes outside, getting louder and louder as they got closer, walking up the concrete path.

John grew more nervous when he heard the clicking change pitch as they stepped onto the wooden stairs leading onto the porch and into the house. There was more than one set of footsteps.

How many? John asked himself.

There was a loud noise as one of them started turning the handle on the front door. At first it was light and gentle as they were clearly expecting it to be open, and then more violently.

It became clear to John that they must have been there before, maybe they lived there?

That couldn't have been true, how would they live there with one of those things running loose in the house?

John carried on listening and after a few seconds the sound disappeared. *Maybe they left?*

The engine of the car hadn't started back up again though, so they must still be outside.

Suddenly there was a voice, loud, rich and smooth. It called out, 'We know you're in there. We saw the smoke rising from the chimney.'

John's face twisted and he scrunched his eyes closed as he thought, *Damn it.*

He snuck over to the window on his knees so he could peer through and take a look how many of them were out there and what they looked like. Maybe he would be able to get an idea if they were friendly or not. If they weren't, then surely they would try and kick the door in, no questions asked.

John pulled the curtain aside slightly thinking that they wouldn't be able to see him, as it was pitch black in the house. He was wrong.

'I see you in there,' the man yelled. 'Trying to gauge whether we're friendly huh?'

The man had a smug grin on his face. He stood amongst a small group of men. John could not see their faces that clearly, but they were all wearing raggedy clothes and holding various weapons including bats, clubs and guns.

The man that was calling out stood right in the middle of them, wearing a leather jacket with shirt underneath and dark trousers.

A cloud in the sky must have glided out of the way of the moon and its luminescent glow cast down on them illuminating the whole group.

The men amongst him looked dirty and grotty. They were different to him, a lot different.

He stood out like a prince amongst thieves. That's certainly what the other men looked like, dirty thieves. But the man in the middle, the one doing all the talking was clean and fresh looking. His teeth were white and reflected in the moonlight, and he had clean wavy looking hair.

'If you come out, I promise we won't hurt you,' he said. 'But…Don't keep me waiting.'

John had no clue what to do, he was making all kinds of promises that they were friendly and that they wouldn't hurt them, but could he trust them?

The thing was, whether he could trust them or not, it didn't change that there were more of them and that they had guns and other weapons.

If he just ignored them there was no telling what they would do.

John reluctantly opened the door. He saw the man a few feet away smiling widely as he looked towards him. John noticed he wasn't holding a gun, but had a machete clipped onto his belt on his left side.

'Thank you,' he said, keeping his eyes locked onto John's.

His men stayed where they were as he walked towards John without asking if he could come in. John stood in the doorway before he got too close and was forced to move out of the way to let him in.

He walked in and straight passed John into the hallway, 'Nice place you got here,' he said. 'Is this *your* house?'

John remained standing by the door, holding it open as he watched the man look around, always keeping his back to John.

John still had the club in his hand and on his way in the man looked at it and smiled.

'No,' John replied.

He turned around, now standing just inches away from the dead thing that had attacked him when they got in.

The man looked at it and shook his head slowly, 'Mmh...mmh...mmh, friend of yours?' he asked.

'No,' said John.

The man looked back up locking eyes with John again, keeping his arrogant smile.

He walked over slowly towards John, his shoes making a dull noise against the wood as he walked. He only stopped when his face was mere inches from Johns.

'What's wrong old man?' he asked. 'Relax...Close the door, they can wait outside'.

John stared him right back in his eyes, almost shivering from his intimidating presence.

'What do you want?' asked John.

The man didn't respond and slowly moved his left arm and reached up, John's entire body tensed expecting him to do something to hurt him. But the man's hand went straight past him and landed gently on the wooden door which John still held open, and a second later the man slammed it shut.

The sound of it echoed all through the house and John's eyes immediately shot to look up the stairs involuntarily, worrying that it might have woken Abe and that he would come downstairs any moment now.

He saw him look and said, 'What's wrong, someone else here?'

John swallowed with unease and said, 'No.'

The man let out a small puff of air from his nose with a subtle laugh and his grin widened.

He turned around and walked straight into the living room, looking at all of John's and Abe's belongings. John was anxious as he did and just hoped that he didn't see anything that was obviously not belonging to him.

'Come on,' he said as he sat down on the couch. 'Take a seat...*John.*'

<u>Chapter 7</u>

'How do you know my name?' asked John, sitting opposite the man with his back to the living room window.

The man had opened the curtains and the room was lit by the moon light.

John could feel the gaze of his men, watching through the window on the back of his neck.

'Your friends told me about you.'

John at first was confused, not knowing what friends he was talking about, and quickly realised who it was he meant.

He was referring to Zoe and her people, they had for some reason told this man about them, but why?

'And...They told me, that there was someone else with you,' he said. 'A young boy.'

John bit his lip and held back his anger. 'What if I was?'

The man smiled, 'You were lying before...He's, here isn't he?'

There was no point in trying to deny it, all it would take was for him to walk upstairs and he would see a sleeping Abe in a bed.

'Yes, he's here...What do you want with him?' John asked.

The man was sitting back on the couch, completely relaxed. He had both arms on the back of the sofa and he had unclipped his machete and let it balance on the arm of the chair.

'Oh...it's not just him that I want, I need you as well. I need both of you.'

'Who are you?' John asked.

The man leaned forward reaching out a hand, 'How rude of me,' he said, 'I'm Decan.'

John looked at his hand without reaching for it, as Decan leant forward smiling and looking John in the eye.

After a few tense moments, John yielded and shook Decan's hand.

Decan leant back to his relaxed position with his arms resting on the back of the sofa.

'I need the two of you to do me a favour,' he said, standing up and beginning to pace around the room.

'Now we both know where you're going. You're going to the base where everyone is locked up, safe and sound. Now… unfortunately, me and my people can't just walk up to the gates and ask to be let inside. No. I need you two to go there, knock on the door, and once you're in you're going to do what I tell you to allow *me* and my people to get in as well.'

As he finished explaining he had done an entire loop around the sofa where John was sitting back to the couch and sat down back in his position.

'Seems fair right?' Decan asked.

'Why do you need *us*?' John asked. 'Why can't *you* just go?'

'Trust me, if I could, I would have already. But they're not going to just let *me* in. I'm just a strange man, but *you*…an old man and his grandson. They'll be sure to let you two in.'

'And what do *we* get out of this…*arrangement?*' John asked.

Decan laughed and crossed his arms, he was amused by John and his attitude, 'Hmm,' he said. 'You'll get to where you're headed safe and secure, and for your *loyalty,* you'll also be well fed.'

It seemed like a good deal, John got what he wanted, getting back to Adelyn with Abe safely... but what about when Decan and his people got inside, what would happen then?

They sure as hell don't look *trustworthy*, John thought.

Once Decan got what he wanted, he wouldn't need them anymore, and once they were no longer needed there was nothing to keep him or his people from simply killing them.

'What if I say no?'

Decan's smile dampened and his face turned serious. He tipped his head to one side and looked at John.

'If you do,' he said taking a breath, 'you're going to regret it.'

There was a stiff silence, and then John said. 'No.'

A half smile reappeared on Decan's face and chuckled through his nose.

'Then I guess...you better walk me out,' he said, as he stood up straight.

John was shocked to say the least and expected a greater argument, and so he stood up too to walk him out.

As his body rose from his seat, a swift fist thumped John in the nose, knocking him back down onto the couch.

Blood started streaming from his nose, drenching his upper lip and dribbling down like a half-closed tap.

John's vision was completely gone as his eyes watered from the blow, and he could smell a distinct smell that resembled copper.

Decan's men saw the altercation through the window, and immediately rushed for the house, before Decan raised his hand, stopping them in their tracks.

He hovered over John who huffed and puffed in shock and trembled from the shock of the blow and held his nose.

Decan placed each hand either side of John's head on the back of the couch and lowered himself down, so he was near his right ear and whispered, 'I don't want to kill you John... I need you to do something for me, and you can't do that if you're dead.'

Decan crouched down so that he was looking up at John and pulled his hands from his face, so he was forced to look at him.

'Look at me,' he said. 'What I'll do to *you*...and your boy, will be worse than death, *far* worse. You have *no...idea.*'

'I can keep you alive for as long as I damn well want, until you agree to do what it is, I need and if you don't and I find someone that will...Then I'll kill the both of you.'

He stood back up and John's eyes followed, '*However.*' He stopped briefly fiddling around in the pocket of his jacket, to reveal a handkerchief which he threw at John to help with the blood. 'If you do as I say, then I think we're going to be just fine.'

John had the hankie held to his nose, and it already was drenched with blood staining a once perfectly white piece of fabric with dark red.

John tried to speak, but Decan interrupted smiling arrogantly. 'Uh...uh...uh,' he said. 'No more talking from you. You need some time to think about what it is you want to do.'

Decan waved his hand in the air again signalling for his men to come inside.

'Now let me tell you something,' he said, still looking at John. 'If you cross me or don't do what I want, then I'm gonna hurt the kid and there's nothing you can do about it.'

His men came in through the door, but it was only a few of them, the rest remaining outside.

Decan turned to pick up his machete off the arm of the couch, 'Get upstairs and bring that boy down here,' he said, pointing upstairs. 'But be nice. *Don't* hurt him.'

Two of the men headed up the stairs, footsteps thundering as they went up.

'I'm a man of my word John, and I promise not to hurt your grandson or let anything happen to him, as long as from here on out, you do every damn little thing I say,' said Decan.

He pulled an apple out of his jacket and started eating it with a small knife he removed from his trousers.

'What was his name?' he asked. '*Ade*, was it?'

'Abe,' John responded with a muffled tone as he spoke through the hankie and his hands.

Decan just responded with a smile, and a second after there was sound of struggling from above and muffled voices. John's eyes widened and he grew worried. His body jolted forward as he almost tried to jump up to go after them.

Decan quickly pointed the little knife he was using to eat the apple at him, smiling as he sat on the arm of the chair John was sitting on.

'I wouldn't even think about it if I were you.'

Then there was the sound as if a sack of potatoes was being dragged down the stairs, one of the men had Abe locked in his arms at his chest as he dragged him down the stairs, and Abe's feet were hitting each step letting out a thud on each one.

Abe was struggling and trying to break free as he yelled at them to get off.

When the man dragged Abe to the door of the living room, Decan looked at him staying seated and turned to John, 'This is him huh?' he said. 'He's smaller than I thought he would be...Skinny too.'

Decan stood up allowing Abe to be able to see his grandpa sitting there with a face full of blood.

Abe was immediately enraged and panicked, and all rational thought was lost. He ran forward to try and get to his grandpa, but the man who had dragged him down the stairs quickly grabbed him by the neck of his shirt, abruptly stopping him.

Abe turned around fast and shoved his fist through the air and punched hard into the man's face, knocking him too in the nose, and sending a mist of blood into the air.

The man looked shocked, as if surprised something so hard came from something so small and feeble looking.

His eyes were covered in a blanket of water, impairing his vision. In anger he pulled Abe forward and returned the punch hard, into Abe's cheek, knocking him down onto the ground with a great thud.

Abe was now on the floor weeping and in pain, it was a miracle that a blow from a full-grown man that was so big didn't knock him clean out.

Decan witnessing the altercation, stared at his man now standing there red faced and heavily breathing in rage.

'What on earth do you think you are doing?' Decan asked him.

The man didn't respond and just looked at Decan with a sheepish look on his face.

Decan stepped slowly one foot after the other until he was standing right in front of him, so close that their noses were almost touching.

The man had begun to hunch over and avoided looking at him, instead keeping eyes on the ground.

Just as he started to open his mouth, Decan's gruff voice interrupted, 'I said, *not* to hurt him.'

'I'm sorry Decan,' the man whimpered, 'but, he hit me.'

Decan looked down at Abe and back up at the big man standing there with a bloody nose, cowering in Decan's shadow.

Even though he was hunching over like a scared dog, he was still much taller than Decan, but that didn't seem to matter.

'Did he hurt you?' Decan asked in a patronising tone. 'That little kid on the ground? Did a little twelve-year-old kid beat you up?' he said, his voice raising to a furious yell. He somehow now seemed taller than the whimpering man.

Silence fell as the man was too afraid to respond. It was broken by Abe who said, 'I'm *fifteen.*'

Decan, looking surprised that he said anything at all, turned to Abe and smiled. Then he turned back to the man with a slight chuckle, showing his white teeth.

'Does that make you feel better? he asked, 'That you got beaten up by a fifteen-year-old instead of a twelve-year-old?'

'He didn't beat...'

Suddenly, Decan leant back and brought his head forward with all his might and head butted the man clean in the face knocking him down on the ground.

Decan still had half of an apple in his hand, he took a big chunk out with his teeth and threw the rest on the ground. 'Let's get this show on the road, shall we?'

Decan waved his hand in the air, signalling his men to move out.

Two of his men grabbed John and dragged him to his feet, followed by Abe and pushing and shoving them out of the door.

'Where are you taking us?' John demanded.
Decan walked out of the house after the last man and closed the door behind him, 'You'll find out soon enough.'

Abe and his grandpa had bags shoved over their heads making everything black, and they were forced into the back of a vehicle.

Chapter 8

Sometime later, everything was still black, and their hands were bound behind their backs. They had been thrown around by the careless driving and the bumps in the road, sending them rolling around and occasionally crushing one another, but Abe was impacted more, as John was much heavier.

John would have apologised every time it happened, even though it wasn't his fault, but they had both been gagged the only noise they would make came out as pure nonsense. By the end of the journey, their bodies would be covered in bruises.

The vehicle they were in came to an abrupt stop, and with it came the sound of the tyres skidding and the breaks screeching, sending them both rolling and knocking into each other.

They heard doors opening and slamming shut a few moments before there was a sound of the sliding door to where they were laying, and they were dragged out by several people.

There was a slight light that peered through the fabric of the dark bags that were over their heads as it must have been daytime now, and they could feel the hot sun beaming down on them.

They thought that they might have taken their bags off now, but they were wrong. They didn't. There was someone on each side of them guiding them forward to wherever it was they were being taken.

Abe and his grandpa had no idea where they were or even when they were.

Being locked up and with the bag over their heads, Abe had no way of telling what time of day it was.

The only thing he could do to try and guess where they were, was to feel the ground with his feet and listen carefully to the sounds around him.

When he was initially dragged out, his feet were met with what felt like gravel crunching under his shoes. As he were forced forward, Abe heard what sounded like the screeching of metal gates, and the sound of people muttering and the occasional person joking or swearing at one another.

There was even the sound of dogs barking, which brought up memories for Abe.

After they had passed what he assumed was the front gate, it felt like they walked past a fire as he could feel the warmth against his skin and the smell of oil.

It became clear when they had entered a building when the floor changed. It was carpet instead of gravel. Thin carpet, though, nothing like in a house, something more industrial like what they used for offices, as the floor was hard.

The air was much warmer inside, and as he walked, they went through several doors and even climbed a few stairs, until eventually he was pushed into a room, separate from his grandpa. As he was, the bag was removed from his head, along with the gag and bounds around his hands.

The room outside of theirs was square and the size of a small café.

It was just, plain and empty with bright lights above and a small desk in the middle, facing their cell-like rooms. Abe's vision blurred and his eyes stung for a while after the bag was removed as he adjusted to the lights. His mouth was painfully dry from being gagged and having no water. By the time his eyes were clear enough for him to look around, the men that had brought them in were long gone.

The small holding cells that Abe and his grandpa were confined in were clearly not meant to keep people for long periods of time as there was no sink or toilet in the room, and the only furniture was a bench like bed. However, it was clear that this was to be their new home, at least for a little while.

Abe and John weren't able to see each other, but Abe's face now had a massive bruise from where the man had hit him, and it covered his cheek and left eye, it was as purple as a plum. The bruise felt hot and kind of heavy. Each time he tried to touch it he would flinch and let out a quiet whinge of pain.

John had a mark too, but it was his nose. It was still stained red but seemed a lot messier than before as it had been spread across his face from the sweat that gathered from the warmth of the bag.

Each time he tried to touch it, it was agony. He dreaded to think what it would feel like if he sneezed, and it was a likely event to happen with the room they were stuck in. It was if it hadn't been cleaned in ages, it was dusty as anything.

The silence in the room was awkward, John didn't know what to do or say. He certainly couldn't do anything to help them escape. He felt like all of this was his fault. He after all was meant to keep guard.

How could I have been so stupid to light a fire, he thought to himself.

Maybe he should have just agreed to do what Decan wanted? But if he did there was no telling if he would have treated them differently even if he had agreed.

By giving in straight away, maybe they would have given up their only bargaining chip.

John needed to be sure of what Decan had planned for when he and his goons were inside. For the sake of Adelyn and everybody else in there, he had to be sure if he was going to get out of that place and go there to find Adelyn, that he wasn't going to bring their doom with him.

If Decan truly was a man of his word, then John needed to get him to agree to not harm Adelyn as well as Abe, if they did what he wanted.

He at least had to get that and, if he could, ensure the safety of the others as well. But Abe and Adelyn came first.

'Are you okay?' John asked Abe.

There was a brief pause before a quiet voice responded, 'Yeah.'

'Why are we here?' Abe asked. 'Who are these people?'

John told Abe about what happened and that while he was asleep, he lit a fire to keep them warm and it brought the attention of Decan and his men.

'Zoe and her people told them about us Abe. They were looking for us,' he added.

Abe had a hard frown on his face, mixed with anger and confusion. 'Why were they looking for us?' he asked.

'Why would Zoe do that? She wouldn't, she wanted to help us and travel together, we should have gone with her, like I said.'

John shook his head, 'No Abe, she didn't want that, she probably just wanted to bring us straight here. She probably works for him,' said John. 'Decan needs us to get into the base where your grandma is and let him and his people inside.'

'*No,*' said Abe, 'I don't believe that. Zoe wouldn't do that to us. What about *her* family?'

John said that she probably wanted to bring them to Decan so that he would repay her by taking her to her family and promising to keep them safe.

'Then what did Decan offer *us*?' Abe asked.

'The same thing, he said he would take us there and keep us safe as long as we get them inside.'

'What's so wrong with that?' Abe asked, only seeing that they would be getting to *their* goal and not thinking what the consequences might be if they let them in.

'These kinds of people can't be trusted Abe. We have no idea what they're capable of and what they will do if they get inside,' John explained. 'We need to be sure that you and your grandma will be safe.'

Abe was sat on the floor as he stared at the joining wall with his grandpa's cell, listening to him speak.

'How do we do that and make sure that everyone else there will be safe as well?' he asked.

John had the same amount as answers as Abe did. *None.*

Neither of them knew these people or how many of them there were.

'I don't know Abe,' John responded. 'We'll be lucky if we can guarantee your grandma's and your safety, let alone everybody else's as well.'

'We can't just let everyone else die and save ourselves'

'I know, but you can't save everyone Abe.'

'We can try,' said Abe. 'We have to.'

An hour later, they heard the slow sound of footsteps coming from a nearby hallway, echoing and getting louder as they came closer to the room.

The door opened slowly as someone leant against the wall on the outside. It was Decan, and just a few seconds after it opened, he walked in with a grin on his face admiring, the two of them in their little rooms. Neither of them spoke a word to him but looked in his direction.

'Afternoon gentlemen,' he said loudly. 'How are we doing?' Decan asked as he walked over to look at John in his cell.

John had no answer for him and kept his silence. Decan kept smiling and walked over to the cell that Abe was in.

'What about you kid?' He asked him, 'How are you doin'? Did your grandpa here fill you in on everything?'

'Yes,' Abe said bluntly.

Decan walked into the middle of the room, so he was in the sight of both of them but kept looking at Abe.

'And don't you think he was a little rude to decline my kind and gracious offer?'

Abe only stared and gave no response.

Decan walked back over to him and crouched down so he was the same height as him, as Abe sat on the floor of his cell and met eyes with him.

'And what do you say, huh?' Decan asked him.

Then there was a voice from the other side of the room,

'Leave him out of this,' John yelled. 'He's just a kid, he can't make that kind of decision.'

Decan turned his head to the sound of John's voice and walked back over to his cell, 'What did you say? He asked, 'That's not fair John... I think he's capable of making his own decisions.'

John stood and put his hands on the bars of the door so he was looking right at Decan, 'He can, but he's *my* grandson and wherever I go he goes. He follows *me!*' Decan's smile had disappeared as John gave his speech, but by the end he started to smirk, as if an idea had just crept inside his head.

It was Abe who he had to get through to, not John. But he couldn't let John's bravery go unpunished. Decan picked up a fire extinguisher that was hanging on the wall not too far from the cell and before John could realise what was happening, Decan smashed the bottom of it hard against one of Johns hands that was wrapped around the cell door, crushing his fingers.

There was a dull thud and a crack, followed by the intense wail from John as he cried out from the pain.

He fell backwards onto the bench in the room and then stumbled off onto the ground landing on his side. He clutched his hand against his chest and whimpered in agony.

Abe yelled out in a panic, 'Leave him alone!'

He jumped to the door of his own cell and clutching his fists around the bars, clearly not learning from what had just happened.

Decan still had the extinguisher in his hands and walked over to Abe, so he was only a metre away from his door and stared at him, but with no smile on his face. He could have easily done the same to him, but he didn't. He looked at Abe and placed the extinguisher on the desk in the middle of the room.

'Now, what do *you* think about my proposal?' he asked him. 'Do you want to help me?'

Abe's lips had gone white from pressing them hard together in anger.

'Why would I do anything to help you?' Abe asked. 'I hate you!'

Decan pushed his lips together now and his head bobbed back and forward as he thought about what Abe had just said.

'You hate me, huh?' he asked. 'Hmm...alright then.'

Decan glanced over at John to see him still lying on the floor clutching his hand and back at Abe before he turned around and walked out of the door, turning the lights off and closing the door behind him, leaving them in the dark.

Then Decan walked away just like he arrived, the sound of his footsteps echoing in the hall, but this time getting quieter the further they got away.

Abe tried to console his grandpa and ask if he was okay, but he got little to no response. John was still on the floor groaning in pain.

Abe was really worried for his grandpa; his mind was racing as he tried to think what he could do to try and help him. He would do anything.

A couple more hours had passed, and as they sat there in the dark, they started to realise how hungry they were. Abe more so than his grandpa, as John was still pretty distracted from the pain.

Just as Abe's stomach started to growl, one of Decan's men came in and brought them some food. He was holding two tins with plastic forks sticking out of the top.

He placed them down just outside of their cells and then threw a bottle of water on the ground for them to share. The man said nothing and walked straight back out, but he left the light on for them.

Whether he did intentionally wasn't clear, but it was a good thing that he did, because when Abe picked up the tin of food, he noticed that it was *dog food.*

Abe was starving, his stomach hurt he was so hungry, but he couldn't eat dog food. He wasn't quite that desperate. He hoped that he never would be. It was starting to become too much for Abe. It was all piling up - he was hungry and had no food, he was stressed, he was worried for his grandpa, and he missed his grandma.

That's when he remembered Bud again. He really thought that nothing was going right for him and that he was doomed.

He felt completely hopeless now and felt like maybe he was even cursed, not that he ever believed in such things before, but maybe he was.

His grandpa was no luckier than Abe was, they had given him dog food as well, and they only had the one water to share between them, and there was no telling when they were going to bring more.

John didn't much fancy eating dog food either, they just decided to share the water and hope that that would line their stomachs a bit, so the hunger was less noticeable.

They couldn't tell what time it was, but they were both tired, they were both worn out, so they sat there until they fell asleep.

Chapter 9

The next day, they had a visit from Decan, but it was a little different, and not something that Abe expected.

Decan came in just after one of his men had brought in their breakfast.

It was cold, lumpy, and pasty porridge - thick enough to use as glue.

'Good morning, gentlemen,' said Decan.

Abe and John remained where they were, trying to eat their food. Decan walked up close to the front of Abe's cell and watched as he tried to force down the horrible food as his face turned at every gruelling bite.

Then, the next thing Abe knew, Decan had fished out a set of metal keys from his pocket and opened the door to his cell.

The cold metal door screeched loudly as he opened it. John, watching him do this became anxious and edged towards the door of his own cell.

'What are you doing?' John asked.

Decan ignored him, and gestured Abe to get out of his cell. 'Out you come,' he said.

Abe was wary about it though. *What does he want me for?*

'Relax,' said Decan. 'Let's get you some proper breakfast.'

Is it a trick? Abe thought, as he puckered his brows in confusion.

Abe put down his small metal bowl on his bed, still half full of uneaten porridge.

He stood up slowly and walked out to the cell door. His cell was dark and as he stepped closer to the room outside of it, the bright lights that filled the room stung his eyes.

When he came out, Decan stepped towards him and Abe immediately flinched and jumped back an inch, pulling his hands to his chest in a cowering position, expecting to receive some kind of blow.

However, he opened one of his closed eyes and saw that Decan had only stepped into his cell, to pick up the bowl of half-eaten porridge, and then threw it down in front of his grandpa's cell.

'Where are you taking him?' John pleaded.

Again, Decan ignored him as he placed his hand on Abe's back and guided him towards the door.

Abe turned his head to try and look at his grandpa, but Decan stopped him, turning his head back to the door and said, 'You like waffles?'

He took him down a long hall from their holding room, and on both the left and right wall was door after door. They had writing on them, but he didn't have a chance to read them as Decan was stealing his attention by talking to him the entire way.

'I want to get to know you a little Abe,' said Decan.

'Why?' he asked.

'Because...I don't know you that well, and you don't know me either. I think, once you get to know me and find out what I want and what I'm doing then you'll understand why I need you.'

Abe looked up at Decan, 'What about my grandpa?' he asked. 'Wouldn't it help to get to know him?'

Decan had a reluctant look on his face. 'I know him already Abe, and he has already said "no" for the both of you. You haven't had a choice yet. It's not fair that you should be punished, is it?'

'No...I guess not,' said Abe.

Abe was feeling stuck, Decan was right. He hadn't been given the chance to consider his offer yet, his grandpa had said no, without really asking him, and he hadn't told him why.

It made him think of what happened with Zoe. He had wanted to go with them, but his grandpa didn't listen and just said no, and made them leave on their own.

If they had gone with them, then maybe they wouldn't have been there in the first place. Although, his grandpa said that it was because of them that they were there; that Zoe told Decan about them.

Abe thought that he could use this as his chance to find out who told them about him and his grandpa, and where they were.

'How did you find us?' Abe asked.

Decan frowned, 'I'm surprised your grandpa didn't tell you already,' Decan said in an accusing tone. 'Although...it was his fault. It makes sense that he has lied to you to cover it up or hidden the truth from you.'

Abe scowled, 'What do you mean?' he asked, confused. *He wouldn't lie to me. How could it be his fault?*

'Why, the only reason we knew you were there was because of the smoke from the chimney, it was like your grandpa had lit up a big sign letting us know you were there.'

Abe turned his head and looked straight ahead trying to hide his frustration. *He did lie!* he thought to himself.

Decan could not read Abe's thoughts, but he knew exactly what he was thinking.

I can't believe Grandpa would lie. I knew that Zoe wouldn't have done what he said she did.

While Abe was lost in his thoughts, he hadn't been paying attention to the world around him and he had been taken to a large room, it was mostly empty, but it was really big.

It was square, and had white walls all around, in the corner to his left was a red sofa and a small table in front of it.

Decan sat him down on the sofa and only a few seconds later a lady came in holding two big plates of hot steaming waffles.

She was quite pretty, she had long brown hair with slight curls at the end and wore a long sleeve black top and dark jeans.

She placed them down on the table and smiled at Abe. Abe was a bit reluctant to eat the waffles, thinking that it might be a trap. *Why is Decan suddenly being so nice?* Finally, the smell overcame him, and he gave in, and after he saw Decan take a bite, he figured that it must be safe.

When they were both done eating, Decan asked Abe what he liked and what he enjoyed doing.
When Abe told him that he liked video games and collectables, Decan asked what kind of video games he liked and talked to him for a while about it.

Abe had completely forgotten who it was he was talking to and was too busy telling him about the different games he liked playing, and that he used to play those games with Ash. Decan asked about Ash, and whether he knew where he was.

Abe told him that they went to his house, but he wasn't there, and they were hoping to find him in the base when they got there.

Maybe I shouldn't have told him that? Abe thought.

'Would you like to see your friend again?' Decan asked him.

'Um...yes, I would.' Abe responded.

Decan looked at Abe with a smile on his face and said, 'I can make sure you see him, all I need is for you to help me. And if you do help me Abe, if you agree, then you won't have to go back to that cell. You can stay here with me. I'll make sure you have things like video games, and waffles for breakfast. I can make sure you see your friend again, and anyone else who is there.'

'But why me? I don't understand why I'm so special,' said Abe.

'Because Abe, you're a kid, and no one sees you as a threat. They'll let you in.'

Abe could see sense in what Decan was saying, and everything he was offering was what he wanted, *but why did he want to get into the base so bad and have to get someone else to get him in?*

'What about when you're inside, what happens then?' asked Abe.

'*I'm* going to tell you the truth Abe, but this is a secret you have to keep between just you and me,' said Decan, looking Abe in the eye. 'My wife and daughter are in there. I need to get inside to get back to them.'

If that was true then Abe really had nothing to worry about, 'But why all these people then? Why have you got these people following you?' Abe asked, *if he is just trying to get back to his family, then it doesn't make sense why he has these kinds of people following him.*

Decan stood up from the couch gently and walked over to the door that they had walked in through and twisted a small metal knob on the door to lock it before he walked back over.

'I need them to make sure I can get there, with the monsters that are out there, I need people who can protect me, and who better to do it than criminals and thugs?' Decan explained.

'I don't know why. Why them? They're horrible,' Abe replied.

Decan had lowered his voice into a hushed tone, 'That's exactly the point Abe, they do the grunt work, they're just pawns. I'm using them to avoid using the good people, the people who don't deserve to die.'

Abe pushed up his bottom lip as he thought about it, thinking that it made sense to use those sorts of people for what he was explaining. It made sense, if they're there and you can get them to do it to save the people that should be saved, then why not?

'So...what do you need me for now?' Abe asked. Now that Decan was done telling him the secretive information, he got back up and unlocked the door.

'Now, I need you Abe, to convince your grandpa to help me.'

'Okay,' said Abe.

Decan pulled a small radio from his belt and called through it, 'Anna, could you come here and take Abe back to his grandpa please?'

A staticky voice came through the radio. *Sure thing. Will be right there boss.*

'Now remember, don't tell anyone else about this, this is between us. Nobody else here can know the real plan, okay?'

Abe was a bit concerned, 'What should I tell them then?' He asked. 'What should I tell my grandpa?'

Decan lowered down to his knees and placed his hands, on Abe's shoulders.

'It's your decision, you can tell him the truth if you want but if anyone but your grandpa asks, it is as I told him, I need to get into the base with my people so that *we* can stay there.'

A few seconds later and there was a firm knock at the door, and it was Anna, the lady who had brought the waffles earlier.

'Hi Abe, how were the waffles?' she asked.
Abe smiled up at her and said, 'They were great, thank you.' He thought that Anna looked nice, she was really friendly and had a warm smile and beautiful green eyes. He wondered if maybe she *knew* about the real plan, seen as she was one of the only other nice people he had met there and who wasn't a thug.

'Am I taking him back boss?' she asked Decan.

'For now,' said Decan as he turned and winked towards Abe, 'but before you do, take him by the stores and find him a fresh set of clothes.

'Will do,' she said, and then opened the door for Abe to walk out and then walked off down the hall.

John was sitting in his cell, anxiously waiting for someone or Abe to come back. Every minute that passed was nail-bitingly tense.

He felt sick, even more than he had already. When the door opened, he shot up from his sitting position, and moved towards the door, hoping that it was Abe and that he was okay.

But it wasn't Abe, it was Decan. He stepped into the room slowly and walked up to the front of John's cell.

'Where is he?' John yelled. 'What have you done with him?'

Decan had a grin on his face and laughed through his teeth.

'Relax...he's fine, probably better than he has been in a little while. I fed him and now he's gone to get a fresh pair of clothes.'

John frowned, *this doesn't make any sense*, he thought.

'Why would you do that?' he asked.

Decan pulled the chair from the desk in the middle of the room and sat down in it in front of the cell, holding his machete in between his legs.

'It doesn't matter why John, but you'd be interested to know that Abe has agreed to help me, and I suggest that you do too, it'll make things a hell of a lot easier on the both of you.'

John frowned hard in irritation, 'What did you tell him?' he asked.

Decan tittered and shook his head slightly at John, 'I told him the truth as I did, to you, we're just trying to survive like you are, we want in as well,' said Decan. 'If you help me get in, and me and my people are safe, you'll be rewarded for your loyalty.'

John was sceptical, he still didn't trust him.

'How do I know that you're not going to kill everyone, all those innocent people?'

Decan stood up and stepped closer to John, 'Oh there are bound to be a few casualties, especially those who *resist...*or get in my way.'

John scowled. *How has he gotten Abe to agree to this?*

Then suddenly, as John was about to say something, the radio on Decan's belt made a noise followed by someone speaking. *All sorted boss, taking him back now.* It was Anna.

'Ahh...that's my cue to leave,' said Decan. 'See you later John.'

John was enraged as he saw Decan walk away, 'Where are you going? Come back!' he yelled. 'Where is he?'

A few moments later, when Decan was gone, Abe came walking back in with a smile on his face and freshly clothed.

'*Abe,* are you alright?' John exclaimed.

Abe was fine, he had a full stomach, fresh clean clothes and a light ahead, and now his worries and doubts were gone.

'I'm fine Grandpa,' Abe replied.

'Decan said you agreed to help him.'

'Yes, I have. He asked me to talk to you about it,' said Abe.

Abe looked so relaxed about the whole situation and John was confused.

'He's already talked to me about it,' said John. 'He was just here.'

Abe frowned, and so did Anna who was stood beside him, 'What do you mean, he can't have been, I just left him,' said Abe.

Then Anna chimed in, 'No, that can't be right. I spoke to him on the radio, he's nowhere near here.'

John was glancing at them both, his head moving from one to the other.

'He's lying, and your lying,' said John pointing at Anna. 'He was just *here.*'

Abe looked at his grandpa and felt frustrated at the way he was acting, he knew that Decan hadn't just been there because he had just been with him, and he had heard Anna speaking to him on the radio.

Besides, who is he to point the finger and call people a liar after what he did, Abe thought.

'You're the liar,' Abe said pointing at John, 'You lied about Zoe... you were the one that lit the fire, it was all your fault, and *you* stopped me from saving Bud, that was your fault too.'

John stepped back in shock at first and then frowned at Abe.

'What do you mean I'm the liar?' John said back with his voice heightened.

Abe was feeling incredibly annoyed now that his grandpa was making it worse by denying it and yelling at him. 'If you had given me the opportunity to make a decision, instead of treating me like a child, we wouldn't have been stuck in these cells.' Abe yelled back.

Anna interjected and said to Abe, 'I'm sorry Abe, but I have to put you back in your cell until you have spoken to your grandpa, and he has agreed as well.'

Abe was breathing heavily, and his face had gone all red after getting worked up. 'I don't want to. Can't I go back and speak to Decan?' he asked.

Anna had a sad look on her face when she said, 'I'm sorry, but you can't. I will speak to him, but I have to lock you in your cell for now.'

What has Decan done to make Abe want to be with him instead of me? John thought, sadly.

Anna had opened the door of his cell and Abe walked in obstinately and said, '*Fine.*'

Anna closed the door and locked him in. She looked at both of their cells, and they both were sitting on their beds with their arms crossed in silence, frowning at the ground.

She walked out and as she got a few metres down the hallway, she lifted up her radio, 'Did you hear all that? she asked.

Decan responded, *'Perfect.'*

Chapter 10

Abe didn't speak to his grandpa at all. He had been frowning with his arms crossed tight ever since he had been made to get back into his cell.

His grandpa didn't say anything either. Occasionally Abe heard breath coming out of his mouth as though he had opened it to start to say something but changed his mind.

Now that he had been out of the cell, seen the light outside of it and had some nice food and been given fresh clothes, the putrid smell of their cells was even more noticeable than before.

The smell came from the buckets they had been forced to use in place of a toilet, and the stench had started giving them migraines.

I don't want to be in here...I hope Decan comes back soon, thought Abe.

Just as he thought that the door opened. He got up hastily from his seat, thinking that it was him.

He hadn't been able to convince his grandpa to do what Decan wanted yet, he hadn't even tried.

There's no point, he thought.

He hoped that even if he hadn't, that Decan would let him out of the cell just for *him* agreeing, like he promised he would.

Besides, Abe hadn't done anything wrong, he didn't deserve to be punished. He *wanted* to help.

The person that came through the door was familiar, but it wasn't Decan, it was Anna. Abe was glad to see her anyway. She had been nice to him.

She came in holding food in both hands. Two medium sized bowls with steam rising from them.

She brought the food over to Abe first. 'Hi Abe,' she said quietly.

'Hi,' he replied. 'Have you spoken to Decan yet?'

'No not yet, he's gone out to get something and will be back soon.'

Abe was disappointed, he hoped he would be able to get out of the cell, he didn't want to spend another night there.

'Could you let me out anyway?' Abe asked with a hopeful tone.

'I can't,' she said. 'I know better than to make a decision for Decan'.

Abe looked down at the ground and his smile disappeared.

Anna passed him the bowl of hot food; it was some kind of stew.

'*Here,*' she said. 'eat this'.

A small smile reappeared on Abe's face, 'Thanks,' he said, *at least it's not dog food, or cold porridge.*

Anna grabbed something else from a pocket wrapped in tissue and passed it to him, 'Here, I brought you this as well.'

Abe opened it, it was soft and spongy feeling through the tissue.

It was bread, to go with his stew, and it was nice and fresh.

'Thank you,' he said. That little bit of bread was going to make the meal ten times better.

'That's not all,' she whispered as she pulled something else from the inside of her jacket and passed it to him.

Abe grabbed it carefully and angled it in the light so that he could see it. It was a comic book, one that he hadn't read before, which was a shock because every penny he saved up often went on comics and he had hundreds of them.

Anna smiled at his response as he looked at the comic with joy. 'Hope you enjoy it,' she said as she stood up, placed the bowl of food down at John's door without speaking to him, and left.

Abe was pleased when he first tasted the stew, it was actually quite nice.

He was sat leaning against the door of the cell, so the light could reach his comic book, and he could read it, when he saw his grandpa's hand reaching for his bowl of stew, in the corner of his eye.

Abe was just about to dip a piece of his bread into his stew, and it made him think...*Grandpa would really like some bread.*

He was mad at him, but he still loved him. Abe tore the bread in half, sending crumbs tumbling down onto his front and onto the floor.

He put down his food and carefully put his bit of bread on his comic book and reached out of the cell door to pass the bread to his grandpa.

'*Here,*' said Abe.

There was no sound at first, and then his grandpa's hand came out to meet his and took the bread from him.

'Thank you, Abe,' said John.

Abe couldn't see his face, but he imagined him smiling. He chose not to respond, as he was still mad and didn't want to talk to him all that much.

Instead, he dug back into his food, mopped up every last bit with the bread he had remaining and read his comic book.

A couple of hours later and Anna came back in. Abe was surprised to see her; it must have been late seeing as the meal they had just eaten was meant to be dinner.

Mealtimes were the only way they knew roughly what time of day it was. There was no windows or clock in the room.

Anna walked to Abe's cell. 'I've got good news,' she said.

Abe smiled slightly. 'What is it?' he asked.

She took the keys from her pocket, jangled them around as she looked for the right one and opened the door to his cell.

'I spoke to Decan on the radio, he has to stay out for the night and won't be back until tomorrow, but he said you can come out now. You'll get to spend the night in a nice cosy bed.'

Abe's smile turned into a grin, 'Really?' he said. 'That's great...but what about my grandpa?'

He stepped out of his cell and looked at his grandpa. He was fast asleep.

Anna stepped beside Abe as he looked into the cell. 'I'm afraid he has to stay here, that is until he agrees, like *you* have,' she said. 'You can speak to him in the morning. You should let him rest.'

Abe didn't hesitate, his grandpa looked like he was in a deep sleep, and he didn't want to disturb him. *Maybe a good night's rest is just what he needs so I can speak to him tomorrow and make him see sense*, Abe thought to himself.

'Come on, I'll show you to your room,' said Anna, as she walked Abe out of the room and down the hall.

A short while later, a sudden wave of ice stung and covered John's body, rushing him awake fast and sending him into shock.

He woke up with a loud gasp and made an *eek* like noise in the form of a yell. His whole body was shivering, and his clothes were sopping wet.

He looked up and saw Decan standing outside his door with two of his goons, one either side of him.

One of them was holding an empty bucket which he had used to throw cold water onto John.

'What do you want *now?*' John said through gritted teeth.

Decan smirked. 'It's time for you to go,' he said.

John knitted his eyebrows in confusion. *'What? Go where? Where's Abe?'* he asked, and then called out, *'Abe?'*

No one answered. He wasn't in his cell.

'Where have you taken him?' John asked.

Decan didn't answer and he picked up a bag from his side and threw it down in front of his cell and said, *'Change.'*

John put his hands through the bars and opened the bag to see that inside were some raggedy clothes.

'Why?' he asked. 'If you hadn't had thrown water on me to wake me up then I wouldn't need to.'

Decan pulled something out of his jacket pocket, it was a small plastic bottle and he showed it to John.

'*Sleeping tablets*. When you're on these, it's the only way to wake you up,' he said. 'Couldn't have you waking up when we took Abe and have you talking to him now could we?'

John stood up, still in his wet clothes and dropped the ones he had been given on the floor.

'*Where* have you taken him?' John demanded again.

'He's sound asleep in his own bed. He's mine now,' said Decan.

John was silent, he had all kinds of rage bubbling inside of him, but instead of yelling, he just stared daggers at Decan.

Decan turned to the man still holding the bucket and said, 'Give me your knife.'
The brute of a man smiled and let out a small but evil laugh and passed it to him.

John grew frightened as Decan stepped forward with the knife in his hand looking John dead in the eye with a smile on his face.

He felt his stomach knot as he gulped with unease. He grew pale and his forehead began to sweat. *This is it,* he thought.

Then, just as he stepped forward, Decan swung round, his boots making a scratching noise against the floor as he did and forced the knife straight up into the man's neck. The one that had *given* him the knife.

It went straight into the centre of his throat and into his windpipe as blood spurted out and the man gargled and gasped in shock.

His hands were clambering around as he tried to save himself somehow, but it was too late.

The man soon lost all consciousness and dropped to the floor like a damp sock, soon as Decan let him go.

The other man still standing there was pale and in shock but remained still, like a statue.

Did he know that was going to happen? John thought.

John felt the blood drain from his face, and he was almost sick. He was also confused. *Why would he do that to his own man?*

Decan turned to look at John, his hand was covered in blood and his face was spattered in small drops.

'Got to make it look convincing, now, don't we?' said Decan.

John was still pale, and he was trying to stop himself from throwing up as he kept looking and the blood gushing out onto the floor from the man's open throat.

'What do you mean?' John asked, having no idea what he was talking about.

It dawned on John...*He's trying to make it look like I escaped and killed that man in the process.*

Decan turned to the man that was still standing there and told him to drive him far away into the middle of nowhere and *kill him.*

Chapter 11

It was early hours in the morning and Abe was wrapped up in a bed bigger than he had ever slept in. It was soft, warm and cosy.

He had been sound asleep for hours in a sleep deeper than he had been in a while. He couldn't remember the last time he had been this comfortable.

Suddenly, there was a loud shrieking siren that echoed through every room, including the one Abe was in.

It took a few seconds, but he was soon awake. His room was dark, and all he could see was a light that was peering under the door from over the other side of the room, and occasional shadows rushing past as the sound of footsteps stomped.

Is it a fire? he thought.

No one had come for him, and he was worried. He hoped that Anna was somewhere near, and she would be able to look after him and tell him what was going on, she was the only other person there that he knew and could trust.

The siren was still screeching, and Anna hadn't come for him, so he jumped out of bed and hurried for the door. There were several of Decan's men running through the hall holding their guns.

The hallway cleared, but then someone else came running down the hall.

It was a little far away to tell who or what it was at first and it was too blurry to make out if it was man or woman, but Abe thought they looked short.

They were walking fairly fast and as they got closer, Abe could see that they were looking left and right as if they were looking for someone.

Finally, they got just far enough away that Abe could make out that it looked like a young boy, and then it got close enough so he could see its face.

It's one of them! Abe thought frantically and started to panic.

They must have gotten through the gates and into the building... that's why the alarm is going off! he thought.

Abe stumbled and fell backwards as he tried to back away and landed on the floor, and the thing that was running towards him got to his feet and Abe closed his eyes in fright and used his arms as a shield over his face, waiting for it to try and bite him.

But then a voice said, 'It's okay, I'm George,' it said, but *George* sounding like it started with a *D*. 'I didn't mean to scare you.'

Abe slowly opened one of his eyes and saw the boy standing over him and its shadow casting over Abe. He peeked through his arms and saw his face.

Now that he was standing in front of him and he spoke to Abe, he could see it wasn't one of *them,* and was just a boy, except he was missing his nose. Instead, he just had two big triangular like holes there flat on his face where his nose would have been.

Abe felt a twist of guilt in his stomach as he realised his mistake. If he had just taken a second to look before running the other way, it would have been obvious it wasn't one of *them.*

George reached out his hand to Abe, 'Here...let me help you,' he said smiling.

Abe took his hand and George pulled him to his feet.

Abe brushed himself off and caught himself staring at him and his face that was missing a nose. Abe still hadn't said anything.

'What's your name?' George asked.

Abe shook his head to shake himself out of the stare, 'Uhm...I'm Abe,' he said, 'I'm sorry I...that I was scared of you. I thought you...'

'Were one of them?' He butted in, finishing the sentence for Abe. 'It's okay, a lot of people here have done the same. At least you didn't run away screaming or throw something at me.'

Abe saw the sad look on his face and felt awful for doing what he did, 'People actually throw things at you?' said Abe.

George nodded, 'Yeah, and a lot of the people here call me names, like *zombie* and freak...Not everybody though, there's one or two that are okay.'

'That's horrible,' said Abe.

George stood there with a sad look on his face, and there was a silence that hung in the air for a while until Abe said, 'It's okay, you can be my friend if you like?'

George smiled, but before he could say anything, they were both interrupted by someone running around the corner and up to the both of them.

'Are you okay?' It was Anna. She was speaking to Abe. While George and he had been talking, he had forgotten about the alarm that was going off.

'Anna, what's going on?' Abe asked.

Anna looked at George and then back at Abe, 'It's nothing too bad, there's no fire or anything, but you better come with me,' she said, and then turned to George. '*George*, what have I told you? You should stay in your room. You're just giving people a chance to pick on you.'

George had a sheepish look on his face, 'I'm sorry Anna', he said, 'I was scared by the alarm. I tried to ask someone what was going on, but nobody would talk to me.'

Anna had a sad frown on her face, 'It's okay George, you have nothing to be scared about. Just go back to bed.'

George looked at Abe and then back at Anna before he said, 'Okay', and then turned around saying, 'Goodbye Abe...It was nice to meet you.'

His voice sounded funny to Abe, because it was so nasally, it sounded like he was swapping a lot of his letters with D's.

Anna gestured for Abe to follow her and said, 'Come with me'.

'Is there something wrong?' He asked, worrying about what could have happened.

Anna was walking in a fast pace down the hall as Abe followed, 'It's your grandpa,' she said. 'He's escaped.'

Anna took Abe to a small medical wing. On the way there he had got to see a lot more of the building that he was in. It was a lot bigger than he had thought. On the way there he asked Anna what the place was, and she told him that it was some kind of government building before, and it had been abandoned when everything happened. It was a good place to use because it had good fences and security measures around the entire building, it even had it's own back-up generators and water pump.

She said that the facilities they had there were incredible, they had their own little doctor's surgery, a couple gyms and a sports hall, they even had a bar, a laundrette with shoeshine, and a hairdresser.

When they were in the medical wing there were mostly empty beds and then Anna walked Abe around a corner through some privacy curtains to see a man in a long white coat, who he assumed was a doctor.

Then he realised who the doctor was attending to. It was *Decan*.

He was sitting on a bed, with his leather jacket to the side of him, and his t-shirt was covered in blood. He had a knife sticking out of his left shoulder.

Abe's eyes widened as he was shocked by what he saw.

'What happened?' Abe asked with a gasp.

Decan looked tired, but pretty well for someone who had obviously just been stabbed in the shoulder.

'It's okay kid, I'll be fine,' he said.

Who's done this? wondered Abe.

Decan told him that his grandpa had escaped, and to do it, he killed one of his men. He told him that he cut the man's throat and took his keys to get out.

Then he explained what happened to him. He said that he had just gotten back from his mission, and he was on the way to speak to John.

'You know to tell him *the plan*' he said with a wink.

He asked Anna to leave them and to take care of things and then he said that when he was on his way to speak to John, is when he caught him in the hall.

He said before he could even try to speak to him that John tried to go for him and cut his throat too, but only got him in the shoulder, and then ran off and escaped.

Abe had a blank look on his face. He was in complete shock.

'He's gone?' Abe asked.

Decan was tired and drained, both from his trip and his wound, 'Yes,' he said, 'I'm sorry Abe...I tried.'

Abe hung his head in sorrow and began to tear up.

He just left me here, he thought, as he began to sniffle to himself.

By now the doctor had removed the knife from Decan's shoulder and placed a square bandage on the wound. He had a look of remorse on his face as he watched Abe cry to himself, and he shuffled down the hospital bed and placed his hand on Abe's shoulder.

'It's ok Abe,' he said as he pulled him in for a hug. 'I'm here for you.'

Abe felt comforted by his support, but he was still distraught. *What has happened to my grandpa?* he thought.

He was gone, and he left him there without a second thought. *Now* Abe was alone and had no family or friends with him.

I can't believe he would do something like this, it doesn't sound like anything he would do... but what other explanation would there be for Decan's shoulder?

Decan passed him a hankie from his pocket and Abe wiped his tears away and then blew his nose.

'Come on,' said Decan. 'I've got a surprise for you.'

Decan took him to the same room he had taken him to before, where he had the waffles.

However, it wasn't just a white room and a sofa this time. It was full of all kinds of things that he loved, and as he looked closer, he realised that it was the *actual* things that he loved.

It was everything from his house that he owned. Every single one of his collectables, action figures and comic books.

There were even some arcade machines that Decan must have gotten from somewhere else and brought there especially for him.

He had all his favourite games, Space invaders, Pac-man, Galaga, Donkey Kong.

Abe was elated. His mouth was half open as he gawked at the things, he thought that he would never see again, things that he cherished so much.

Decan walked in ahead of him and towards the end of the room where there was a massive TV, which had Abe's game console next to it.

'I thought that I would leave your TV there and bring you an even bigger one.'

Abe now had a smile on his face instead of drying tears. It was possibly one of the best surprises he had had yet, but he realised something.

He would probably have to leave them all again, and soon.

'Won't I have to leave it all here...like I did before?' he asked.

Decan frowned, 'Why would you think that?' he asked.

Abe thought it was obvious, 'Well...when we leave to go to the base, won't I have to leave it all here?' Decan smiled and walked over to Abe, 'No, we'll figure something out,' he said with a wink, 'and...we won't be able to go at least for a little while, so you'll have some time to make the most of it.'

Abe knitted his brows in puzzlement, 'What?' he said. 'How come?'

'Because winter has just arrived and it's too dangerous to travel that far. We'll have to wait a while and we'll go then.' Decan explained, 'Plus, we don't have everything we need quite yet to make the journey. It'll give us enough time to gather everything.'

Abe looked to the window on the right-hand side of the room.

He's right, he thought. It was snowing outside, and it was heavy, really heavy, he could barely see out of the window.

Chapter 12

The next morning, Abe woke up clean and fresh. He looked around the room, and before he opened his eyes he had forgotten where he was.

He had never had such a big room to himself before, and as he looked around and admired all of his things and the arcade games, it brought a smile to his face.

It was almost a good enough distraction to make him forget what was lurking outside.

Luckily, he had some pyjamas that he was able to get from the clothing supply they had there.

Anna told him that they had been to several malls on supply runs and taken as much as they could, so he wasn't going to have to worry about not having anything to wear.

It made him think though. *Why were there so many people walking around in tatty clothes?*
He asked Anna and she said that if they want something, they are welcome to it so long as they have something to trade or work for Decan.

Abe asked why he got it for free, and Anna said because he was special and close to Decan. He also had agreed to do something for him, and in return he was allowed to take whatever he needed.

Abe was happy that he didn't have to worry about having to find things to trade for food and clean clothes, *But why can't we just share everything with everyone here that needs it?* he thought.

When he hopped out of bed and looked around the room and realised how empty it was...not of things but of people. It was incredibly quiet.

What do I do now? he thought.

He wasn't used to having nothing he had to do. He usually had school or work or his chores. He decided that he would just play some video games, like he used to do on his weekends.

When he sat down on the sofa and turned on the TV though, he remembered how he used to play with Ash, and it made him feel lonely.

Maybe I can get George to play?

Just after he got changed into some normal clothes and went to head for the door, someone knocked on the door.

'Come in,' said Abe.

It was Anna. She came in and said good morning and asked him what he would like for breakfast.

He took a moment to think, and his mind was completely blank, but then he had an idea.

He thought seeing as he was planning on going to find George anyway, that maybe he could invite him to have breakfast with him and then spend the day playing video games together.

'I was thinking maybe I could spend some time with George,' said Abe. 'Do you know where he is?'

Anna pursed her lips as she thought, 'He should be in the main atrium having breakfast, like everybody else.'

Abe hadn't been there yet and hadn't really had a full tour of the whole place so he figured that this would be a good chance to have a look around.

'Do you think it would be okay if he came here and had breakfast?' he asked.

Anna touched her face as she looked to be pondering over the idea. 'I don't see why not,' she said. 'Do you need me to come with you?'

Abe shook his head, 'No thank you,' he said, 'I should be fine.'

Anna pulled a small radio off her belt and handed it to him. 'Okay, great. Just make sure you call me on this if you need anything,' she said, 'and once your back, let me know what you want, and I'll have it brought up here for you.'

Abe smiled as he took the radio and grabbed a backpack to stash it in.

Maybe I'll take some other things too, he thought, and he grabbed a bunch of candy and some soda and put it in the bag before throwing it over his shoulder.

It took him a little while to find it, he was walking around for almost twenty minutes, and he realised that there were still signs everywhere pointing in the direction of where all the places were.

All the buildings that connected to each other seemed to be named after something, but he didn't know what they were or what they meant.
When he eventually got to the atrium, he was surprised to see how big it was.

He walked through the big double wooden doors with flat metal handles, and he looked up at the high glass ceiling.

All the walls to the left were made of glass, and the to the right he could see every level as it went up.

There were four floors including the ground floor. It reminded him of a shopping mall in the way it looked, and how much glass there was.

There was even an escalator, and what looked like an old cafeteria on the ground level, which he was standing on.

He looked around, and saw that the room was extremely crowded, he had no idea how many people there were. Most of the people in the room were normal people, and the others were the people working for Decan. They were standing on most of the doors holding guns and other weapons. As he looked up at the other levels, he could see some walking around.

As he started to walk through, he saw that there had been row after row of tables set up, with heaps of junk, food and other supplies where there were people trading and selling their goods.

Where did all these people come from? he thought. *Were there this many people left behind?*

Abe walked through the people and the rows of tables, on his way through he noticed one stall in particular that caught his eye.

It was a comic book stand, heaps of them, and books. He wanted to go and look, but he decided it could wait until later.

Abe reached the far end where the cafeteria area went into a kind of little cave where there was a serving station, and a massive queue of people waiting for their breakfast.

As he looked there, he saw that it was nowhere near the level of food he had been eating. It was a huge vat of porridge, and there was a row of people on the other side spooning a small ladle into the people's bowls as they came up to the counter.

Abe looked at every person in the queue, but George was nowhere to be seen. They were all tall adults. In fact, Abe couldn't see any other people near his age.

He walked through until the queue stopped and he was at the tables where people were eating and he couldn't see him on any of the tables that he passed, and he even talked to a few people and asked them if they knew him and if they knew where he was, but they either said no or just grunted at him with a mouth full of food. Then as he asked someone and they gave him nothing but a mean stare, someone opposite him spoke up.

'The ghoul looking kid is over there, where he belongs,' he said, pointing.

Abe gave him a hard look and turned around wondering why they would say such a thing.

Abe walked around the corner where he had been told George was, and they were right. He was sitting in a small corner hidden behind a wall next to a fire exit.

George was sitting on the ground with a small bowl of food that had something sticking out of it.

What's that? Abe thought.

'Hi George,' said Abe.

George was startled and jumped a little, before he turned and saw Abe standing there.

'Hi Abe!' he said with a happy smile on his face. 'How are you?'

Abe smiled back as George stood up off the ground to meet him.

'I'm good, thanks,' Abe responded. 'What are you doing?' Abe asked, pointing to the thing he had put into his porridge.

George turned slightly confused and looked at his bowl and then turned realising what Abe was talking about.

'Oh...it's my birthday,' he said. The thing that was sticking out of his porridge was a little candle.

Abe felt incredibly sad for George, as he sat all alone eating in the corner.

'Happy Birthday,' said Abe with a smile.

George looked like he had been given a gift and his face lit up slightly.

'Thanks,' he said. 'You're the only person here who has said it.'

'Why are you sitting over here on your own?' Abe asked, 'Don't you have anyone here who you can sit with?'

George started to look sad and looked down at the floor, 'No... I tried for a while sitting at the tables, but people made me get away and someone kicked me over here one time and said I was making them feel sick.'

Abe wished he hadn't asked, because it had made his smile disappear and now, he looked sad.

'Don't worry about them,' said Abe, 'They can sit here eating their horrible porridge, you can come with me and have breakfast in my room.'

George's smile returned, 'Really?' he said. 'You can do that?'

Abe smiled back, 'Sure, we can have waffles or maybe pancakes.'

'How?' he asked, with an amazed look.

'I know Decan,' he said. 'He looks after me.'

George looked surprised.

'Really?' He asked.

'Yeah, come on, let's go.'

Abe showed George back to his room, and while they walked, everyone stared and occasionally Abe could hear them whispering and making comments. He couldn't hear what they were saying, but they were probably not nice things. He was just glad that George couldn't hear them properly.

When Abe opened the door and let George in, George's face lit up and his mouth dropped in amazement.

He was particularly impressed with the arcade machines he had there.

'Are these all yours?' George asked.

Abe had a wide grin on his face as he walked over to them, 'Yep, and you can play on them if you like.'

Abe smiled at how happy it seemed to make him. He was even more excited than Abe was when Decan gave it all to him.

George walked over as quick as he could, and started playing the space invaders game, keeping his smile the whole time.

Abe and George played on the arcade games together until their breakfast arrived. They both had a stack of pancakes with maple syrup smothered all over them.

Anna brought them up for them, and when they came in the smell was mouth-watering.

Abe thought that pancakes were a good choice seeing as it was George's birthday.

Anna didn't stay, she just dropped off the pancakes and left them to it.

George ate them like he hadn't eaten in weeks, although by what Abe saw, it might have been close to nothing with the rations of food he had been getting. They both carried on eating their food until the plates were almost clean and George asked Abe a question.

'Is Decan your dad?' he asked.

Abe frowned slightly and thought. *Of course not.* It made sense why he would think that though, as there didn't seem to be many people there that had the same privileges as Abe did.

'No, he's not my dad,' he said.

George frowned and looked a bit confused, probably wondering why he was getting treated by him so well if he wasn't his father.

It made Abe wonder and think about George and where his parents were.

'What about you?' Abe asked. 'Where are your parents?'

George scooped the last bit of pancake into his mouth after mopping up the syrup on the plate with it and put it in his mouth just as Abe asked.

'I don't have any,' he said. 'I was an orphan and I've been alone for as long as I can remember.'

Abe could relate slightly as he didn't have a mom or a dad when he was growing up, but at least he had his grandma and grandpa.

'I'm sorry,' said Abe.

George just smiled at him, 'It's okay,' he said. 'What about you, where are your family?'

Abe was quiet for a minute as he thought about his grandma and grandpa. He felt like it had been ages since he had thought about them.

It made him feel sad when he thought about it, remembering that his grandpa escaped and left him there.

'I don't have a mom or dad either,' he said, 'but I lived with my grandparents and when everything broke out, my grandma was evacuated, but my grandpa stayed behind for me.'

George watched Abe's face slowly turn sad as he explained.

'What happened to your grandpa?' he asked.

'He left me here,' said Abe.

'Why did he leave you here?' George asked, confused.

Abe looked sad, 'I don't know', he said.

'Was he not very nice?' he asked.

Abe took a moment thinking how ridiculous that question was, *no I thought he was the best grandpa ever,* he thought.

'No, he was really nice. He was like my dad. He did everything for me.'

George was even more confused now. *That doesn't make any sense,* he thought.

'Are you sure he left?' he asked, 'Who told you that he did?'

Abe was looking at the ground as he thought.

'Decan did,' he said.

George didn't respond but looked over at Abe.

Abe started to question things. *Did he run away?* he thought. *He must have, why would Decan lie, and how else did the guard get killed and who stabbed Decan in the shoulder? Where could he be if he didn't escape and run away?*

Abe had been silent for a while and was lost in thought, before George put his hand on his shoulder and shook him softly.

'Abe, are you okay?' he asked.

Abe blinked his eyes fast a few times like he was shaking himself out of a dream and then looked at George.

'Yeah...thanks.'

Abe and George were playing video games together as they sat on the sofa, and had been for hours, but they were having so much fun that they hadn't realised how long they had been there at all.

George at that time was one of the happiest he had been in as long as he could remember. *This is the best birthday I've ever had,* he thought.

'You're so lucky to have all this cool stuff in your room,' said George. 'I wish I could play games in my room; I have to spend pretty much all of my time in there and it gets really boring. It makes me miss my old home and I thought I would never say that. At least I had books there to read.'

That gave Abe an idea, he had the perfect gift for him. He stood up off the sofa and ran over to the corner of the room where there was a load of his boxes, and he went rifling through one as George watched from where he was sitting.

Abe found what he was looking for and told George to close his eyes. George covered his eyes with his hands, excited, and wondered what it was.

Then Abe said that he could open them, and he was holding out a present in his hand for him. It was Abe's old Gameboy.

George was amazed by what Abe had given him, 'Thank you,' he said, holding it like it was treasure. 'And it's my favourite colour, *Purple!*'

Chapter 13

Abe was in the atrium looking at the stall where he had seen the comics being sold the day before.

He was trying to see if there were any good finds, like a first issue, but he didn't find anything quite like that.

He did, however, find a few special editions that he wanted, but he soon realised that he didn't have much to trade with.

He asked the small man wearing a dark green top and big grey trench coat how much they were, and he looked at him funny.

Why is he looking at me like that, thought Abe. It sort of looked like he was mad at him for asking, which didn't make any sense. Surely, he wanted to sell them.

'No charge,' he said, in a gruff voice.

Abe turned his face in puzzlement. *No charge?* he thought.

'Excuse me, did you say...no charge?' Abe asked him.

The man snapped, 'Yes...yes, that's what I said, now please don't take anything else, this is all I have.'

Abe was even more puzzled now; he was speaking to him like he was holding him up at gun point. Abe walked away and put the two comics in his backpack with his candy and soda, before he walked off to find George.

Abe hadn't been to George's room yet, and he didn't know where it was, so he had to spend some time looking for it.

304a, is what George had told him. Abe soon realised that it was on level three and section 04 that he was in.

The section where he was headed looking for George was quite dark and dingey. It looked like there were windows on both the left- and right-hand walls all along, but now there were boxes taped all over them, Abe assumed to block out the light so people could sleep. It made it harder to see how cramped and unwelcoming the place was.

There were people's sleeping bags and cots laid out all over the floor. There were little camping lanterns on the floor and dirty food containers left lying around. There were people sitting around smoking and drinking out of cups and bottles staring at him as he walked past, most of which looked mean and unfriendly.

There were some that didn't look that bad though, there was a woman that was hanging up some clothes on a piece of string she was tying between some windows. She smiled at him, which made Abe feel a little better.

Abe kind of hoped that he was in the wrong place and that George wasn't there. He had no idea he was living somewhere so horrible, it made him feel bad for all the space and nice things that he had in his room.

Abe got to the end of the long stretch and came to a dark corner where there looked to be a little kitchen that was used by the staff at one time, and he hadn't seen George.

Phew, he thought, *maybe he's somewhere much nicer than this,* and then he heard someone call out his name.

He recognised George's voice easily, but he couldn't see him.

Then he heard the squeak of a door hinge and he turned around, he was standing in the doorway of a small utility closet.

'George?' Abe said. 'What are you doing in there?'

George called him over and showed him the inside. It wasn't too small and seemed almost cosy.

'It's my room,' he said.

'Do they make you stay in here?' Asked Abe.

George shrugged his shoulder, 'Yes and no,' he said. 'I like it, it's closed off from everyone else and it's nice and quiet. It's also easier to keep warm, and I have my own little sink,' he said pointing.

George switched on a light, so it illuminated the small square room with the sink on the far wall ahead. There was a box in the middle of the room, with fabric coming out of it.

Abe felt a little sad for him, 'Is that your bed?' he asked.

George had a smile and said, 'Yeah, but it's not as bad as it looks, It's really comfy. Plus, look at this.' George opened the flaps on the box so Abe could climb inside.

He's right, it is cosy, thought Abe. There were two small pillows at the end and a couple of blankets on the floor that were nice and soft.

George told him to lie down and look at the roof of the box.

Abe led on his back and looked up, there were holes in the top and the light was coming through.

'See, it kinda looks like the stars,' he said.

Abe climbed out and wanted to say something reassuring, but George really didn't seem to mind it and had a big smile on his face.

It made Abe think how lucky he had been and how he took things, even now for granted. He thought that if he were in his situation, that he wouldn't probably be able to smile.

'You wanna come to my place and play some video games?' Abe asked him.

'Sure,' said George. 'That would be great.'

On the way there, Abe decided to tell him what happened in the atrium when he was trying to buy the comics. He wanted to know if George had seen anything like that happen before and why the man reacted the way that he did.

George told him that he didn't know and that he had seen something slightly similar happen when the guards that work for Decan go through there looking for stuff.

George said that they take what they want from the stalls and don't have to pay, and the traders rarely argue. If they do, they get a beating or worse.

Abe frowned and thought how horrible it was.

'Does no one ever complain? Surely, he doesn't know this is going on, why would he let this happen to the good people?' Abe asked.

George looked at Abe with a questioning look, 'I'm sure he does know, a lot of the time the guards take stuff for him and to him as well,' he said.

Abe stopped and looked back at George, 'Really?'

'Yeah, I've seen him walk through and take things as well, not as often as his guards but a few times.'

That doesn't make any sense, why would he do that? Abe thought.

'Have you ever spoken to him?' Asked Abe.

George kinda went a little pale and shook his head.

He looked scared, thought Abe.

'No...I always hide when I see him coming, I'm afraid of what he might do if he sees my face.'

They started walking again and Abe had a lot of questions running through his head.

'Decan is always really nice to me,' said Abe.

George didn't answer and they carried on walking until they got to his room.

On the way there, Abe had a lot of questions running through his mind. He decided he would try and visit Decan later to get some answers. He needed to find out what was going on.

Abe and George spent a few hours playing video games, but Abe kept thinking about what had happened earlier and what George had said. He had loads of question he wanted answering and it was bugging him.

Abe told George that he was going to go and find Decan and talk to him.

George looked at him like he was joking, but he wasn't.

'Okay,' he said. 'Thanks for having me over, I'll go back to my room.'

The sight of the place where George was living flashed into Abe's head.

'No, it's fine,' said Abe. 'You can stay here.'

George had a doubtful frown as he fumbled his hands nervously.

'Are you sure?' he asked. 'What if somebody comes?'

Abe shook his head. 'It's fine, nobody ever comes here. The only person that does is Anna, and she knows we're friends.'

George smiled, 'Okay...thanks Abe.'

George watched Abe walk off out of the room and he sat back down in front of the TV.

The game they had been playing was paused, so he decided he would wait for Abe to come back so he didn't miss any of it.

Abe walked up to the highest floor in the main building where Decan's office was supposed to be.

That level was really big and there was nobody allowed up there unless Decan specifically allowed it. Not even all of the guards were allowed there.

When Abe got to the elevator, he thought that he was going to have to explain who he was and who he wanted to see, but he didn't. The guards just opened the elevator, pressed the button and allowed him up there with no questions.

One of the guards even spoke into his radio and said, *He's on his way up.*

Abe thought it was strange, *but I guess it's good that they know I'm friends with him.*

That made him realise something. *That's why that man at the stall let me take what I wanted for free, without taking anything from me. It was because I'm friends with Decan, and they think I work for him.*

The thought of it made Abe feel kind of bad - like he was a criminal, like a lot of the people that were working for Decan.

Abe shook his head and muttered to himself, '*No,* I'm a good person. It's different.'

Abe walked into Decan's office. The guards that were waiting on the door opened them for him. They both were holding big guns in their hands, and each had a small handgun clipped to their belts.

When Abe walked in, he saw how big the room was. It was even bigger than his, which wasn't really a surprise, since Decan was in charge of the place.

It was square like his, except there were shelves all along the left and right wall with books and files on them. There were a few sofas and big fridges, a TV and even a tabletop oven on one of the counters.

The room smelled of cigar smoke, and someone must have been smoking one recently because the air in the room still had clouds of blue smoke hovering.

Abe could see Decan standing in the middle of the room in front of a big table where he was rolling up and folding loads of different pieces of paper. He was doing it quite quickly, like he didn't want anyone to see what was on there, or at least Abe.

'How're you doin'?' Decan asked without turning around. He knew it was Abe.

'I'm fine,' said Abe.

Decan pushed all the rolls of paper and half folded sheets and carried them over to his big wooden desk and locked them away in a draw as he looked at Abe still standing near the door.

'Come in,' he said, waving his hand towards himself.

Abe walked over in a leisurely pace, looking around at the room, trying to get a good look at the books and files that were on the shelves, trying to see if he could read them without making it obvious that he was trying to.

'I'm sorry I haven't been down to see you,' said Decan. 'It's been busy trying to prepare everything ready for the long journey.'

Abe turned his attention to Decan away from the shelves when he spoke to him.

Decan walked over to one of the sofas in the room which was big and dark brown leather.

'Anna said that you are happy though.'

Abe sat down on the sofa beside Decan before he answered and then let out a subtle smile.

'Yeah, everything is good,' he said.

Decan smiled. 'Good.'

Before Decan could say anything else, Abe jumped in, 'I had a couple of questions,' he said. 'I hope that's okay.'

Decan sat back in the sofa, 'Of course,' he said. 'What's up?'

Abe felt nervous, 'I was in the atrium earlier looking at the stalls and there were some things that I wanted, and when I tried to ask the man how much they were, the man just yelled at me and told me to take them,' said Abe. 'Do you know why?'

Decan frowned and said, 'Well...you're my special guest here, if there is something you want, you get it.'

Abe's worry was right, he did just give him the comics because he was forced to and was afraid. Abe felt terrible.

'Well...can't I just pay him anyway, I already have loads of nice things, it wouldn't hurt to let me pay.'
Decan leant forward and let out a little laugh through his nose, 'You're a good kid,' he said. 'I've never had someone complain about getting stuff for free before.'

'So...can I just pay him?' Abe asked. 'I feel bad after what he said.'

'Sure, but don't worry about that guy, I'll see that he is taken care of.'

Abe smiled and said, 'Thanks.'

Decan placed his hand down on his knees and said, 'Was that it?'

Abe took a minute to think, now that he was there, the plethora of questions he had had seemed to all disappear.

'No actually, there was a few more,' he said. 'Now that my grandpa is gone, what's the plan?'

Decan smiled as he sat up off the sofa, 'I'm glad you asked.'

He walked back over to his desk and opened the drawer he had just been in and ruffled through all the papers he put in there and pulled just one of them out.

'Come over here,' he said.

Abe walked over to the big table, he saw once he was close enough that it had a big map over it, built into the table.

It reminded him of one he had seen in an old war movie with his grandpa, and they used it to plan their attacks and movements.

The questions about his grandpa came flooding back, but he didn't know how he would ask Decan.

Abe didn't think that it made sense that his grandpa would escape and leave him there, especially if he had to kill or hurt people to do it. *He wouldn't even kill those monstrous things that were trying to eat us,* thought Abe. *He wouldn't even kill the fish they caught on fishing trips; he always threw them back.*

Decan unfolded the piece of paper and showed it to Abe. It was a satellite picture looking down, but it was just a picture of the desert, and a small building.

'What's that?' Abe asked.

Decan pointed at it with his finger, '*That is* where we're headed,' he said.

Abe knitted his eyebrows in bewilderment, 'That's it?' he asked. 'But that's so small, there's barely enough room for a street of people.'

Abe was really worried now, *what's going on?* he thought.

Decan laughed in amusement and said, 'Not exactly. They're tricky you see, it may look like that is all that there is, but there is far more.'

'What do you mean?' Abe asked.

Decans smile of amusement continued as he explained, 'The building you see there isn't just a building, it holds the entrance to a bunker. A bunker that is underground. It's designed so that it will keep everybody safe no matter what kind of disaster hits the world, though it's primary design was in case of a nuclear war.'

Abe looked at it and was a little dubious, 'And this bunker is big enough to hold everyone?' Abe asked, picturing the small bunkers he had seen in movies.
He had no idea the kind of facilities and capacity this thing had.

Decan said that it was bigger than he could imagine and that it had everything that they needed. It had clean and recyclable water, they had the facility to plant and grow food, and they had an air filtration system meaning that they could all breath clean air, far away from the thing that had taken hold of the infected, far beneath the ground.

It all sounds a bit too good to be true, thought Abe.

Abe noticed that there was what looked like co-ordinates written in the top left corner, and then there was a scrap piece of paper just a few inches away from where Decan had the satellite picture, and there were ten or more other co-ordinates written down.

Abe went to grab it and said, 'What's this?'

But before he got close, Decan grabbed it in a hurry and crumpled it before shoving it into his pocket.

'Oh...that's nothing, don't worry about it,' he said.

Abe felt like that wasn't true, *why did he panic so much? It was just a piece of paper*, he thought.
There was a silence that awkwardly hung in the air.

Decan looked at the clock that was on the wall above one of the set of shelves, 'It's just about lunch, why don't you run along and get something to eat?' he said. 'I'll have Anna bring you something.'

Abe wasn't really ready to go, he had a lot more questions to ask, but he felt like he should, as Decan was pushing him to.

'Ok, thanks,' said Abe.

On the way back to his room he was kicking himself, thinking that he should have pushed more to find out about his grandpa.

Maybe Anna would know? he thought.

Abe didn't know where Anna stayed, but he still had the radio that she had given him, so he called to her on it to ask her to meet with him, and she came back quickly, telling him where to go.

Abe felt a little more at ease around Anna, like he could just about ask her anything without worrying. Abe asked her about the night his grandpa escaped, and if she knew anything about it, but she was quick to tell him no.

She said that she was in Decan's office that night working on something while he was out. She only knew what she had been told by him.

'Why do you ask?' asked Anna.

Disappointed, Abe said, 'I just think that it doesn't make sense that my grandpa would leave me here. How could he do that?'

Anna had a sympathetic look on her face as she sat down next to Abe and placed her arm around him.

'Sometimes people aren't who we think they are.'

They were both quiet for a bit before Anna asked, 'Who else have you talked to about this?'

'No one but you really,' he said.

'Then why suddenly all the questions?'

'I was talking to George about my life before, with my grandparents, and I mentioned that my grandpa left me here. He asked if my grandpa wasn't a very nice person, but he was the opposite.' Abe explained. 'So George said that doesn't make any sense...and he's right. I don't think that he would.'

Abe glanced up and saw Anna looking at him with a still face, but when she noticed him looking, she quickly turned a smile back on.

'Why don't you run along back to your room and I'll bring your food up for you in a minute,' she said. 'And try not to think about that, play some video games to take your mind off it.'

Abe felt like he was being ignored, maybe he shouldn't have bothered asking at all. No one else seemed to agree with him, except for George.

Chapter 14

When Abe got back to his room, he saw George there and he was pacing back and forward in the room looking worried.

George had his back to the door when Abe walked in and didn't notice him until the door creaked shut behind him.

'*Abe!*' he exclaimed. 'You're okay.'

Abe frowned and said, 'Of course I'm okay.'

Abe was confused. George had been fine when he left, but now he looked panicked, like something had happened.

'What's wrong?' Abe asked.

George gestured for him to come and sit down on the sofa as he lowered his voice and started to whisper.

'When you left, I waited here for a little while and then I remembered what you said about that man in the atrium, and that you felt bad about him not getting paid,' he said. 'So, I had an idea. I took the candy and sodas that you gave me and took them down to the atrium to give the man as payment.

Abe smiled, it was an incredibly kind thing to do, especially, considering George probably had less than the man did.

'So, what's the problem?' Abe asked.

'When I went down, I went searching for the stall, and as I got close, I saw the man being dragged away and he was being beaten,' said George.

Abe was shocked, '*What?* Really?' he said, his voice full of concern. 'By who?'

George paused, like he was struggling to say their name. 'Decan,' he said, 'I saw him and some of his men dragging him out somewhere.'

Abe was both confused and worried. *That doesn't make any sense, I was with him for a while,* he thought.

'When did you see it?' asked Abe.

'Not that long before you came in,' said George. 'I was worried that he might have hurt you.'

Hmm...I guess that he could have gone there after I left and went to see Anna, thought Abe, *but why would he do that?*

Abe asked George if he heard them say anything about why they were doing it to that man, but he said that he couldn't hear anything and that he was too far away.

'What did you say to Decan?' George asked.

Abe took a moment to think. 'Not much really. I just told him what happened, that I had tried to buy some stuff and the man got mad and yelled at me and said to take them for nothing.'

All of a sudden, it hit him. 'It's my fault. Decan thinks that he was rude to me and that he yelled at me,' said Abe.

'No Abe don't think like that. You never meant for this to happen,' George replied comfortingly.

Abe still felt bad. *What if they kill him?* he thought.

Suddenly, the door opened, without being knocked. It was Decan. He had a big flat tray on one hand, that he was holding in the air.

Both Abe and George were quietly panicking, they weren't expecting him to come in. Anna was the one who usually brought the food.

Decan placed the big tray he had in his hand down on the table. It was a big pizza.

'Hey boys, I thought that I would pop up and bring lunch for you.'

George was trying to hide his face from Decan.

Decan looked at Abe, 'I'm sorry our chat was a bit short earlier bud, I felt bad, so I thought I'd bring you an extra special lunch. There's some stuff I gotta do off base tomorrow, but we can catch up after and talk, how about that?'

Abe looked at the pizza and then back up at Decan, he was being just as friendly as he was earlier and even was smiling. It was as though nothing had happened.

Decan looked at George acting shy and turning to one side with a hood over his head, 'This is your friend, George huh?'

Abe just nodded quietly.

Decan smirked, '*Well,* hope you kids have fun and enjoy the pizza, I'll see you later,' he said winking as he walked out the door.

Abe placed his hand on George's shoulder after he walked out.

'Are you okay?'

George nodded as he lowered his hood, 'Yeah,' he replied in a strange tone.

'What's wrong?' Abe asked.

George was staring suspiciously at the door where Decan had left. 'It's just that, I've never seen him act that way before.'

Abe looked at the door and then back at George with a puzzled look, 'What do you mean?' he asked.

'The few times that I have seen him he always acts arrogant, mean and just generally seems different and more threatening,' said George.

'So...do you think that maybe he's just pretending?' Abe asked. *It could all be an act.*

George looked at Abe with an apprehensive look and nodded. 'Yeah, I think he must be,' he said.

Abe looked down as he thought about it and then said, 'But which one do you think is real?'

It had become clear to Abe now that he didn't know everything and he had to get some real answers, but he had no idea how. They couldn't make it look like they were on to something; they had to just play along like everything was normal.

That night Abe tried to convince George to stay with him in his nice big room. He did, after all, have plenty of space, and that way George wouldn't have to go back to that dark and dirty place he had been staying. However, George said he should just continue to stay there, so as not to draw any attention.

George said that they would meet like they had been the next morning and figure something out.

Abe agreed that it was a good idea.

The next morning, Abe woke up earlier than he had in a long time, and he wanted to go and find George right away but thought that that would look suspicious. So instead, he decided to just sit there.

Abe thought that he could play some games to pass the time, but he was too anxious, *and someone might hear them and know that I'm awake*, he thought.

Suddenly, Abe felt like he was being watched, and he knew that there was nobody else in the room, but he looked around left and right looking for any prying eyes.

He even looked in each corner of the room, just in case there were cameras that he hadn't noticed, but there were none he could see.

The next few hours were painfully slow. Every time he thought it had been an hour, it had only been ten minutes.

Finally, it was time to go, so he hopped out of bed, already dressed and shot off in a hurry to head to George's. It was quite a walk and was going to take at least fifteen minutes to navigate through all the floors and people.

He tried no to walk too fast, so he didn't get noticed by any of the guards, but when he got close to the end of the long walkway that led to where George's room was, he started to power walk until he was at the door of the room.

Abe knocked on the door and opened it slowly calling out quietly, *'George.'*

There was no response, Abe quickly turned on the light and his box was missing, and so was everything else. The room had been cleaned out and George was *gone.*

Chapter 15

Abe could hear a sound like a loud beating drum. It was his heart thumping in his chest as he paced around the small utility closet that had been George's room.

The room was cold, but he felt hot, and his forehead was wet from sweat.

Where is George? he thought, panicking and thinking about the worst-case scenario.

He looked around the room helplessly for clues, but there were none, his box was gone and everything else with it. There was no trace of him.

Abe started to tear up. *What if they've killed him?* he thought. *Who took him? Is this my fault?*

Everything around him had been silenced by his increasingly worrying thoughts.

He didn't know what to do now, he needed George, and he was realising now how *much* he needed him. He was his only friend.

Abe shook himself to try and bring himself to sense and calm his heavy breathing.

I need to find out what's happened, he thought.

He quickly walked out of the room looking for people nearby to try and figure out who he could get information from.

I have to be careful who I ask.

He walked a few paces away looking around for someone to help, but he was met by many unfriendly faces. Then he heard a soft voice humming.

It was the lady he had seen before that smiled at him when she was hanging up clothes. He saw her again pegging material up on the line and hurried over to her.

Abe hadn't realised, but he must have looked like he was in distress because when the woman saw him, she immediately asked if he was okay, with a genuine look of concern on her face.

'I'm looking for my friend,' he said. 'Have you seen him?'

She looked around with her eyes in a way that suggested she was checking for prying ears and eyes. She didn't answer him right away, instead pouring something out of a grey metal kettle on a camping stove and telling him to sit down.

'Here,' she said. 'Have a cup of this. It'll make you feel better.'

Abe was in a bit of a hurry, but he sat down and listened.

She sat down in front of him after pouring them both a cup of the hot tea and started to whisper to him.

'Who is it that you're looking for?' she asked. Abe had to take a big gulp to hold back his tears before he could answer.

'It's my friend George, I think he's been taken.' The woman sat up straight with a look of sympathy.

'I know that little boy,' she said. 'He was sweet.'

'Have you seen him?' Abe asked, stammering.

'I saw him early this morning, the people that dragged him away woke me when they made the racket that they did.'

Abe's stomach felt like there was a bowling ball inside of it and it had just dropped to the bottom.

'Did they hurt him? Do you know where he is gone?' Abe asked, his voice getting louder as he grew more concerned.

The woman shushed him softly. 'Keep your voice down,' she said, 'I don't know where they have taken him, but I did see them drag him away, and I heard him try to fight them, but by the time they left I think he was unconscious.'

Abe's tears started to fill up his eyes, worrying that he wasn't just unconscious. *What if they just killed him?*

The woman took a tissue from her pocket and helped him to dry his tears from his face as if she were his mother.

'I know you're upset, but if I were you, I wouldn't go searching for your friend. It's too dangerous,' she said.

Abe took a sip of his tea as he stared at the air.

'Have they done this to someone here before? Do they ever come back?' he asked.

The woman paused and looked like she was trying to think of something comforting to say rather than the truth.

'They have,' she said. 'And I'm sorry, but I have never seen anyone come back.'

Abe's tears started to trickle from his eyes as he cried into his cup.

Why does everyone I love and care about go away or die? he thought.

First Grandma, then Bud, then his grandpa and now George.

What do I do? he asked himself.

Then there was an abrupt static noise coming from Abe's radio. It was Anna calling through.

'Abe...can you hear me? Where are you?' she asked.

The woman passed Abe a tissue and closed it in his hand and said, '*Go,* pretend everything is fine. Just do what they ask, and it'll all be better in the end.'

Abe heard what she said, but he didn't want to. He wanted to find out where his grandpa was *and* George. He felt like he had been so stupid to trust these people.

The woman helped him up and guided him away from her small living space and told him to run along. Abe picked up the radio and held it to his face to talk back to Anna, but he took a second to try and steady his voice.

'I'm just heading back to my room,' he said.

Anna took a while to come back and there was crackling for about twenty seconds, 'Okay, I'll meet you there,' she said.

Abe's stomach knotted with anxiety. *Are they coming for me now too?* he thought.

He was breathing heavily again as he walked slowly not knowing what to do. Should he hide? Should he run away and try and escape? Or should he go and see her and do what the lady said - pretend everything is fine and see what they want from him?

Does Decan definitely have a part to play in this? He thought, *and did he have something to do with George's disappearance?*

Abe was struggling to decide what to do and who to trust, but he had to get answers somehow, and he decided the only way was to go back acting normal and try and talk to Anna or maybe even *Decan.*

When he got back to his room Anna was waiting for him outside.

'There you are,' she said. 'What took you so long?'

Abe forced out an innocent smile, 'I just went on a little walk around, trying to stretch my legs,' he said. Abe wondered if he sounded suspicious. He was always most comfortable in his own space left alone with his things, and Anna knew that.

'It's about George,' she said.

Abe's stomach became even more tangled in nerves, and he felt himself becoming flustered and frightened.

He could see Anna's expression change like she knew something was wrong with him.

Does she know that he knows?

'What about him?' he asked, his voice stammering with unease.

Anna placed her hands on her sides in a relaxed stance and said, 'We better go inside and sit down.'

Abe took a big gulp to try and contain his nervousness as he followed her in behind.

Oh no, she's going to tell me that he's dead, he thought, struggling to keep his face neutral.

Anna sat down on the sofa and looked at him with a gentle look. 'I don't know how's the best to tell you, but...'

Abe started to sweat and tried to shake his top to cool himself down.

'George has had to be locked up,' said Anna, 'he was caught stealing, and his room was searched, it looked as if he had been doing it for a while.'

Abe taut his eyebrows in confusion, thinking, *That's a lie!*

Abe knew better than anyone else, he had seen his room and its entirety, there was nothing there that he could have stolen.

'What?' he said. 'That can't be true.'
Anna tried to comfort him by placing her hand on his shoulder.

'I know he was your friend Abe, but the evidence was found. We had no choice,' she said. 'The punishment could have been a lot worse.'

Abe was looking around frantically, 'Well...what happens now?' he asked.

Anna pushed her lips together into a hard line and said, 'I'm sorry, but I couldn't say.'

Abe watched her as she stood up and walked out of the room without looking back at him. He was left sitting there worried and having no idea what he could do.

Maybe I could speak to Decan? Maybe I could try and work something out? He thought.

Abe quickly jumped up and ran after Anna, opening his door and bolting after her.

'*Anna,*' he yelled.
Anna turned around and saw him running after her.

'What is it?' she said.

Abe took a few seconds with his hands on his knees as he panted and tried to catch his breath.

'Where is Decan?' he asked. 'I need to speak to him.'

Anna had a look of uncertainty on her face, 'He's not here,' she said. 'I don't think that speaking to him will help.'

Abe looked at her almost desperate and said, 'Please, can I just talk to him?'

Anna looked at him for a couple seconds as she thought about it.

'Okay, but you'll have to talk to him on the radio...but not the one I gave you, it won't reach him. You'll have to use one of the main ones.'

Abe had a slight smile of relief, 'Thank you,' he said.

Anna smiled back at him and placed her hand on his back to guide him. 'Come on, we'll go there now,' she said.

Anna took Abe to one of the security offices up on the third floor near the atrium.

The room was quite small and had a table in it with drawers and filing cabinets behind it. There were no windows, and a lot of TVs with pictures of where the cameras were looking.

The radio was in the middle of the desk, next to a piece of paper on the wall that was advising of what all the buttons did in the office, like the water pump, the air vents, and the alarms.

Anna showed him to the door and passed him her keys, saying, 'It's a little cramped in there, so I'll just wait out here.'

Abe thought that it was a little weird that she was trusting him with her keys and being in there alone, but he soon saw that she would probably be able to hear everything anyway and would know if he tried to do something he shouldn't.

Abe sat down on the small metal chair that was under the desk and clicked the little knob on the radio to "on".

He picked up the mouthpiece and pressed the button to call out to Decan. The channel was already set to the correct one and all he had to do was speak. A few minutes passed and there was only static.

Anna called through the door and said, 'Just wait a little longer and call out again, he'll answer sooner or later.'

Abe nodded even though she couldn't see him and waited for him to come back.

He looked around in the room while he waited, looking at the screens that were showing the different areas of the base. Then he saw a little cabinet beside the desk, it had a sign on it saying *Keys.*

He looked around making sure that there wasn't a camera, and that Anna wasn't peeking through the door as it was still open ajar. *No*, he was alone.

Quietly and gently, he pulled Anna's keys down towards it, trying not to jangle them as he put one in the lock. Just as he did, the radio blasted out and made him jump and dropped the keys letting out a loud clang as they hit the floor.

Oh no...what if Anna heard that, he thought.

Decan was calling out on the radio, '*Abe...is that you?*'

Abe waited a few seconds and edged back and forward between radio and the keys, trying to decide which to go to first. Anna hadn't come in so she must not have heard the keys fall.

'Yeah, it's me,' he said.

Decan took another few seconds to respond, 'What's up kid?'

Abe pressed the button on the mouthpiece but all that came out was a squeaky noise from his throat as he was trying to force out his words.

He let go of the button and then Decan said, 'Is it about George?'

'Yes.'

Decan came back just a second after, 'Look kid I'm sorry. I know you were friends, but I didn't just choose this, I have to treat him the same as I would anyone else for stealing.'

Abe pressed the button down hard quickly after he had spoken with an angry frown, 'He didn't do it, I *know* him. I know he didn't,' said Abe.

There was just static for a little while, as Abe panted in frustration and his face had gone a little red while he frowned.

'Okay, well if that's what you think, we can talk about it when I get back,' he said. 'Just try and relax and chill in your room until I get there...okay?'

Abe was really mad at all of it and he had reservations about Decan now after everything had happened but at this moment Abe thought he was being relatively reasonable.

But I can't let that trick me... Not until I know which side of him is real.

It had been some time before Abe had responded and he was staring at the ground with his arms crossed when he saw the keys lying there. He had almost forgotten them. He quickly picked them up softly, and as he did Decan called through again.

'You still there?'

Abe was quickly testing a bunch of the keys and then he noticed that one of them said, *p39,* and it matched up with a label on the locker.

He opened it as he spoke through to Decan, 'Yeah, sorry...I'm here.'

Decan came back straight away, 'Okay good, just take it easy and play some games, I'll be back in the morning.'

While Decan was talking, Abe was able to see what was inside this little cabinet, there were lots and lots of different keys on hooks.

However, in the back there was a big set on a ring that had even more than the ones that belonged to Anna. He quickly grabbed them, holding the keys still with his hand so they didn't jangle, and he pushed them into his left pocket.

He jumped back up and spoke back to Decan, saying, 'Okay, will do. I'll see you when you get back.'

Abe quickly closed the little cabinet and locked it as he shut off the radio with a click and walked out with a slight grin.

Finally, I'm getting somewhere, He thought. *Maybe I could use these to find some answers or free George.*

Anna was still standing there with a smile as she saw him walk out seeing that he looked happier than he went in and tussled his hair with her hand.

'There we go,' she said, 'did that help?'

Abe smiled back at her and said, 'Yeah, thanks.'

Now all I need to do is try and get into Decan's office while he is away and try and find out what is going on. There must be something on those papers he was hiding...

Chapter 16

Abe was in his room sitting on the floor in front of his TV, playing the game that he knew that would take the least amount of concentration, so he could think about the matter at hand.

I need to try and be quick as possible, he thought, *at least I know where George is because I've been in one of those cells.*

He remembered how horrible they were and now he just felt embarrassed that he could have thought someone who locked him in there was nice and trustworthy.

It was clear to him now that he needed to find George and escape...but how was he going to do it without help or without hurting somebody?

The first thing he was going to have to do was sneak into Decan's office. On one hand nobody else really lived on that floor so he was less likely to be seen, but it was high up and further away from an escape, and there were a load of guards there last time.

Maybe if I go when it's late, there won't be any guards? he thought.

Then he had an idea. He remembered that in the security office there was a screen that told you where the fire was if there was an alarm.

If I set it off somehow then the guards should be distracted, he thought, *but I can't just start a fire. People could get hurt.*

Suddenly, something clicked in his head and he ran over to a bag of his things and started to hunt through, pulling something out.

It was a small metal aerosol can. *If I spray this somewhere then it should set off the alarm*, he thought.

It was the best idea that he had that was unlikely to arouse suspicion. It could just be looked at somebody being careless.

That was it, he had a plan, *I have to do it later tonight when it's dark,* he thought. *Now I just have to wait.*

The sun crept away slowly as Abe watched it set. Nightfall couldn't have come quicker. It was time for Abe to sneak out and try put his plan into place. While he was waiting for the sun to set, he couldn't help but think about George and how he must be feeling. He was all alone there and probably scared. He wanted so badly to go there and tell him that everything was going to be okay, but he couldn't yet. He had to follow the plan.

He sneaked out of his room quietly and looked down each end of the hall, left and right looking for any guards or even Anna.

Anna had always been nice to him and done things for him to make sure he was happy, but he couldn't risk seeing her and getting caught.

Abe decided to wear a hoodie so he could hide his face and put on some boots that had slight heels on them to try and make himself look taller, thinking, *people might not recognise me.*

He made quick work of getting somewhere to set off the alarm with the aerosol. He made sure that there was nobody around the surrounding room and that it was on the lowest level, far from where he was heading.

Hopefully it would give him enough time to get to where he needed to be and get out.

The room was an old shower room, the perfect choice and easily excusable for it being an accident. Abe sprayed the aerosol near the alarm...and it didn't go off.

Oh no, is the alarm broken?

He was about to think about plan B when suddenly the alarm blurted out, screeching loudly and tearing at his ears. It was louder than he expected, and he covered his ears with his hands to try and drown out the horrid sound as he made a run for it through the door and towards the stairs, he hoped that the guards would be taking the elevator.

He got all the way to the top floor without seeing a single soul and when he peeked out of the door of the stairs, he could see that there was no one guarding the room either.

Finally, Abe was having some good luck.

The alarm was still screeching, and Abe was wishing that there was another way because the alarm was affecting his concentration.

He walked up to Decan's office door. It was unlocked.

A good start, he thought.

He carefully closed the doors behind him. The room was empty, and it was lucky that it was because he stupidly forgot to look through the keyhole first before going in. He quietly cursed himself for being so stupid.

I have to be quick, he told himself.

He rushed over to the desk and saw the drawer; he knew exactly which one it was, he had been picturing it in his head for the last few hours.

There must have been over fifty keys on the set he had picked up, and he knew he may not have much time to figure out which was the right one.

Do I just break it open? he thought. *No, that's a bad idea, if Decan comes back, he'll know that someone has been in here.*

Abe tried key after key and after five minutes he still hadn't found the right one. His hands started to get clammy and making it harder to grab the individual keys and push them into the lock.

Then the alarm stopped and so did his breathing as he let out a little *eek* in panic. He heard the clicking of footsteps outside and a muffled voice.

His heart was getting faster by the second as he looked around not knowing what to do. He looked left and right, hoping there was another exit, but there was none.

The door swung open and in came Decan. He had a fat cigar in his mouth and the plume of smoke that came from it floated up and into the air above him as he walked into his office.

Abe had jumped under the desk to hide before he had come in.

Decan was mumbling to himself as he walked around the office and then shouted at someone, Abe couldn't tell if they were in there or outside.

'Find out who it was that set off that damn alarm and beat them so hard that they piss themselves.'

Abe was sweating profusely now. *What if he catches me?* he thought.

Hearing what Decan had just said, gave him the answer he needed about who Decan really was. He had just been playing him the whole time.

He had no idea where Decan was in the office, but he was far away in the room somewhere and he could hear him talking. Abe wasn't sure but as he listened it sounded like he was talking to himself.

It was too quiet and difficult to figure out what he was saying. *Maybe he's just practising some kind of lame excuse for locking up George,* thought Abe.

Abe kneeled down so he was peering under the desk, his face pressed against the scratchy carpet.

He couldn't see any feet, so he had to get out *now*.

But what's in the drawer? he thought. *Do I have enough time?*

He crawled out of the desk quickly and pulled the keys back out, taking calming breaths.

Looking at it from this angle, he noticed for the first time that the keyhole was in the shape of a 'V', like a bird when its wings were up.

There were only two keys like it on the set he had and the first one he tried unlocked it straight away.

He opened it carefully trying not to make a sound, and there they were - all the rolled up and folded pieces of paper that Decan had in there before.

That's not all that was in there, there was also a gun, and some car keys. Abe didn't like guns at all. His Grandma had always told him how dangerous it was to hold one. But he knew that he might need it, so he swiped it along with the keys and the papers.

He stuffed it all into his bag and ran as quickly and as quietly as he could, looking behind him every other second to make sure that Decan wasn't running after him. As he ran out, his body felt all tingly at the fear of being chased.

Luckily there was no one in the hall when he got there, but when he looked ahead he saw that the numbers above the elevator were lit up and headed up to where he was.

He made a dash as quick as he could, this time not having to try and be as quiet, and just as he got to the door of the stairs next to the elevator there was a *ping!*

The elevator opened and Abe watched through the crack of the door to see who it was. It was Anna, she was headed for Decan's office.

I wonder if she knew he was here the whole time, he thought, *or has she been lying to me as well?*

Abe bashed his way back into his room using his shoulder like a battering ram to open it, he was breathing heavier than ever as he tried to calm down and his body was rushing with adrenaline.

I can't believe I made it back without seeing anyone, he thought, *I need to get out of here...Now!*

He ran to the middle of his room and grabbed, as much food and drink as he could force into the bag.

He took a second to look around at all his stuff. His whole life was in that room, and he was having to leave it behind for a second time.

A tear gathered in one eye. *Maybe I can get it all back one day,* he thought. *Somehow.*

Now for the hardest part. He was going to have to get to George and break him out, and then escape together without getting caught, and hopefully without being seen. It almost felt impossible, but he had made it this far.

It was much later in the night now and Abe was worried that if he went walking through the halls and he was seen walking alone that people might become suspicious and tell Decan or Anna.

This last run might be his downfall, and he considered the idea of pretending to sleep for a few hours until it was early hours of the morning and going then, but the risk was too great.

By then Decan might have realised that the stuff in his drawer was missing and he might come looking for it.

All it would take is for him to go to his room then and search Abe's things, and then he would be done for. Abe took a deep breath and opened the door and walked straight out at a confident pace, heading right for the cells where he and his grandpa had been held before.

I hope that's where he has been taken, he thought.

The halls on the way there were long and well lit, not ideal but not a place people hung around either, as there wasn't reason to be there.

Abe passed one of Decan's men a few minutes later and he grew nervous, but he hid it well and avoided eye contact, and headed straight for the way he was headed. The man didn't even glance at him. Then he passed another two that were busy chatting and swearing at one another arguing about something, but Abe was too preoccupied to listen to them.

The cells now weren't too far away from where he was, and it took every fibre of his being not to break into a run.

If someone saw him running, then they would be sure to know who he was and what he might be up to.
That last corner was the scariest and as Abe approached it, the halls around him were so silent. All he could hear was his own breathing and heart beating away in his chest.

This is it, he thought.

He carefully peeked around the corner to make sure no one was guarding the last door at the end of the hallway, and he ran up to it.

He remembered this time to look through the keyhole. There was nobody in sight, though it was too dark in the cells to see who was in there.

Abe opened the door, expecting to see George, and preparing himself to get them both out of there.
He looked at the cell that had been his and it was empty, nothing in there but the bench like bed he had slept on, and the cover hanging over the side of it.

Then he walked over to the other side of the desk to look into what was his grandpa's cell but... there was nobody in there either.

Abe's entire body went stiff with anguish, he jumped forward so his hands were wrapped around the bars of the door and saw the empty cell.

Oh no, he thought.

He saw a massive pool of blood drenching the centre of the cell floor. Too much for anyone to have lived through. As he looked closer, he dropped to his knees and began to cry out. He noticed the blood was smeared and the body had been dragged from out of the cell and that the trail led off to a hatch on the wall to his left.

Abe's lip began to tremble as tears tumbled from his eyes.

George was dead. *They killed him and threw his body down the garbage shoot.*

Chapter 16

Abe's head was pressed against the cold metal bars of the cell door as he kneeled on the ground, closing his eyes.

There was no glimmer of hope left, as far as he was concerned. His grandpa was gone, his dog was dead and so was his friend.

Who do I have left? he thought.

'My grandma is out there somewhere, and I have to find her,' he said to himself. 'Now I have these maps, I can go there myself.'

Suddenly, there was a noise to the right of the room, like someone was crawling on the floor and making mumbling noises. Abe stopped and held his breath as he turned to its direction. He looked and the rest of the room was empty, and the door was still closed.

What if it's one of the guards? he thought, as he panicked and looked around for an escape.

Abe crept towards the middle of the room and then someone called out.

'Abe?'

Abe was startled and was looking in the other direction. He turned towards the voice. It was coming from the cell he had been in before.

It was *George,* he was lying on his stomach half out of underneath the bed that was in the cell with the sheet hanging over the side.

Abe was ecstatic, he rushed towards the door and quietly exclaimed, 'You're alive!'

George was still lying down looking up at Abe. He had a great big bruise over one side of his face, covering almost his entire left eye.

'Yeah,' he said. 'Did someone tell you that I was dead?'

Abe wiped his face dry and crouched down closer to George, 'No, I saw the blood in the cell next to you and thought that this cell was empty, so I figured you were,' he said. 'Why are you lying under there?'

George was rubbing the sleep out of his eyes, 'It was too bright, so I laid under here. I'm used to sleeping in a box and It's normally much darker.'

Abe let out a small laugh, he was thrilled that George was alive and almost unhurt.

'Come on, we have to go,' said Abe.

George had a slight frown and stood up from the floor, 'What do you mean?' he asked. 'Where?'

Abe grabbed the keys back from his pocket and vigorously searched through them trying to find the right one, this time not being careful about jingling them around.

We just need to get out and fast. I have a plan; I know where we have to go!'

Abe was trying key after key, but there were so many that it was taking forever.

George put his hand out to take the keys and said, '*Here* give them to me, I saw them use theirs, I know what it looks like.'

Abe passed him the keys and it only took George a few seconds of looking before he found the right one.

Just as he opened the cell door, the room started to flash, followed by a great harrowing siren that echoed through the room, and probably the entire base.

Oh no, thought Abe. 'They know what's going on. We have to go.'

George and Abe were now both standing in the middle of the room looking around helplessly wondering what to do and how they could escape.

'What do we do now?' asked George.

Abe was just as clueless as George, he had no idea where to go, now that they knew what was going on, it was going to be even harder.

'I don't know,' said Abe frantically.

A sound of footsteps started somewhere nearby, and they could hear voices yelling and dogs barking. George was trembling in fear and looked to be on the brink of crying.

Abe was kicking himself, thinking that anything that happened now was going to be his fault for not having a better plan of escape.

Hearing the footsteps running, Abe panicked and reached into his bag for the gun. He pulled it out and George's eyes widened.

'Where did you get that?' he asked.

Abe gripped the gun in his hand not really knowing what to do with it or whether he even could.

'I stole it from Decan's office,' said Abe.

George looked worried, 'You can't use that, it'll kill someone,' he said.

Abe frowned, 'If we don't then they will kill us.'

Suddenly, the door shot open and Anna appeared, closing the door quickly behind her. She looked right at them and looked like she had just run a mile. There was no smile on her face now. She looked furious as she marched towards them both, with her hands open like claws.

Abe panicked and started to walk backwards pushing George back and quickly raised the gun at Anna.

Her eyes widened. It was clear she hadn't expected him to have a weapon. She started to slow and opened her mouth to speak, but Abe was too quick and he had already pulled the trigger, pointing it straight at her with his eyes closed.

George saw Abe start to shoot at her and yelled, 'No!'

He jumped forward trying to push the gun away, but it was too late. The gun fired with a *bang,* and the bullet flew out of the gun and hit Anna straight in the shoulder, knocking her down onto the ground.

She let out a moan as she clutched her shoulder in agony. Abe was stood there with his mouth open in shock, and unable to move.

There were more footsteps nearby now, *they must have heard the gunshot*, he thought.

George grabbed Abe by the shoulder and said, 'Quick, this way.'

He dragged Abe towards the garbage shoot, opened the hatch and said, '*get in.*'

Abe threw his bag in and heard it thunder down the shoot and then jumped in after it.

The sounds of people nearby got close, and the barks of the dogs were nearer too. George's entire body was tingling with fright as he jumped as quick as he could into the shoot, the hatch door closing behind them.

Abe landed at the bottom on a huge heap of stinking garbage. The journey down was luckily short but dark and not kind to his body, he was covered in scratches and soon to be bruises.

He was lying on his back letting out a groan as he tried to recover from the long fall, when he heard the echo of George's yell as he came down the shoot. Abe gasped as he rolled away in a hurry, dragging his bag out of the way.

A second later George came crashing down onto the heap of garbage. As Abe stood up, he saw who the trail of blood belonged to, and it was a horrifying sight.

It was the man from the comic book stall that had been dragged away and beaten, his limp corpse was now lying at the bottom of this shoot. He had been carelessly disposed of like a piece of trash.

This is all my fault, Abe thought feeling terrible.

The sound of George's complaining reminded him he was there, and he turned around quickly to check on him.

'Are you okay?' he asked.

George stayed lying where he was and nodded, 'Yeah, I'm okay,' he said.

Abe and George looked around and noticed that they were now outside. It was lucky that the skip they had landed in was almost full.

They could hear the voices of the people that were running from the room echo through the shoot.

'Do you think they know where we are?' George whispered.

Abe stared up at the shoot, 'I don't know, but I'm sure Anna will tell them if she saw us climb in. Why did you stop me?' Abe asked.

George, looking sheepish, pulled himself up said, 'It's not right to kill people.'

Abe had a half frown. He agreed normally but these people were dangerous, and she could have stopped them from getting away.

'Come on,' said Abe. 'We have to go quickly.' Abe walked over to George, trying hard to keep his balance as his feet sunk in uneven ways on the trash, and held out his hand to help up his friend.

George took his hand and smiled.

Abe made his way to the furthest end of the skip from the shoot, aiming to jump off and onto the ground. The air was freezing and luckily there was a little snow on the ground, because it was going to help break their fall. However, before he got the chance to jump, he saw something...it made him freeze. He thought he had gone through as much as he could stand, but seeing his grandpa's clothes, he knew he had been wrong. He recognised them straight away. They were just lying there in amongst the trash and had blood stains on them. He stepped up to it and kneeled down, George saw him and called out asking if he was okay, but Abe was too upset to respond.

He didn't run away, he thought, *they just killed him.*

George grabbed Abe's shoulder. 'What's wrong?' he asked. 'We gotta go.'

Abe stayed still for a second and had tears in his eyes, 'My grandpa is dead,' he said.

George looked down at the clothes and at Abe, wanting to console Abe, but they didn't have any more time to waste.

He placed his arms around Abe and pulled him up, 'I'm sorry Abe we got to go, otherwise we might be killed.'

He's right, Abe thought, *I need to survive so that I can kill Decan.*

Chapter 17

The next ten minutes were some of the scariest Abe had ever experienced. While he and George ran from wall to wall, crouching and crawling, avoiding spotlight and every person running around the base, he clenched his fists with stress and tried to stop himself from breathing so heavily.

He worried that the dogs might find them by picking up their scent, but since they had just been rolling around in literal garbage, all they smelled of was rotten food and waste.

Abe hadn't really seen much of the outside, and wasn't too sure where they had to go, but they were able to see a clear way out. There was no fence to climb but there was a wide moat, frozen over, cast in a soft white glow from the moonlight reflecting off the snow-covered surface.

Is it thick enough to walk over? Abe thought.

Abe jumped down first to check the ice with his feet, it didn't crack and seemed quite thick, so he lowered himself to his hands and knees and started to crawl across, waving George to follow.

The ice held out and as soon as he and George were over, they hurried towards the pile of cars that were parked just metres away from the barriers that lead to the open world.

Abe had only driven a car once and was not something he had thought about. He was determined to find the car that belonged to the keys he had swiped from Decan's desk drawer.

Abe clicked the button on the keys, but nothing happened right away. He kept clicking it as he walked up the stretch of cars until eventually he saw the orange lights flash.

He rushed over, hurrying George along with him, looking back to make sure that he was keeping up.

If it wasn't for finding his grandpa's clothes, he would have thought how lucky they had been so far.

It was a big jeep, and had huge tyres on it, it was going to be just what they needed to get them out of there.

He opened the driver door, which activated and turned the light on inside the truck, allowing him to see George's face in the light.

George had gone almost blue, and he was shivering in the cold, his clothes were wet, and he was freezing.

George hurried as quick as he could and climbed into the truck with his cold stiff body.

Abe was worried for him, but at the moment he had more pressing things to worry about.

We need to find a way out of here. Then we'll find a way to warm up.

George turned to him from the passenger seat and said, 'Do you know how to drive?'

Abe, with a doubtful look replied, 'Yeah.'

George heard him say yes, but his body language said no.

He wanted to ask Abe some follow up questions, but he was too cold. Each time he opened his mouth, his teeth chattered loudly.

Abe put the keys in the ignition and started up the engine. The truck roared as it turned on and George could feel the vibrations in the seats.

Abe took a deep breath as he put it into drive and pushed his foot down on the pedal, the truck shot off much faster than he had expected it to. The truck went smoothly through the ice and snow, spraying it on the nearby cars as it pushed it out of the way.

He saw the barrier just ahead in the beam of the headlights, and just as he could taste freedom, he saw two guards that had run to the centre of the road on the other side of the barrier holding guns and aiming them at the truck.

Before he would have panicked, trembled with fear and been drenched with sweat, but he had had enough. He wasn't going to let them stop him, so he slammed his foot down on the gas pedal and headed straight for the barrier without a second thought.

As the truck's engine grew louder and they bolted for the exit, the guards moved as if to open fire. Out of nowhere, a silhouette darted at the guards and knocked them out of the way and stopping them from shooting.

Abe was relieved and shocked. They had another stroke of luck. If the guards had started firing there was no telling what would have happened.

He had no idea though who saved them, and when looking in the rear-view mirror, he could still only see the person as a dark silhouette, and the guards looking up at it from the ground with puzzled faces.

Abe drove as fast as he could for another ten minutes until he was sure that nobody was behind them, without looking at George.

He hadn't realised how quiet he was until those ten minutes had passed and he knew they were safely away.

Abe looked to his right and saw George sitting in his seat with his head leaning to one side. He was out cold.

Abe brought the truck to a halt and grabbed George.

'George...George, we did it, we're free!'

George didn't respond.

Oh no, thought Abe. 'Not after all this. You have to be okay.'

Abe shook him, but he didn't wake, and he felt his face with his hand, he was ice cold, and it was only then that Abe realised he was cold too.

George was only wearing a thin top now, and not his normal dark green hoodie. The guards took everything he had when he was locked up.

Abe quickly took off the hoodie he was wearing and wrapped it around George like a blanket. Then he looked frantically on the truck's dashboard and at all of its buttons, trying to figure out how to turn the heater on.

Every second that passed he got more and more annoyed with himself, and worried for George.

He saw the big button with the little picture above it saying *max* and pressed it, turning the truck's fans on full. He cranked up the heat dial to the thick red line so it was as hot as it could get and then waited, hoping that George would warm up and be okay.

Abe waited for a while sitting there and watching him, hoping that he was going to wake up soon, but he didn't. He hadn't thought about how dangerous it was just sitting there though, if Decan had sent his people out looking for them then they could have been caught straight away.

As soon as he realised that, he tried waking George up again by calling his name and shaking him softly.

George didn't wake up, but when Abe tried to wake him, he felt that he was warming up, which was a good sign. *He is still alive*, he thought, a slight hint of a smile touching his face.

He had almost forgotten about what else was out there, until he looked up through the windshield and saw *them*.

They were frozen solid, some standing in the snow, in the middle of the long narrow road he was parked on, and some were lying on the ground, mostly covered and hidden by the snow. His heart started to beat harder when he saw them, and it was only when he realised that they were frozen still that it started to calm. Abe let out a sigh of relief and put the truck back into drive so he could carry on going and get further away from Decan and his men. He needed to keep going until he was sure that they wouldn't catch up.

When he was close enough to see the frozen remnants of *them*, it looked like some of them had been shot at, while they were frozen.

It was almost like someone had taken the opportunity of them being frozen to go around and make sure they were fully dead. If the freezing didn't finish them off, then the bullet would.

Chapter 18

Abe drove continuously for the next four hours into the night. Every twenty minutes he would look to his right checking on George, making sure he was okay.

Every passing hour, his face became more and more like its normal colour, and Abe grew less worried. By the third hour, he received the confirmation that he needed that he was okay, when George started to snore.

When he did, Abe smiled with relief and turned down the heaters on the truck.

After hours of driving down a long highway Abe was tired and his body was aching almost everywhere from sitting still. He decided to pull over and have some rest. However, he was reluctant as they were in the middle of an open road, alone in the night and in a big truck. There were a couple abandoned cars every now and then, but no sign of living people.

The floor was still covered in snow, and the sky was throwing more down as he looked around, for anything that might be a danger.

As he looked, he saw *them* here and there, only a few, but all stuck like solid statues in the ice. It was like they had been frozen in time just for him to finish his journey in relative safety.

But the snow wouldn't keep them safe forever. The place where the bunker was meant to be, was in the middle of some desert area, which was unlikely to have any snow at all.

He hadn't thought about how much gas they had, but the vehicle they were using didn't seem the most efficient for fuel, it's not something he had practice in checking, but by chance he happened to look at the dial when he was looking at the time. Their tank was just under half full, and he had no idea how much farther he had to go. He didn't even know if he had been driving in the right direction, the only thing he was interested in at the time was making sure they were far away from that place.

His eyes were starting to feel heavy as he felt himself suddenly get hit by a wall of sleepiness.

He thought he would recline the seat back and have some sleep for a few hours until the sun was up, and they could see where they were going.

Maybe then George will be awake too, he thought.

There was a loud rustling that echoed in a deep black space. Abe could hear it getting louder and louder and then he felt a hot glow on his skin.

His eyes shot open as he realised he had been asleep, and looked to his right to see an empty seat where George had been.

He sat up quickly and he heard, 'Morning.'

Abe turned around and saw George on the back seat looking through one of the maps he had pulled out of Abe's bag.

He had pulled out the food as well and laid it out on the seat. From what Abe could tell, he was checking how much they had and trying to figure out how they were going to make it last.

Abe rubbed the sleep out of his eyes with his hand, 'George?' he said. 'You're awake.'

George smiled at him, 'Yeah. Where are we? I don't remember anything after we got to the car.'

Abe too climbed into the spacious back seat, beside George so he could get a look at the maps.

'I don't know where we are,' he said. 'I just drove most of the night to get us out of there.'

George put the map back down on the seat in front of him, 'I can't believe we got out,' he said.

Abe smiled back at him, 'I know,' he said. 'It was close at the end, I didn't think we were going to make it, and when we did, and you were passed out. I thought you might be dead.'

George bowed his head slightly. 'I'm sorry,' he said, feeling bad for worrying Abe, and feeling like a burden.

Abe shook his head and gave him a hug. 'Don't be sorry, I'm glad you're okay.'

George was relieved that Abe wasn't mad or annoyed. He was happy to be out of that place and somewhere safe with Abe. He had never had such a good friend as him. It was hard for him to make friends wherever he went, because people didn't like to look at him.

'So,' said George, 'What was your plan? Where do we go now?'

Abe looked through the pile of papers and hunted for the little satellite picture that Decan had shown him before. He pulled it out and showed it to George.

George had almost the same look of confusion as Abe did the first time he had seen it, 'What's that?' he asked. 'We're not going, there are we?'

Abe nodded and told him all about the bunker and all that it had there. He said that it was going to be their new home and that they would be far away and safe from *them* and Decan.

Abe told him about his grandma and how she used to bake for him and his grandpa, and that once they got there and saw her again that maybe she would be able to bake them all kinds of treats, and George looked excited and had a glowing smile.

'How are we going to get there?' George asked.

Abe pressed his lips together as he thought, making them go white as he picked up the map George had been holding.

'The only way we can really. We're going to have to drive,' he said. 'It's too dangerous to walk, and it would take forever.'

Abe hadn't had a lot of practice using maps, the only time he had used them was when he was with his grandpa, and he had almost always drawn a line on the map of where they started and where they needed to go. But this map didn't have that, and his grandpa wasn't there to help him now. He could feel himself falling into despair.

George looked up, noticing the look on Abe's face, and asked, 'What's wrong?'

Abe lowered the map and said, 'I was thinking about my grandpa. I miss him.'

George's smile had dampened as saw Abe in pain.

'It's okay Abe,' he said placing his hand on his shoulder. 'We might still find him. If your grandma is where you say she is, then maybe he has gone there.'

Abe smiled slightly at George as he tried to cheer him up, but he doubted what George had said. *Why would he have left without his clothes?*

Abe kept staring at the map, which was just of a small area, and while it didn't have a line saying where to go, it did have a lot of circles and notes, with different markings.

He looked at them, trying to figure them out and, when he squinted his eyes, he started to figure out what some of the places on the map were.

A lot of them were gas stations from what he could tell, which meant that they must have been the places that Decan and or his men went out and raided. That meant that he had pretty much all of the supplies and fuel in the majority of the surrounding area. There was also no telling in how far he ventured out to go and raid the shops, supermarkets and gas stations to scavenge everything.

As George was watching Abe pull the map closer and closer to his face, and as it got higher, he noticed something on the back.

'What's that?' he said, pointing.

Abe snapped out of the deep focus he was in and turned the map over. It was a handwritten key to the map with details of what the different symbols meant.
This is great, Abe thought, *but it really is just as useless as before. Decan's either been to all these places… or he will soon.*

Then Abe realised they had an even bigger issue. 'Uh oh,' he said.

George looked at him, his eyes widening, 'What is it?'

Abe lowered the map from his face and said, 'I don't know where we are.'

George frowned, 'That's okay, that's why we got the maps,' he said.

Abe shook his head and put the map down on his lap, 'Yes, but...if we don't know where we are, then we can't find where we are on *any* of these maps and look where to go.'

'Have you ever used a map before?' he asked George.

George shook his head and said, 'No.'

What are we going to do now? Abe thought, fed up that nothing was ever simple, and getting more and more worried.

'Maybe if we look through the rest of these then we will be able to figure it out,' said George, trying to be helpful and make light of the situation.

Abe's face still looked as if he had little hope and folded the map, he had in his hand so he could look at the others.

George grabbed one of the maps that had been rolled up and was the biggest out of all of them. It had a big rubber band around it to hold it together

'Maybe we should start with the biggest one first,' he said.

Abe took the paper from George's hand and rolled the elastic band to the end with his hand, before taking it off and opening the map as wide as he could in the limited space he had.

The map was so big that it was like a curtain between George and Abe, and neither of them could see the others face now.

Abe's eyes widened and he said, '*Oh, crap.*'

George couldn't see the expression on Abe's face, but he had a good guess of what it looked like by the sound of his voice.

'What is it?' he asked.

Abe turned the map so it was leaning against the back seat and they both shuffled out of the way so they could see it together.

George looked at it too and saw what Abe was so shocked about.

'Is that...?' asked George, his voice trailing off.

Abe nodded with a smile and said, '*Yep.*'

The map that they now had rested against the back seat was staring them both in the face, a map of the entire country. It had markings all over it with numbers one to twenty. On the back, next to each number were co-ordinates, and the co-ordinates for number *three* matched exactly with the ones on the satellite picture of the one they were headed to.

George turned to Abe, 'Does that mean that they are all...'

Abe turned with a happy look on his face, 'Yeah,' he said. '*They are all bunkers.*'

End of Part I

Chapter 19

The room had filled with steam, and the walls and ceiling had become damp as its clouds settled.

There was a big silver metal tub in the middle of the room, filled with hot water.

An old man was carrying a small body, freezing cold, and still. He lowered the body into the warm metal tub of water and let it lay in there with its head just above the water.

It was Abe. More than three days had passed since they had discovered that there were more bunkers, and they had tried to continue their journey, but with little fuel and no idea where they were, they were soon lost in the ice and snow.

They were able to find a city nearby, but there were no signs of living people who they could ask for help to use a map. By the time they knew what city they were in, they were out of fuel, low on food and water, and had no way too keep themselves warm.

They planned to try and get into a building where they could keep safe and warm themselves up, and then make a plan, but nightfall came too quick. They decided to camp in the back of the truck until the morning, but the night was cold. The snow fell hard, and the ice became thicker than it had been that winter, covering the windows of the truck and nearly creeping inside.

The truck almost became like a freezer and by the morning they had fallen into an icy coma, lying next to each other for warmth.

Around 6am, a red pick-up truck was driving through the street. It had driven around those same streets for weeks, and the driver hadn't seen this jeep before.

The old man in the truck thought, *It doesn't have as much snow on it as the other cars around,* and decided to take a look. When he scraped ice off the window with the cuff of his sleeve, he saw two young men inside. He couldn't tell if they were dead.

The old man dragged his feet back through the snow to his truck to get some tools, before he jimmied his way in the locked vehicle and carried both Abe and George, one at a time, back to his truck and put them inside.

Abe awoke with a pounding in his head, and a bright light glaring down at him. He thought he might be dead, until he looked around and noticed he was in somebody's living room after his blurry eyes became clear enough to see.

It was small, and to his right he could see the kitchen and a wooden table with chairs in the middle of it.

Where am I? he thought.

He sat up and noticed he was lying on a sofa, wrapped in a scratchy woollen blanket.

There was a sudden whistling noise that came howling from the kitchen. Abe covered his ears and jumped a little when it started so suddenly.

He heard footsteps and the sound of humming as they got closer, followed by the opening of a brown wooden door in the middle of the room. Somebody walked in over to the kitchen stove, moving a kettle and silencing the whistle.

Abe saw the old man and kept quiet, he hadn't realised that Abe was awake yet, and Abe watched him. He was tall, had a denim jacket on from what Abe could see and he was wearing a hat. Abe frowned and thought that the shape of his body looked familiar.

He opened his mouth in a gasp, *Is it...?*

Before Abe could say anything, the old man turned around and then he saw his face.

Abe's hope vanished.

It wasn't who Abe thought it was, *how could it have been*? He thought, feeling disappointed.

'You're awake,' said the old man.

Abe wasn't too sure what to say, the man had definitely saved his life, but he had no idea who he was. He had had issues with trusting people he shouldn't have before. He wasn't going to be making that mistake again.

The man walked over to Abe and stopped just in front of the sofa.

'Mind your feet,' he said.

Abe looked at the man in a puzzled way, having no clue what he said.

'Your feet,' the man repeated.

Abe's eyebrows raised quickly as he realised what he meant and brought his knees up to his chest and placed them down on the floor.

The man passed him a steaming hot cup of tea, 'Here drink this,' he said. 'Sorry it's not coffee, I don't have any.'

After Abe took the cup, the man reached for his forehead and felt it with the palm of his hand. Abe thought it was strange at first, but he was clearly just checking he wasn't sick.

Now Abe was closer to him, he realised how silly it was to have thought that he was his grandpa. This man was easily twenty years younger.

'How are you feeling?' the man asked him.

Abe was sipping at the hot tea, and as he did, he felt like a big weight had been lifted. He couldn't remember the last time he had tea, and only now realised how much he had missed it.

'Umm...okay I guess,' Abe replied.

The man didn't respond and just let out a puff of air from his nose and stood back up before heading over to the kitchen.

'You must be hungry,' he said.

Abe took a moment to gather his thoughts and realised the man was right, when he felt the ache and grumble in his stomach as it yelled at him for not answering the man sooner.

'Yes, I am,' he said.

Abe was still having a tough time figuring the man out, but realistically, would he have saved him and brought him back to his home if he had bad intentions?

The man was moving around pots and pans in the kitchen making all kinds of clinking and clunking noises, and then the sound of the gas stove flicking on.

'Do you like stew?' he asked.

Abe nodded, but the man didn't see because he was stood over the stove, so Abe answered, 'Yes.'

'Good,' said the man, 'I hope you like beef and potatoes, your friend seemed to enjoy it.'

Abe's face expression grew wilder as he heard him mention George and he stood up fast, knocking the blanket to the ground.

'Where is he?' he asked desperately.

The man turned around to see Abe standing there in a panic.

'Shh,' he said, placing a finger on his lips, 'He's fine, and he's asleep. He's not gotten as much sleep as you did, and he has pretty much been waiting by your side ever since he woke up.'

Abe sat back down and picked up the blanket from the ground, it was then that he realised he was wearing somebody else's pyjamas.

'How long have I been out?' Abe asked.

The man had turned back to the stove as he prepared the food for Abe, 'Since I found you' He said, 'No more than a couple days, but no idea how long before that.'

Abe looked around and stared at the window, realising he had no idea what time of day it was. The curtains were drawn, and he couldn't see outside to tell.

'What time is it?' he asked.

The man lifted his wrist to look at his watch and said, 'It's 9 'o'clock, in the evening.'

The man started humming again, and then tapped the wooden spoon he had in his hand as he finished scooping the stew into a bowl. He walked over to Abe dragging a small wooden coffee table over in front of the couch he was sitting on and placed the food down.

'Here, eat up,' he said. 'Sorry, I don't have any bread.'

Abe smiled and the smell of the stew was mesmerizing.

'Thank you,' he said.

The man began to walk out of the room, before Abe looked up from his bowl and quickly asked, 'Where are you going?'

He stopped and looked back at Abe, standing just before the door he had come in through. 'Bed,' he said. 'I'll see you in the morning.'

Abe was left sitting there on a stranger's sofa and a room he had never been in, he looked around and it was quiet. He had loads of questions that he wanted to ask the man, but they were going to have to wait until morning.

He scooped up every bit of the stew that he had on his spoon and when he was done, he laid down and tried to sleep, forcing his eyes closed.

I'm too awake, he thought, *I'll never get to sleep,* but before he knew it, he was flat out, back into the dream world.

Chapter 20

The sun had risen, staining the sky pink and George was sitting on the armchair opposite the sofa where Abe was still asleep.

The chair was large and made of brown leather, George was small and didn't even fill the gaps between the arms.

George woke up early to check on Abe. He was still worried, and he didn't know that he had already woken up. He was pleased to see that there was an empty bowl of stew left on a coffee table beside the couch he was lying on.

George took it upon himself to wash the bowl in the sink before the man woke up.

The man thanked George when he came into the living room, by giving him some of the hot chocolate he had left. George savoured every delicious sip; it was like sweet liquid gold to him.

He felt he could relax a little now, that Abe had woken up and had something to eat. The man told him that he was going to be fine.

George was shocked, but happy when the man didn't seem to react to the fact he looked different. He just spoke to him normally and treated him like he would anyone else.

Abe woke up, his eyes opened slowly seeing the sun beaming in through the open window.

He saw George sitting in the armchair opposite him, a cup resting on the arm and the man sitting on a wooden chair next to him, showing him something in a book and pointing to things.

George was sat there looking at the book with a smile on his face.

The sun was in Abe's eyes and he couldn't see what the book was about, but as he tried to use his hand to shade his eyes from the sun, the man snapped it shut in his hand and passed it to George, giving it to him as a gift.

George was looking at the book in his hand, and then looked up and noticed that Abe was awake.

'*Abe!*' he exclaimed as he ran over, giving him a hug. 'You're awake.'

Abe smiled, 'Yeah,' he said. 'Are you okay?' George stood in front of where Abe was laying.

'Yeah,' he said, 'I'm good.'

Abe then realised that the man was still sitting on the wooden chair, drinking from a steaming mug. Abe was still suspicious. He didn't know enough about the man yet to decide whether he was trustworthy.

George noticed Abe looking over and introduced him. 'This is Frank,' he said. 'He's the one that saved us.'

Frank stood up from his chair and walked over to the kitchen and filled the kettle up with water before placing it on the stove.

'Tea?' said Frank.

'Yes please,' Abe replied.

Abe was looking at Frank as he had his back turned and he was grabbing a clean mug from the kitchen cupboard and a tea bag.

'Did you tell him?' Abe whispered.

George frowned, 'Tell him what?' he asked.

Abe sat up, 'About where we're going.'

George shook his head and started to lean in closer to say something, but was interrupted by Frank from across the kitchen.

'I can hear you whispering,' he said.

Frank was turned around with his arms crossed looking in their direction.

'You don't have to worry about me,' he said, 'I wouldn't have brought you back here, and shared my limited food supply with you if I had bad intentions.'

Abe looked sorry and felt bad after Frank had fed them both and saved their lives.

'Sorry,' he said. 'We've just had issue with trusting people before.'

'I know,' said Frank, 'I could tell by the big bruise your friend has on his face there.'

Abe looked at George at the mention of it. It still looked quite sore.

'Maybe you could tell me what happened?' he asked. 'George said he didn't want to say anything until you woke up.'

Abe looked at George waiting for approval, and as he nodded with a smile, he started to tell Frank everything about Decan and how they held them at the base they were held at. He told Frank about what they did to George and about their escape.

Abe left out the part about the bunker and the maps.

Frank got a sense that Abe was leaving out something important, but he didn't blame him after all he had been through.

'Where were you planning on going?' he asked.

'There is a place where my grandma was taken, we were trying to head there,' said Abe.

Oh no...the truck, Abe thought in a panic.

'Where's the truck?' he asked. 'The one you found us in.'

Frank walked over with a cup of tea in his hand and passed it to Abe, telling him to calm down.

'Relax, I went and towed it here after your friend woke up,' said Frank, 'he said that there was something really important in there and made me promise not to look if I left him here with you.'

Abe took the cup out of Frank's hand, 'And the bag?' he said, looking from Frank to George.

'I've got it,' said George. 'It's in my room.'

Abe let the air out of his chest in a sigh of relief.

'Okay, good,' he said.

Frank walked back over to the wooden chair and sat back down.

'You want to tell me what's so special about the bag?'

Abe was a bit dubious about telling him, but he mustn't have looked in the bag, just like he promised. *So maybe we can trust him*, thought Abe.

Abe looked at George and just nodded. George quickly ran off to retrieve it from his room.

There was an awkward silence while George was gone, neither Frank nor Abe said anything. They hadn't talked that much yet, not like he and George clearly had.

'It's *Abe,* right?' asked Frank.

'Yeah,' Abe replied.

Frank smiled. 'Well, it's nice to meet you,' he said. 'You did well to get out of that place, and to bring George with you, he's a nice kid.'

Abe smiled responding to the compliment and agreeing with Frank about George.

George came back in the room walking quickly and stood back next to Abe as he placed the bag down on the floor, beginning to grab everything out.
Frank stood up and said, 'Why don't you take it over to the table, while I get us something to eat for breakfast.'

Abe stood up and George passed him the bag as they both walked over to the small round table in the centre of the room.

It was then that Abe was able to see out of the window and noticed that they were at least one story up. It became clear that it was an apartment that they were in. He wanted to ask George how much they should tell Frank, but it was difficult with him there in the room.

Should I tell him about all of the bunkers? he thought. *Or just the one?*

He took out the satellite picture of the bunker they were headed too, the map that had details of all the places Decan had raided, or was going to raid, and another one where it showed they needed to go. He left the main one with the list of all the bunkers in the bag.

George looked at Abe, clearly wondering why he had left the possibly the most important one out. It was easier for George to trust Frank, because he had spent a little more time with him, but Abe wasn't there yet.

Frank came back over a little later with some bowls of porridge, sparking some rough memories for the both of them. However, this looked a lot different - it wasn't clumpy and thick like paste. It was perfect, and when they each took a mouthful, they were surprised to find that there was some kind of sweet taste that made it actually enjoyable.

'What's in this?' Abe asked.

'Cinnamon,' he said bluntly.

They carried on spooning it into their mouths as they all sat around the table, and Frank looked at the maps they had put on the table.

It took a few seconds before he looked round and saw the satellite picture.

'What's this?' he asked.

'It's where my grandma has gone, to be evacuated,' said Abe, and before Frank could say anything about it being small to hold a lot of people, Abe jumped back in and told him that it was a bunker.

'So that's where they took them all,' said Frank.

Abe and George stopped eating and turned their attention to Frank.

'Did the trucks come here too?' Abe asked.

Frank had a sad look on his face, 'They tried to,' he said, 'but the city was full of *them,* they barely got in and took a hundred people, there's no telling where they are now.'

Abe and George looked at each other, they had no idea it was so bad here.

'Did you have any family? Did they get out?' Abe asked.

Frank shook his head softly, 'No, no family,' he said. 'It's just me.'

Frank continued eating, Abe and George followed. George looked at Abe meaningfully, trying to tell him to show Frank the other map.

Frank was looking at how far away the bunker was. 'It's a bit of a journey to get there,' he said. 'It's going to be a while before we can go with this weather. Not safe to go before.'

He told them that they had been a lot closer before but had driven in the opposite direction. Abe looked down at his food, feeling like an idiot, for how much time he had wasted.

Abe bent down to where the bag was and pulled out the other map that was rolled up.

'There's one more,' he said.

Frank looked at the map in Abe's hand, looking curious.

Abe glanced at George and said, 'George seems to trust you, so I do too.'

He rolled the map open, covering the entire table, revealing the markings of the other bunkers.

'What are all these?' he asked pointing at the markings.

'Bunkers, the same as where we are headed.'

Frank's gaze became more intrigued and his eyes widened. 'All of them?' he asked.

Both Abe and George nodded.

But Frank's look quickly dimmed as he sat back in his chair. 'You do realise, that a lot of these might be empty?' he said. 'A lot of these places are near major cities, if they are anything like what happened here, they probably never got there.'

Abe started to look at all the marks on the map and realised that Frank might be right. He started to slouch as he thought that his grandma might never have gotten there, and something might have happened to her on the way.

He had finally thought that he was free and had a clear way to where he needed to be, but now a dark fog started to cover the path ahead.

However, George quickly pointed out, speaking loudly and placing his finger on the one they were headed too. 'Not this one, the one we're going to is in the desert, nowhere near a city.'

Frank just looked down at where George was pointing and back up to the two of them, not really showing them what he was thinking with the expression he had on his face.

Abe lifted his head. 'Can you help us get there?' he asked.

Frank paused and sat there quietly for a minute, glancing back and forth between them and the map.

'There's nothing keeping me here I guess,' said Frank.

Both Abe and George's face lit up slightly with hope, before Frank continued.

'But...like I said before, we can't go anywhere in this weather, it's worse outside the main bit of the city and my truck won't make it,' he said.

George glanced at Abe, both of them looking slightly disappointed.

'What about ours?' asked George.

Frank pondered for a second and then said, 'It would be a lot better, but you know as well as I do that it is out of gas.'

Abe's head dropped in disappointment.

'Can't we use the gas you have for your truck?' Abe asked.

'Yeah we can, but yours will use it a lot faster, and I only have so much,' he said. 'We're going to need to find a lot more food for this journey too.'

There was starting to be more problems than solutions and the things that they needed to do was starting to pile up higher and higher.

Now they needed to get to the bunker and find enough food and fuel to get all three of them there.

'Is there anywhere we can get all that we need?' Abe asked, knowing that almost everywhere had been raided already. At least it had where he had come from.

Frank sat there, rubbing his chin and then he had an idea.

'There is one place I know we can get the main bulk of the supplies we need,' he said. 'There is a distribution centre a few miles away. Your map doesn't cover it, but I wouldn't mind betting that nobody has gone there yet, and if they have, they would have needed a few lorries to get everything out of there.'

'But the longer we wait, the less likely there is going to be anything left when we get there,' said Abe, 'we need to get there now.'

'That's okay,' said Frank. 'My truck will get us that far.'

'But what about the rest of the way?' Asked Abe.

Frank sat forward, looking over the map, drawing on it with his finger.

'Almost half of the journey, we're going to be driving through snow, which is going to eat up the fuel faster than if we were just driving down clean roads,' he said. 'We could get the supplies we need and then come back here and wait out until the weather gets better.'

Abe thought it was a good plan, but there was one big problem.

'What about when there is no snow and ice, won't this place be swimming with *them?*' asked Abe.

The expression Frank had on his face darted from disappointed to annoyed. He was clearly irritated with himself for not thinking about it.

'You're right,' he said.

George looked at the both of them, beginning to worry that they were trapped. They couldn't go now because they couldn't get very far, but if they waited then they would be overrun.

'But they're frozen solid. They'll just die, won't they?' asked George.

Frank looked at him and said, 'I would think so, but we can't be sure.'

Abe remembered the ones he saw before that had been shot while they were frozen. They were an open target.

'What if we shoot them while they are stuck and frozen? Then they won't be able to get us even if they do survive.'

Frank shook his head. 'No, we can't. There are too many of them around, there are thousands.'

They all sat back in their seats, staring down trying to think what their options were. No matter what they came up with, it seemed that there was always something that would go wrong.

Abe looked at the map and the direction they would be going. *If only it was one of these closer ones,* he thought. *Then it wouldn't matter.*

'Wait a minute,' he said. 'How far can we get with the fuel we have?'

Frank had no idea where he was going, but he leant forward looking at the map, doing equations in his head and then pointed, 'Roughly, around here,' he said, pointing just under a quarter of the distance.

Abe looked, and he saw if they drove almost the same distance but further north, there was another bunker.

'What if instead of going straight there, we left now once we get the extra supplies, and go here,' he said pointing at the other bunker.

George looked at him with a strange look.

'What?' he said. 'Why would we do that. That's not where your grandma is.'

Abe had a grin on his face, because he knew what his plan *was,* 'No, but it's not that far from here, and we could go there and wait there until there is no snow, and it's far enough out of the city that we shouldn't run in to too many of *them.'*

George was smiling again. 'That's a great idea.' he said.

They both looked at Frank, but he didn't have the same smile as George, who asked, 'What if it is empty, how do we get inside?'

Abe was quiet for a second before saying, 'If it is, then it will be unmanned, they are bound to have the keys in the base guarding it somewhere.'

Frank had his arms crossed as he chewed his lip, thinking about it. 'What if there are people there?'

'Then that would surely be better, then we could ask them for help getting to the one we are trying to get to.'

Frank still looked a little unsure and looked at George, 'What do you think George?' he asked.

George still had a smile on his face as he glanced at the map and then back to each of them, 'I think it's a great idea.'

Abe looked at Frank and said, 'What do you think?'

Frank looked like he was about to say no and then, 'I guess we better get a move on and get some supplies, and head there as soon as we can.'

Chapter 21

Somewhere, only a few miles away from the distribution centre, stood a factory with great big chimneys that towered into the sky. Once, they had plumes of black smoke gushing out of them, but now they sit silent.

In a small dark and humid room were two young men wearing scruffy unwashed clothes, that had been beaten with dirt and sweat.

One of the men was small and had mouse brown hair. The other was tall and muscular with a shaved head. The taller man, Shaun was speaking quietly to the other.

'What did you get on your run?' he asked.

The smaller man, named Ethan muttered something as he rummaged around in a dirty brown sack he had been using as a bag to carry things.

'Nothing that I'll get to keep,' he said bitterly. 'Just some packs of cigarettes, and a bottle of vodka. What about you?'

Shaun wasn't as lucky. 'Not much, just a small can of gas, and some protein bars I found in a broken-down truck,' he said.

Even if he had found similar items to Ethan, he wouldn't get to keep much if any of it anyway. Most of what they would find on their runs would be inspected on their return and if it was something luxurious like alcohol and cigarettes, stuff that was basically currency. It would be taken from them and given to the leader of the group they were stuck with, *Janus.*

Ethan offered Shaun a cigarette as he shoved one behind his dirt covered ear.

'*Here,* you want one?' he asked.

Shaun took one and placed it in the corner of his mouth as he counted up how many of the protein bars he had in his bag.

'Thanks,' he said.

Ethan pulled out an old flip lighter that had an engraving of a snake on it, and lit Shaun's cigarette before his own.

Shaun was tempted to save just one of the protein bars he had found, he had seven in total.

Maybe I could just eat one? he thought.

It wasn't worth it if they got caught though. the punishment would be cruel and unreasonable. If you were lucky, it would just be one of Janus's trained monkeys that would beat you or force you to fight someone you had no chance against, for their entertainment.

Ethan was putting everything he had back in his sack. Shaun watched him throw each pack of cigarettes in, before he looked left to right and went to slip the small bottle of vodka in his back pocket of his jeans.

Shaun knocked him in the arm, causing him to stumble slightly.

'Hey!' he said. 'What are you doing?' asked Shaun.

Ethan looked at him with an annoyed look in his eyes.

'What does it look like?' he asked.

Shaun tried to grab the bottle from his pocket quickly before anyone came and saw.

'You know what'll happen if Dimitri catches you,' he said. 'Don't be an idiot.'

Ethan tried to back away to get away from Shaun to stop him from taking the bottle.

'No,' he said, 'I'm sick and tired of spending all day out there, freezing my ass off and having nothing to show for it.'

Shaun sighed as he looked at the ground and then took a long drag from his cigarette.

'I like a drink as much as the next guy, but you know what will happen if they catch you,' said Shaun, 'and I can't jump in and fight for you this time, if they catch you with *that.*'

Ethan scowled, looking at Shaun. He didn't care, he wanted to keep it for himself. 'Well I'll just have to risk it. If they do catch me I'll just have to make sure I drink it before the fight'.

Shaun shook his head and tried to ignore him.

Ethan took a drag from his cigarette and blew out a puff of smoke, followed by a cough.

'Besides, we can't give these cigarettes to him, we're halfway through smoking them.'

Shaun looked at the cigarette in his hand and then at Ethan. He quickly grew annoyed. He had no idea that was where Ethan had got them from.

'What the hell is wrong with you?' he said, 'Why didn't you tell me when you offered me one, that was where they were from.'

Ethan smirked, 'Sorry I guess I just forgot,' he said. 'Don't worry. How will he be able to tell?'

Shaun tried to find the cigarettes in Ethan's pockets and said, 'Quick, put them back in the bag. If they find the vodka and find out we smoked the cigarettes, we're both dead.'

Ethan tried to hold the pack of cigarettes he had opened away from Shaun, and tried to hold him back, but he was way too strong and pulled him abruptly forward, taking the cigarette in his hand. Ethan frowned and shook himself off like he was a toddler pouting after being told off.

Shaun took the cigarette and threw it down on the ground along with his own, stamping on them with his huge boots.

Just as Ethan was about to complain, some heavy feet came down the stairs at the end of the room.
It was Dimitri. He was tall, even taller than Shaun, and he wore a long dark coat and had a short dark beard.

'You two! Upstairs, you still need to check in after your runs,' he yelled.

Dimitri saw the two of them standing there and stared at them.

Shaun pushed Ethan along, and when he was in front of him, he sneakily put the cigarettes back in the bag, hiding it behind Ethan so Dimitri couldn't see.

'*Hurry up!*' Dimitri yelled.

As he turned around and headed back up the stairs in front of them, Shaun grabbed Ethan by the scruff of his clothes and snatched the vodka, throwing it into the sack before he passed it back to Ethan.
Ethan wanted to say something, but Dimitri was too close, and Shaun whispered behind him.

'You'll thank me later.'

As they came out of the stairs, it opened into a large hall. Oil drums were scattered around with flames coming out of them, lighting up the room. There were tables all along the far wall in front of them as they walked behind Dimitri. Each table was piled high with mounds of stuff that other people had scavenged and checked in over the last day or so.

Janus had particular people that he trusted, and only they were allowed to say what got taken and what was allowed to be kept by the runners, unless it was him deciding.

When they first started to do the runs, they were told that they would get half, but that soon changed. Some people tried to complain that it wasn't fair, but that didn't end well for them. Occasionally people would try and be smart; they would try and use things like food and alcohol while they were still out, and even stash it for when they were out next. If someone else spotted that they were doing that, however, they had the opportunity to report them and gain a reward - the reward itself differed, depending on who you told and what it was the person had done.

Sometimes it would buy you a few cigarettes, or a candy bar, but nothing worth the beatings you would get from the others living there for being a snitch. Ethan tried it when he first saw someone stashing supplies outside, but he lost twice. He snitched and when he saw how little his reward was, he complained, losing his reward and getting a beating off the back of it.

Then he got a beating from the friends of the person he had snitched on, after they had a few of their fingers removed for being dubbed thieves.

Dimitri stood behind the tables, and Shaun and Ethan hurried over trying not to provoke him.

'What took you so long?' Dimitri yelled, spitting saliva out in front of him.

Ethan wasn't able to look at him, and was instead cowering like a dog.

Shaun was facing forward and said, 'Sorry Dimitri, we lost track of time.'

Ethan remained looking at the ground and dropped his bag on the table, and so did Shaun. Dimitri emptied both bags out onto the table at the same time, mixing up their loot. He looked through the contents, taking the vodka first and then placing it aside, as he looked up at the two of them with a dark scowl.

He took one of the protein bars and put one in his pocket and then slid one to Shaun.

Then he counted the packs of cigarettes, but as he did, he noticed that one of them was open. He picked it up and looked inside, seeing that three of them were missing.

He looked at them with a level gaze, switching from one to the other.

'Which of you brought these in?' he asked, in a suspicious tone.

Shaun could see Ethan in the corner of his eye as he began to tremble from fear.

'They're mine,' said Shaun,' I brought them in.'

Dimitri grabbed the table with his hand and threw it aside so he could walk up face to face with Shaun.

'And can you tell me why this one's open with missing cigarettes and the rest are unopened?' he asked.

Shaun looked Dimitri in the eye and then back to staring forward.

'That's how I found them,' he said.

Dimitri looked to his side with his eyes, not moving his head so he was looking at Ethan.

He grabbed Shaun by his cheeks with one hand, forcing his lips together.

'Why are you lying?' he asked.

'Sorry?' said Shaun, in a muffled and distorted way as he tried to talk.

Dimitri let him go and said, 'Why are you pretending that you found them?'

'I'm not,' said Shaun, acting like he didn't know what Dimitri was talking about.

Dimitri stepped in front of Ethan and used his finger to force his chin up, so he was looking at him.

'What do you say?'

Ethan was terrified, and it was painfully obvious. He was shaking and trying to direct his eyes away, waiting for something horrible to happen.

'*Well?*' Dimitri yelled, becoming impatient and spitting all over Ethan's face.

Ethan closed his eyes as Dimitri yelled and opened them again as he answered, nervously stammering. 'It was me. I found them, but we both had one'.

Shaun gritted his teeth in annoyance trying to keep his face neutral.

Dimitri took a step back and smirked, as though he was amused. He looked Ethan up and down, and then reached out towards his face and throat with his giant hand. Ethan's face scrunched up as he closed his eyes in fear and his entire body tensed.

Dimitri went past his face and took the cigarette that was left forgotten behind Ethan's ear and placed it in his mouth.

'Thanks,' he said, with a smug grin.

He took a little match book out of his pocket, that had the name of a motel on it, and struck it lighting the cigarette in his mouth.

Shaun and Ethan were standing there, waiting to see what was going to happen. Dimitri was playing with them, making them wait there.

Dimitri took a drag from the cigarette, looking at it in his hand as he held a still expression on his face and blew smoke out into the air.

'Seeing as this is the first mistake you've made, I'll let it slide,' he said, standing in front of them and looking down at them both.

Both Shaun and Ethan were relieved, but also surprised.

'Wait a minute,' said Dimitri.

He walked back over towards Shaun and reached down, pulling something out of his pocket.

'What's this?' he asked, talking in his ear and blowing smoke in his face.

Shaun closed his eyes when they stung from the smoke, and tried not to breath it in.

'That's the protein bar you gave me', said Shaun.

Dimitri frowned at his response and took a step back.

'That I gave you?' he said, acting confused and looking towards the other men that followed him, watching. '*Boys,* did you see me give anything to this liar here?'

They all shook their heads and said '*No.*'

Dimitri smiled and turned back to Shaun.

'You just can't stop lying, can you?' he asked him.

Shaun tensed his jaw, and started gritting his teeth again. Dimitri was trying to get him to react, and he was trying hard not to give him what he wanted.

'My my, do you look angry,' Dimitri said. 'You don't like being caught out huh?'

Shaun tried counting in his head to try and calm himself.

'Well, it doesn't matter how angry you are,' he said, stepping back further and pointing at him with the hand that was holding the cigarette. 'You're still a thief and a liar, and you know what happens to those.'

Dimitri walked over to two of his men that were standing in the corner next to three others and pulled them forward.

'Take them upstairs to see the boss,' he said. 'He will decide what happens to you for stealing from him *and* trying to lie about it.'

Shaun's eyes widened in shock. It was rare that someone came out of there un-maimed.

Ethan, starting to panic as well, was panting and started begging that Dimitri change his mind.

'Please *no,*' he said. 'I didn't lie, I told you the truth, why do I have to go?'

Dimitri took one look at him, and kicked him hard in the stomach, winding him and forcing him to shut up. Ethan was down on his knees, clutching his stomach trying to get his breath back.

The men Dimitri had ordered to take them to Janus didn't wait for him to recover, and one of them dragged him to his feet by his hair. The other jabbed the end of his rifle in Shaun's back, making him walk forward.

Ethan and Shaun were walking next to each other with the men marching them to get their punishment behind them.

'I told you, didn't I?' said Shaun. 'Now you have may have gotten us both killed.'

Ethan was still struggling to speak. 'I'm sorry,' he said quietly.

The men behind them kept jabbing them in the back, making them walk faster.

They were walking through a large room, with concrete floor, and metal walls all around. There were big industrial machines dotted around in different places, but had all started to gather dust from disuse.

None of the lights were on where they were, and the only thing that lit their way were the oil drums being used as fire pits. Every now and then they would walk through a bit of shadow, just dark enough that Shaun thought the men behind him wouldn't be able to see him for just long enough for him to turn around and take one of their guns.

But what are the chances I'll get out alive? he thought. There were over fifty men at least on the same floor as them, all armed, and would shoot before he even got close to the door. He could try and fight them, but there was little chance he would win.

There were people watching as they were marched forward, and they all knew where they were going. Some laughed, but some looked more sympathetic.

On the way there, there was a fight going on between two of the residents, both men were the same size and equally matched. There was no way to tell what they were fighting about; it could have been something as small as one of them wanting the others share of lunch.

The guards didn't take any notice, letting them fight. If one was killed, the way the boss saw it was one less mouth to feed.

Within a few minutes and they were standing at the bottom of a set of metal stairs that lead up to a white metal door. It was covered by an unlit hallway, and loud music could be heard coming from behind the door.

The two men were standing behind them still and told them to get up the stairs.

Shaun wondered why they were letting them go up on their own, but then it hit him that they didn't want to see Janus either. Most people tried to avoid seeing him, just in case he decided to pick on you for fun or use you for one of his games.

Ethan was pleased that they had to go up alone and thought that maybe when they took a few steps up that the two men would walk away, and they could run off, but they didn't. They stood at the bottom and waited until they were at the top and Shaun banged on the door with his fist.

A small metal rectangle slid across the top panel of the door, to reveal a set of piercing white eyes on a dark face.

'What are you here for?' he asked, in an incredibly deep tone.

'Dimitri sent us to see the boss,' said Shaun.

The slide was shut, and the door swung open, allowing the music that was inside to boom out and rattle their ears. There seemed to be no words in the music though, it was just an endless mash up of instruments.

The man that opened the door was tall and wide, he was wearing a dark t-shirt with brown suspenders holding up his pants.

He looked behind down at the men standing at the bottom of the stairs and nodded at them, and then they left.

He stood aside and let both Ethan and Shaun walk in through the door in front of him.

Neither Shaun or Ethan had been in Janus' quarters before, and it was much bigger than they expected. It was longer than it was wide, and by the door where they had just come in, was surrounded by the people that directly worked for Janus.

They sat on sofas, and had piles and piles of junk food, alcohol and soda around them. This place too was mainly lit by oil drums, and when Shaun looked over he could see that the men were throwing books into the fire in place of wood.

They're like animals, he thought.

He watched some of them sitting on the sofas, with women by them looking depressed. It was clear that they weren't there voluntarily, and by the looks of them they were taking some kind of substance to try and make their days more bearable.

There was a makeshift boxing ring towards the middle of the room on the right-hand side, and there were two people in the ring. One of them was a man who worked directly for Janus, he was moving around with his fists in front of his tattooed face, wearing no shirt.

The person who he stood in front of was small, maybe half his size. He was just a child, maybe eleven or twelve from what Shaun could tell, and the man taunted him, before knocking him in the face. Causing him to fall flat on the floor of the ring.

Shaun was clenching his fists tight in fury and wanted to jump up and stop it, but it would be worse for everybody involved if he did. Janus was stood at the very far end of the room moving around like a maniac, covered in tattoos, even on his clean-shaven head. He had a great big speaker system on the far wall next to him, and a huge TV next to a poorly made bar that someone had put together for him. All the things he needed power for were hooked up to a big generator, puffing hot air and fumes into the room.

Janus could see Shaun and Ethan from the other side of the room, and from the looks of it he was expecting them. His shaved head and inked face made his eyes bulge out as he stared their way.

The door man walked with them and guided them up until they were stood in front of him.

'Thank you, Luka,' said Janus.

Luka remained quiet, and just nodded and turned around, walking back to the door, where he sat on an old office chair.

'Which one of you is Shaun?' he asked.

Shaun took a breath and said, 'I am.'

Janus walked toward him, Shaun was a lot taller than Janus, who was actually quite short and skinny compared to him.

He stopped around half a metre away and turned to face Ethan, 'That must make you the coward,' he said.

He stood in between them looking at them both. He let out a small laugh as he looked at Ethan and then turned to Shaun.

'You're his friend?' he asked.

'You could say that,' said Shaun.

Janus looked Shaun up and down and then thumped him on his chest, both hands fisted, lightly making a small thud sound.

'Good thing he's got you to protect him.'

Janus turned to Ethan and looked at him, he was shaking and sweating.

'I'm glad your both here,' he said.

He looked towards someone behind them and some metal foldable chairs were brought over and placed them behind Shaun and Ethan so they could sit down.

There were only two, and as Shaun sat and then Ethan, Janus shot forward and pushed Ethan backwards, almost making him fall. He took the chair and said, 'You can stand.'

Ethan's heart was racing as he thought something much worse was going to happen. Janus sat down on the chair he took from Ethan and sat facing Shaun in his chair, and Ethan standing next to him, looking and feeling awkward.

Shaun was on edge. He had no idea what Janus had planned for them.

'I need the both of you to do something for me,' said Janus. 'And if you can get it done, we'll forget about what the both of you have done.'

Shaun felt a sudden wave of relief, thinking maybe he was going to get out of this alive after all, and even maybe without getting hurt.

'Of course, we'll do whatever it is you want,' said Shaun.

Janus smiled and sat back in his chair. 'Good,' he said.

Janus told them that he needed them to go somewhere, a warehouse nearby that they hadn't gone to yet. He said that his scouts reported that there were people living there, using the supplies, and he wanted the supplies for himself.

He told Shaun and Ethan that he wanted them to go there and kill all of them. Shaun was reluctant, he didn't want to kill anybody, especially if they hadn't done anything wrong. Ethan suddenly felt chattier, as he thought they were going to get out of this easier than he thought.

'We can do that, that's easy,' he said nodding. 'Right Shaun?'

Janus turned his attention at Ethan, with a frown. He stood up quickly, and punched Ethan in the mouth.

Shaun saw it all in a blur, as it happened too fast for him to realise what was happening. The next thing he saw was Ethan lying on the ground beside him crying out, and Janus standing beside him.

'I wasn't talking to you,' he said, and then kicked him in the side of his ribs. Ethan let out a whimper as he took the blow.

Shaun was smart enough to know that he couldn't do anything to help, *and if it wasn't for him, we wouldn't be in this mess anyway,* he thought.

Janus sat back down after a few seconds and warned Ethan to stay where he was.

'So?' he said, looking at Shaun, waiting for a response.

'We'll do it,' he said.

'Good,' said Janus.

Janus stood and waved for one of his men to bring him something and brought him a map.
He took it from the man's hands and showed it to Shaun.

'This is where you are going to go,' he said, pointing at a big building in the middle of what looked to be an industrial estate.
Shaun wanted to ask, *Why us and not people he trusted,* but he knew better than to ask questions.

'You can take what you need on the way out,' said Janus.

'Thank you,' said Shaun, as he began to stand up.

Janus stood up with him, and someone came over to take the chairs.

Ethan was still laying on the floor, covering his head with his arms.

Shaun walked over and tapped him on the shoulder.

Ethan jumped as soon as he felt someone touch him, afraid that he was going to be hit again.

'Come on,' said Shaun.

Ethan poked his face through his arms, and looked up to see Shaun standing by him, relieved that it was him. He went to stand up, but before he could Janus stopped him.

'Wait,' said Janus. 'Don't get up.'

Ethan looked towards him, and so did Shaun.

What is he going to do now? thought Shaun.

Janus walked close to him and said, 'Crawl.'

Ethan frowned. 'What?' he asked.

Janus crouched down to his knees. 'Crawl,' he said. 'I want you to crawl out of here.'

Ethan looked up at Shaun as if he was asking for help, but he looked away unable to do anything and walked on, before Janus could decide he wanted to mess with him as well.

Ethan had no choice but to crawl on his stomach, using his arms to pull and legs to push himself along the grimy floor. Janus stood watching and laughing. His laugh was high pitched and sounded like it was coming from a small child.

Chapter 22

Abe, George and Frank were on the way to the distribution centre in Frank's truck.

George was sitting on the back seat, looking through the book that Frank had given to him.

Now Abe was closer he was able to see, by looking back from the front passenger seat, that it was a book about birds. The front cover was just blank and green, but on the inside, there were all kinds of different beautiful looking birds.

George was eating a cereal bar as he flicked through, they didn't want to waste too much time waiting around in the apartment eating breakfast.

Luckily, the snow hadn't fallen too heavily the night before and it was easy enough for the truck to drive through the roads, though they had to be careful.

They saw that someone had tried to drive their car through there at some point but had driven straight into a fire hydrant that had been hidden by the snow. The bonnet was bent into a upside down *V*.

Abe was sitting next to Frank, and they hadn't talked much since they set off, but he wanted to start a conversation. He was bored, and George was happy looking at his book in the back.

'How long do you think it will take us to get there?' Abe asked.

Frank was in a daydream and didn't answer. Abe prompted him by saying his name.

'Oh, sorry...should only be another fifteen minutes.'

Abe just smiled. 'Great', he said, not knowing what else to say. Frank wasn't the best conversationalist.

Abe turned to look out of the window as they drove down the street, looking at all the bodies lying and standing, all frozen solid. There were so many, it was like a sleeping army waiting for the springtime. It was hard to tell if they were all one of *them,* or if maybe some of them had still been human.

'We're almost there,' said Frank. 'This is the last stretch of road and we'll be on the industrial estate.'
Both Abe and George sat up and looked forward, waiting to see the building Frank had told them about.

He told them that it was huge, and it had over seven loading bays where the lorries would pick up and deliver goods. He said that there were big fences all around so they might have a little trouble getting in, but he took some tools and a ladder to help them when they got there.

When they got close enough to see the big grey metal building though, it became clear that they wouldn't be needing any of it, the tools or the ladder.
The gate had been broken open, and the road in front of them had tyre tracks all along the snow that ran off into the distance.

Frank stopped the truck and let out a tired breath and rested his head on the steering wheel.

'What's wrong?' asked Abe. 'We knew some people might have been there already, but you said they would need more than a couple lorries to get the stuff out of there.'

Frank sat up back in his chair and pointed towards the building with his finger.

Abe looked and all he could see was the loading bays with just two lorries sitting there.

'What?' he asked.

George leant forward, looking through a small pair of binoculars he had been hoping to use to look at birds.

'Someone took the other lorries. The tyre tracks lead from the other loading bays, and they took at least four of them.'

Abe looked to where George now pointed too, and realised that they were right.

'There might still be some stuff left,' he said. 'Come on, let's go inside and check, at least we don't need to worry about the gate anymore.'
Frank put the truck back into drive and slowly and carefully drove through the gate.

'Who do you think took it all?' asked George.

'I don't know, but there must have been quite a few of them,' said Frank.

The tracks had already been covered slightly by the snow, which meant they must have left a little while ago. The building looked quiet, but they still had to be careful. The last thing they wanted was run into anyone unfriendly.

They parked the truck outside, near a fire exit where someone had bashed through the door with something, there were footprints still all in the snow.

Abe had been worried that Frank might tell him and George to wait in the truck, but he didn't. He was happy for them to help, and even showed Abe how to use the gun that he had.

Abe was a little worried about George though - he didn't want to use a gun, so Abe would have to look out for them both.

Frank crept into the building slowly, taking the lead, with Abe behind him and George at the back. He was holding some kind of rifle and tiptoed inside the building making sure it was safe.

They came into a quiet hallway, there was carpet on the ground, white painted walls and an old brown wooden handrail that went all along the wall and up the small stairs that lead to the main warehouse. Frank ushered them in with a hand sign. They were all listening intently, checking for the sound of voices or footsteps.

The further they got into the building the warmer it got, and it made Abe start to think that maybe there could be some of *them* waiting inside. When they got up the little stairs and walked through the door into the warehouse, he saw that he was right. There were at least twenty of them scattered all over the warehouse floor, but they were all torn to pieces, lying on the ground. Whoever had taken the supplies came in with their team and shot every single one of *them.*

For a minute, Abe worried that they might have been just ordinary humans, but as they carefully walked down towards them, he could see that they weren't.

Their skin had started to grey, and the hair had fallen out in patches. Some of them still had blood-stained mouths, and then when Abe stepped a couple of steps forward, he noticed a man that wasn't one of *them,* and he had a tattoo on his neck, next to which had a great big bite mark where one of them must have got to him.

'Frank,' Abe called. 'One of these is a normal person.'

Frank walked over, with George next to him, still carrying his binoculars by a string around his neck.

'Do you think he was friendly?' Abe asked.

Frank bent down, still holding his rifle and looked at the man lying there.

'No idea,' he said. 'We can't even be sure he was part of the same group that came and took everything.'

Abe looked back up and scanned the room, there were shelves everywhere, all empty. Completely stripped clean. The room was quite big though, there was a chance that they left something there.

'Let's keep looking,' said Frank. 'Come on George.'

Abe walked off first, followed by Frank.

George saw them walk off and stepped closer to the body looking sad, but then bent down checking the man's pockets. He pulled a wallet out of one of the pockets that was on the coat he was wearing. It was a small leather wallet, and it was thin and light. It was more like a leather credit card holder. George opened it and looked through, looking for maybe ID, hoping that it could help know who he was and maybe where he was from. If he had military ID, then they would know they were friendly and that they could have come from one of the bases. *Matthew Briggs,* George read in his head, looking at the man's ID.

He looks friendly in his picture, thought George, and then he found a little picture in one of the pockets of the wallet of a little girl and a woman. It made him feel really sad and he wondered if they were still alive somewhere.

Then he found something else, there was a hotel key card in the main pocket.

I wonder why he kept this here? he thought.

He put the picture back in the wallet, and then put it in his coat, thinking if they did find them, that he could return it to the lady.

Abe and Frank had walked quite far ahead, and turned a corner out of George's sight.

When they turned the corner, all they saw were more empty shelves and bodies on the ground.

Except at the far end on one of the loading docks, there were a load of boxes.

'Do you see that?' said Abe.

Frank looked, squinting his eyes, and said, 'Yeah, that must be what they couldn't fit in the lorry and had to leave behind.'

George caught up with them, 'Look what I found,' he said.

Abe held up his hand, 'Hang on a sec,' he said, 'we think we have found some supplies.'

Abe hurried ahead towards the loading dock where the boxes were sat.

Suddenly, something came pouncing out from behind one of the shelves and grabbed on to him.

Abe yelled out in fright as it latched onto his arms, pulling his skin and pinching him through his clothes.

This one had been infected for a long time, its skin was greyer than the others and even had patches where there was pus leaking out. It still had plenty of life in it though, it was strong like a normal human, but its eyes were completely black. It stared into his face, screaming at him and gnashing its jaws. Abe tried to get away and throw it to the ground, but instead he was just dancing around it, making it impossible for Frank to shoot at it.

'Abe! Try and stay still,' he said yelling from the distance, aiming down the sight of his weapon.

Meanwhile Abe was staring into the face of this mindless creature trying to bite him, fighting hard with it, and then something grabbed onto it.

George had run up to the back of this *thing* and jumped on to its back with one of his arms clutched onto around its neck. He used his free hand to pull on what hair it had left on its head, trying to pull it away from Abe.

'Get off him' George yelled.

Abe saw George on the back of this thing, and he felt like his heart had stopped beating as his eyes widened.

'George!' he yelled, worried he was going to get himself killed trying to save him.

The creature was trying its hardest swing around and bite down onto whatever part of George it could get to, and as George pulled it back, they crashed into one of the shelves, and both fell to the ground.

George landed with this thing on top of him, the weight of it, knocking the wind out of him, and making him lose his grip.

It turned around on the floor and crawled onto George like a rabid dog, still trying to bite him.

Before it had the chance, Frank came running, yelling and grabbing it. He pulled it off George and threw it forward into some shelves. As it looked at Frank and started towards him, Frank pulled his rifle up, aimed straight at it and *bang.*

Its head lost a chunk as blood sprayed across the shelves behind it and its body dropped almost immediately, its groans and screams disappearing.

Frank hadn't fired yet though, and he looked to his left-hand side and saw that Abe had fired first.

Abe rushed over to George and helped him up to his feet.

'Are you okay?' Abe asked.

George nodded, looking shaken, taking Abe's hand as he pulled him to his feet.

'You two stay here and keep each other safe,' said Frank, as he walked off holding his rifle, checking between the other shelves and around corners to see if there were more of them hiding.

Frank came back a few seconds later saying, 'The rest of the place is clear but we should get a move on, just in case somebody else comes.'

Just as the words left his mouth, they heard the engines of somebody else's car rev from outside.
It was like Frank had jinxed them by saying it. Abe looked up towards one of the metal shutters on the loading bay, listening with his mouth slightly open in worry.

'What do we do?' Abe whispered.
George was standing still looking scared, and Frank was looking from side to side, looking for somewhere to hide.

'We can't fight them', said Frank. 'We have no idea how many of them there are.'

George was hunched over nervously fiddling with his hands, 'What if they're friendly?' he asked.

Abe shook his head. 'We don't know that, and it's too risky to find out,' he said.

'He's right, we need to hide,' Frank said, nodding.

They all looked around for somewhere to hide. Abe pointed at the boxes that were left on the loading dock.

'Quick, let's try hiding in there,' he said.

They rushed over, there was two huge wooden boxes and a couple of small cardboard ones beside them.

They opened one and it was half filled with small parcels, covered in brown paper. The other was almost full to the top of styrofoam peanuts, but other than that it looked like the things inside had been taken.

Abe jumped in and then George, followed by Frank after he had helped him climb in.

Frank lowered the wooden lid and pulled it down as tight as he could. It was horribly dark and quiet inside, not to mention how cramped it was with three of them in there. All they had to do now was wait and hope that they left soon.

Shaun and Ethan parked outside the front of the building, both of them agreed that it was a little worrying when they saw all of the tracks on the road and the broken gate.

'Do you think they're all gone?' Ethan asked.

'I sure as hell hope so,' said Shaun.

They jumped out of the car, next to one of the lorries by the loading bay. Ethan jumped up, trying the door handle on the door beside it, but it was still locked.

Shaun had gone the other way, holding a shotgun in his hands.

'*Hey,*' he yelled. 'Come over here, I found a way in.'

Shaun was standing by the fire exit with the smashed door when Ethan ran over and asked, 'Did you do this?'

Shaun frowned at him, 'No,' he said, 'it was clearly the people that were here before.'

'Shall I wait here and give you back up if you need it?' said Ethan, hoping that he wouldn't have to go inside.

'No, you're coming in, I need someone to watch my back, we have no idea how many of them could be in there.'

Shaun took the lead and Ethan followed behind. They were happy when they went inside that they couldn't hear or see anyone. When they got to the warehouse, Shaun thought that someone had beaten them to it, killed everyone and took the stuff, but then he noticed that the dead were the infected. He lowered his gun and looked around as far as he could see, looking at the still empty warehouse.

'Looks like there might have been a few of them,' he said, 'and they would have had to be well armed to kill this many.'

Ethan looked round feeling nervous. 'You're right, maybe we should go in case they come back.'

Shaun shook his head. 'No, we can't go back empty handed,' he said. 'The punishment would be worse.'

Ethan turned his lip up in disappointment and followed behind Shaun as he walked onto the main floor, and further into the warehouse.

Abe could hear muffled voices on the far end of the warehouse. He wanted to know if the others could hear it too, but he couldn't see their faces, and he couldn't ask them just in case the people that they were hiding from were near and heard them.

Shaun walked down the length of the warehouse, checking every aisle and every corner, slowly with his gun at the ready in case of any monsters that might jump out at him. He didn't really want to shoot any normal people, not unless they shot at him first.

Ethan saw the boxes on the loading dock, and hastily walked up to them.

'*Hey*,' he yelled, standing next to it, 'there are some boxes over here.'

Shaun looked over and saw Ethan next to the boxes as he looked at one and went to open it.

Ethan grabbed the lid and went to open it to see what was inside.

'Don't!' Shaun yelled, startling Ethan.

'What?' he asked.

Shaun hurried over, 'You know what happened after opening some cigarettes, imagine what would happen if you opened this,' he said.

Ethan looked at the box and then back at Shaun.

Hmm, he thought to himself, considering ignoring him and looking anyway.

'I guess your right', he said, after a few seconds stepping away from the box.

Abe, George and Frank were inside and couldn't really hear what it was they were saying, but they could hear how close they were. They had all been holding their breaths in unease, sweating from both panic and the heat inside the box.

Thinking that the box was going to be opened, Abe started to think this hiding place had been a bad idea. Maybe they should have just tried to run for it.

Shaun walked over to the door next to the metal shutter. Beside it was a button that opened it.

'What are you doing?' Ethan asked.

'We need to open this thing if we are going to get this out of here.'

Ethan turned and looked at the box with a puzzled look. 'How the hell are we going to carry that out? It won't fit in the car,' he said.

Shaun turned and started walking off, 'No, but there is a forklift, and we can use it to get it onto one of the lorries,' he said.

Ethan watched Shaun climb on to the forklift, thinking, *it probably won't even work,* but it turned on almost straight away.

Shaun drove it up beside the box. 'Do you think that you can hotwire a lorry?' he asked, knowing that he could do it with a car.

Ethan had his arms crossed, 'I can give it a go,' he said.

Around twenty minutes later Ethan had successfully started up the lorry and opened the back, ready to load the boxes on. While Shaun got into place to pick up the boxes with the forklift, he made sure to tell Ethan to carry the smaller boxes into the back by himself.

Abe, George and Frank could hear the sound of the lorry and thought that they might be leaving and decided to leave the bigger boxes behind, but then they felt the judder of the box as it was lifted up and carefully moved. All three of them knocked into each other, making involuntary groans as they did, and worrying they might have given themselves away, but with the sound of the lorry and the forklift, mixed with the howling wind outside, they were safe from being heard.

'What do we do?' Abe whispered.

'I don't know,' said Frank.

They still had no idea if these people were friendly or not and how many of them there were.

'We should wait until they put us on the lorry and start driving,' said Abe, 'then we should try and get out, and sneak off the back when they are going slow enough for us to jump off.'

'Okay, let's do it,' Frank said quietly. 'Good idea.'

However, only a minute after they felt the box drop onto the back of the lorry, they realised they had made a big mistake. There was a sudden thud on top of the box. Whoever it was that loaded them onto the lorry, put the other box on top of theirs.

Abe saw George's eyes widen as he realised what had happened.

After they heard the back doors close, and the lorry pull off slowly, Abe tried to push the lid off the top, but he had no luck. Frank tried and it wouldn't budge for him either.

'Come on let's all try at the same time,' he said.

They all tried pushing as hard as they could, but it wouldn't move, and all that happened was a squeak from the wooden lid as they tried to force it open.

*Oh no...*thought Abe. 'We're stuck!'

Chapter 23

Shaun and Ethan were both on their knees in front of Janus as he walked back and forth between them. He had blood-stained knuckles and a blood smear across his forehead. For the moment, Shaun and Ethan were unhurt, but there was someone who was lying on their back in the middle of the ring, unmoving, that Shaun had noticed on the way in.

'So,' said Janus, 'you really expect me to believe that the entire place was empty, and there was nobody there?'

Shaun was still, wondering if he should answer. Janus was fidgeting as he walked, looking like a bottle that was about to explode.

'Someone beat us to it,' said Shaun, 'there were tonnes of dead there, whoever it was had killed them all.'

Janus stopped pacing and looked at both Ethan and Shaun, one then the other, biting his bottom lip hard.

'Really?' he said. 'Why should I believe the liar and the thief, that my supplies are missing and that there was no one there to find who could be to blame for stealing it all.'

'We brought back a couple boxes,' said Ethan, nervously.

Janus bent down, with his hands on his knees so he was closer to Ethan. 'A couple?' he said. 'Lucky me.'

He turned around and walked towards one of his men asking for his radio.

The man fumbled around looking for it on his belt, taking too long.

When he handed the radio to Janus, he took it from his hand, and said, 'Thank you,' and then punched him hard in the face.

The man was quite big though and only stumbled from the blow while holding his face with his hands.

Janus walked over to his couch, near the speakers and his makeshift bar at the far end, staring hard at Shaun and Ethan. Both of them, were feeling shaky with fear.

'Why is he so mad?' Ethan asked Shaun, whispering, 'We brought him *some* stuff.'

'Let's just hope whatever is in there is good and cheers him up.'

Then the men that were standing behind them, knocked them in the back of their heads with the butts of their guns, telling them to *shut up!*

All they could hear from Janus and what he was saying on the radio was him mumbling and the static noise from the radio when the other person was talking. Suddenly Janus' face changed, and he somehow looked to be even more annoyed, then angry. His face reddened as he looked at the radio, threw it down and stomped back over towards them, baring his teeth.

Janus marched up to Ethan and grabbed him, pulling him upwards. As he did there was a sudden ringing of an alarm throughout the entire building. All of the men around suddenly grabbed their weapons at the ready.

What's going on? This can't all be just for us, thought Shaun.

Janus shook Ethan, staring him in the face, spitting on him as he yelled. 'You think that you can sneak people in and take me down?' he yelled. '*Huh?*'

Ethan began to cry as he pleaded and said, 'I didn't do anything, I swear!'

Janus threw him down in front of him screaming, '*Liar!*'

He grabbed onto Ethan's arm as he tried to block any blow that was coming. Janus grabbed a hold of his hand, pried open his fingers and slid his smallest finger into his mouth. Ethan began to scream out blubbering like a baby, pleading him to stop.

Janus did not relent, and instead bit down hard, crunching through the gristle, blood streaming down his mouth as Ethan wriggled around yelling in agony.

Janus got stuck on the bone, making him even more furious that a pathetic little cowardly rodent was too strong for him. So, he moved the finger to the corner of his mouth, and bit down a second time as hard as he could, ripping and tearing off Ethan's little finger.

Shaun was trying not to look. He stared straight ahead, knowing he couldn't stop it, but wanting to.

Janus stood up leaving Ethan crying on the ground in a ball and spat the finger down on the floor. He wiped the blood from his mouth with his arm.

'Now take them both to the cells, I want to finish both of them off later, when we kill these asshole intruders.'

A little earlier, Abe, George and Frank were still in the box, still stuck and unable to open the lid. None of them had any clue where they could be, there was no way to tell.

Since they had stopped, and they heard the lorry park, and its drivers leave, it had gotten so much warmer, making it incredibly uncomfortable. George was scared that they might be stuck in there and die. He even started to worry that they were back at Decans.

Abe told him that they were going to be fine, that Decans place was much further away, and if they could escape Decan, then they were going to get out of there too.

Then they heard voices mumbling on the outside of the box, it was hard to know how many, but by guessing it sounded like there were three or four of them. The voices got louder and they heard them struggle to move the box off the top of them. Then, the lid of their box was pried open, casting a light inside and revealing two grotty faces looking down at them.

The two men grinned and one of them, who had a missing tooth, said, 'Well…well…well, look what we got here.'

The other pointed a gun at them and told them to get out with an irritated frown.

The one with the missing tooth saw their guns, 'I'll take those,' he said.

The one aiming the gun at them, as Abe, George and Frank stood there with their hands behind their heads, looked at his mate and said, 'what do we do now?'

Abe looked at the one with the missing tooth, inspecting them with his gaze, his skin was pale, and his back was crooked.

He said, 'Call it in upstairs.'

Abe saw the other man grab the radio from his belt, reporting to someone with a deep voice, that sounded maybe Russian, telling him of the intruders.

The voice came back saying, 'that's not all, looks like they brought some friends too.'

Suddenly, there was an alarm bellowing through the building. Neither Abe nor the others had a clue still where they were, they were still stood on the back of the lorry, beside the box. All they could see ahead was an open room, mainly concrete and lit by oil drums with fire in them.

The man with the missing tooth and his mate looked up as the alarm went off, wondering what was going on.

The one on the radio called back out on the radio, '*Dimitri,* what do we do with them?'

There was an unnerving silence for a few moments before he came back and said, 'lock them up for now, we can question them about their *friends.*'

Abe could feel George shaking beside him, and he looked over at Frank who met his eyes. They all knew they didn't have any *friends* with them.

Who are they? Abe thought.

Just as the two men were about to march them off, Dimitri called back over the radio with a quick order.

'Bag their heads,' he said. 'Don't let them get a look of what the inside of our base looks like.'

The two men looked around for something to bag their heads with, but they didn't just have three sacks hanging around, so they had to improvise.

It became clear to Abe and the others that these two were quite dumb. The one who had been talking on the radio yelled to someone outside of the truck and told them to come over.

He asked them for something to blindfold them with, and they improvised with some dirty rags for George and Frank, and then he forced one of the other men to remove his t-shirt, so he could use that.

When they wrapped it around Abe's head, he could smell the sweat and dirt, it was horrible and made him want to be sick. It was clear that this thing hadn't been washed in weeks, and the way it smelled was like the person who was wearing it hadn't either.

The men quickly marched Abe, George and Frank off the truck, pushing them forward roughly, all three of them nearly falling over.

Abe couldn't see a thing, or really smell anything besides the disgusting shirt that was around his face. He could feel the heat of fires as he walked past them, which only made the smell worse. The alarm was still ringing, and it was hurting his ears. He wanted to cover them, but he had to keep his hands behind his head.

'Open it,' one of the men yelled. 'Quickly!'

Just as there was a sound of screeching of a door opening, there was a sudden bang and crash from the far end of the room from where they were. It sounded like a bomb had gone off and caused a wall to crash down somewhere. Abe felt panicked even more now and not being able to see made it worse.

Abe had no idea what was going on, but there was a lot of shouting and screaming followed by gunfire shredding through the air. He could hear the panic of the men holding them as they shoved them down on the ground. Abe heard a clicking noise come from their guns.

Then one of them swore and a woman's voice yelled out, 'Throw down your weapons.'

It was followed by the loud clunk of their guns being dropped on the ground.

I recognise that voice, Abe thought, frowning as he tried to place it. The woman got closer, and by the sound of it, she was followed by a lot of people.

Abe assumed that there were far too many for the men who had them captive to even try fighting.

Maybe it's the people that raided the distribution centre? thought Abe. *Maybe they followed us here.* Even if that were true, there was no guarantee that they were any friendlier than the people in this place.

The woman said something to the two men that had Abe and the others. 'Who are these three?' she asked.

All of a sudden it hit Abe who the voice belonged to. *It's Anna,* he thought. He felt George prodding him, probably trying to tell him that it was her.

But does she know it's us? he wondered.

The one with the missing tooth answered her, 'They're yours,' he said. 'We caught them trying to sneak inside.'

Anna squinted slightly, confused. She knew full well that they didn't have anyone try to sneak in, but she didn't have time to think about them now.

'Lock them up in there with those two, we'll come back for them,' she said, pointing her gun at them. 'Now lead the way and show us where your boss is.'

The two men nudged Abe, George and Frank into their cell, leaving their arms free.

As soon as they were in there, Frank removed the rag from his head and looked at the woman on the other side, seeing just how many people she had behind her. She had at least fifteen, maybe twenty people, and all of them had big guns in their hands.

Anna looked at him with a suspicious squint and just saw an innocent old man. 'Go,' she yelled at the other men, ordering them to take her to their boss.

Frank didn't know what to make of her. He looked around and saw that George and Abe still had their faces covered. 'What are you doing?' he asked. 'You can take those off now.'

'Is she gone?' George whispered, before Abe had the chance.

Frank was confused why they were asking, 'The lady?' he asked. 'Yeah, she's gone.'

Abe took the dirty top off his face as quick as he could when he knew that Anna was gone and coughed in the process, trying to push out all the disgusting air he had inhaled through that gross smelly thing that he was forced to wear.

There was a murmuring in the dark corner of the room.

They soon realised that the "cell", they were in wasn't that much of a cell, and was really just some metal fences that had been attached to the opening of a small enclosed sitting area.

It was dark and dirty in there, and they could only see that there were two figures at the end of the room.

'Hello?' said Abe.

Frank had his hand up to his eyes, trying to focus who was there.

'Hey,' said one of them.

Abe stepped closer, followed by Frank and George.

'What happened to your friend,' asked Abe, looking at a young man huddled in the corner.

'Our psychopath leader bit his finger off when he found out that you had snuck in,' said the man sitting down.

Abe and the others felt slightly concerned at that point, thinking that if they were hurt because of them, they might try retaliating against them.

'At least your people will probably kill him and the rest of the scum that's here,' the man continued.

George walked ahead of Abe and Frank and introduced himself to the man. 'Hi, I'm George,' he said.

The man was a little startled at first when he saw George walk forward and saw his face, but he recovered in time to shake his hand, 'I'm Shaun,' he said.

'These are my friends, Abe and Frank,' said George, pointing to the both of them.

'Hey,' said Shaun, 'this is Ethan, I don't suppose any of you are doctors?' Mainly looking at Frank. Abe and George were clearly way too young.

Frank looked at the rag in his hand that he had had over his head, 'I can try and help,' he said. 'I know a little first aid.'

He kneeled down in front of Ethan and pulled his hand away from his chest, his skin and face was pale, and his clothes had a lot of blood on them.

'This will help for now, but he really needs to see a doctor,' said Frank as he wrapped up Ethan's hand in the rag.

Ethan was exhausted and moaning quietly on the ground.

All of a sudden, there was the sound of more shooting in the distance that echoed through the halls, and then the alarm was silenced a few seconds after. That either meant that Anna had won and taken over, or Janus and his men had beaten them, and now were going to come for them now too.

Shaun heard the alarm silence and stood up saying, 'We need to get out of here.'

'How?' asked Abe.

Shaun stepped up to the front of the cell and looked at it up and down. It was poorly made. 'We should be able to break this down with all five of us, but we have to do it now, before they come back.'

Abe didn't know who their leader was, but by the way he had treated Ethan, it was clear that he was psychotic. He didn't know who was left and who had won, but even if it was Anna, and she came back and found him and George there, it might be just as bad.

'Okay, let's do it.'

Chapter 24

Night had fallen, making it even harder to see, with no lights working in the building. Abe, George and Frank had no idea where they had to go to get out. The place was much bigger than they expected, they had to rely on Shaun and Ethan now to show them the way out.

Shaun had Ethan on his shoulder as he tried to run as fast as he could through the halls of the buildings, keeping to the shadows in the corners, whilst making sure that the others were keeping up.

Abe was trying to talk to George as they ran for the exit, both questioning how Anna knew they were there.

'Is she here for us?' George asked him.

'I hope not,' said Abe.

Frank had no idea still who this woman was, 'Who is she?' he said, as he tried to keep up with them, talking quietly.

They all stopped around a corner behind Shaun, hiding in an unlit area.

Shaun was peering round, looking down a short passageway that lead to the cargo bay.

'I'll tell you later,' said Abe.

Shaun turned around to Abe and the others, and said, 'We're almost there, we need to run as fast as we can and take one of the trucks.'

Abe nodded and said, 'Okay.'

He turned around to make sure that George and Frank were ready. They checked left and right to make sure that there was no one around, and once Abe saw Shaun make a run for it, he followed and so did the others behind him.

The closer they got to the exit and to the cargo bay, the more bodies they saw. There was easily over twenty bodies just in this one area, their weapons still lying on the ground or still gripped in their hands. They had been no match for Anna and the force she had behind her.

Shaun got to the end of the passageway and held the door open for them all to run through, before he followed in behind Frank and dragged over a burnt-out oil drum to barricade the door to stop anyone that was following them to get them.

Abe, George and Frank were standing in the middle of the cargo bay looking around. It was empty. Shaun ran up beside them and saw that all the cars and trucks were gone.

Oh no, thought Shaun.

Abe pointed at something in the far end in one of the openings of the loading area.

'What about that?' he said.

From a distance it just looked like a metal shutter in the opening of the loading bay, but it was a big lorry that had been left.

Abe started over towards it, 'Come on,' he said. 'We'll have to take that.'

Frank and George quickly followed behind him, and Shaun was last to follow.

'It won't take all of us,' he said, 'It will only take three.'

Abe and the rest of them kept running. 'We'll just have to squeeze in,' Abe yelled.

As they all ran up and went to jump down the other side onto the snow, Frank stopped at the back.

'Wait a minute, the door is open slightly on the back,' he said, as he walked over to close it.

He pulled the shutter up, intending to pull it down with more force to make sure it shut properly, and as he did, he got a glimpse of what was in the back. He was shocked to see what was there. He closed it tight and made sure it couldn't open, before jumping down off the bay and onto the snowy ground, and running over to climb into the driver's seat. They were all squeezed in together, and it was incredibly cramped.

This is worse than the box, thought George.

Within just a few minutes they were headed out of there. Frank had his foot down on the pedal, with the headlights on and drove as fast as he could out of that place, while Shaun tried to direct him the right way.

On the way past they saw where Anna had broken into the building. There was a great big hole in one of the walls with loads of jeeps and cars outside, their doors left open from where Decan's men had jumped out and run into the building.

Abe watched the place growing smaller and further away in the mirror as he wondered who had won the fight. Did Anna overthrow Janus, or did Janus beat them somehow? It sure looked like he was both out-manned and out-gunned.

Maybe he realised that and bailed, and that's where all the cars and trucks went, Abe thought. *Maybe he took whoever was left and made a run for it.*

Suddenly, Abe was shaken out of his deep thought as someone grabbed his arm.

'Are you okay?' asked George.

Abe turned to look at George and smiled, 'Yeah thanks, I'm fine.'

Abe, Frank and George had a plan and knew where *they* were headed, but Shaun and Ethan had only just met them. They had no idea who they were and if they could trust them with their plan.

Frank headed to the only place he knew that was safe, *his apartment*. It was dark, so dark that it made it hard to drive as fast as he wanted to. Thankfully the lorry was big and could get through the snow easier than if they just had a little car.

It wasn't going to be ideal for the whole journey, though, especially if Shaun and Ethan went with them.

If it wasn't for them, then we might not have gotten out of there, thought Frank.

Frank pulled up to the front of his building and stopped outside. 'We're here,' he said.

Abe opened the door on the passenger side, letting almost all of them fall out onto the snow.

Frank hopped out, closing the door behind them and walked over to where the rest of them were standing.

'Where are we?' Shaun asked.

'Somewhere safe...for now,' said Abe.

'This is my apartment,' said Frank, 'It's a little small, but it will do for the night.'

Shaun looked around and then back at the lorry. 'What are we going to do with this?' he said, pointing to it. 'What if someone comes looking for it?'

'We could dump it somewhere,' Abe suggested. Frank shook his head, 'No we can't do that,' he said.

'Why not,' asked Shaun.

'Because, before we left, I closed the back of it and saw what was in there. There is a bunch of supplies in there, which we desperately need.'

Ethan was on the ground and Shaun had almost forgotten about him until he stirred and made a noise.

'We have to get him inside,' he said.

Frank looked at Ethan on the ground, with Shaun holding him up.

'Abe, take him upstairs,' said Frank, looking at him. 'George, you help me hide the lorry, open the gate on the side.

Both Abe and George nodded and said 'okay', each heading to do their tasks. Just as they moved there was a noise from inside the truck. Abe noticed it first and quickly spun around, making a crunching noise as his feet turned in the snow.

'What was that?' he exclaimed, as he thought, *Is it one of them?*

They all looked at each other as it sounded like whatever was in there was trying to get to the door at the back of the lorry.

'What do we do?' Abe whispered.

They didn't have their weapons anymore; they were taken when they were caught hiding in the box.

'*Here…*someone take this,' said Shaun as he removed a pistol from his pants.

Frank took it from him, 'Where did you get this?' he asked.

'I took it from one of the people dead on the ground while we were escaping,' he explained. 'It's all I could carry with Ethan on my shoulder.'

Frank looked at him feeling slightly suspicious that he hadn't mentioned anything up until this point, and then he was snapped back to what was important by the juddering of the metal door on the back of the lorry. Whatever was in there was trying to get out.

Frank headed to the back of the lorry, with Abe and George behind him, just in case he needed their help. They didn't have any weapons, but if there was only one of *them*, and it managed to grab onto him, then the two of them could easily pull it off.

Frank stepped up to the back of it, gulping with unease, not knowing what was on the other side. The noise had stopped, and Frank told George to slowly open the latch on the door while he aimed at the ready for when it opened.

George pulled the latch to the side, unlocking the back, and the door went flying up into the air as it opened, while George dashed backwards. It was too dark inside to see what was in there right away, until Frank's eyes started to adjust. Whatever it was immediately tried to hide as soon as the door was opened. Frank lowered his gun, realising that it must be someone that was alive.

'Hello?' he said, calling out to whoever was in there.

Abe stepped closer to Frank, 'Did you see them?' he asked.

'No,' said Frank, and then they saw it.

Someone crept forward to the back door of the truck, almost on their knees. All they could see was a dark figure at first, until they came close enough that they could see them in the moonlight.

It was a girl, and she slowly came to the door looking at them all with a sceptical look.

'Who are you?' she said.

Abe and Frank looked at each other, and then Abe stepped forward slightly.

'We just escaped from Janus' base,' he said. 'It's okay, we're not going to hurt you.'

She sounded quite young, but without seeing her face clearly, it was hard to tell.

When Abe spoke to her, she turned her head towards him and looked to be interested in him.

'I know you,' she said, causing everyone to look at Abe, as though accusing him of something.

Abe looked back at them, confused before turning back to the girl.

'What's your name?' he said.

She jumped down off the truck, making her face clear and easy to see. Abe recognised her instantly and froze.

It's Abbie, he thought.

His chest became tight, and his palms started to sweat.

Abbie was standing there wearing clothes that looked like she had been wearing for weeks. Her face and hair were dirty, and she had some cuts on her face.

Abe didn't notice any of that. He could see her how he remembered her from before. She used to work in the shop where he used to buy all his video games. He purposely went there every time, even though the prices were slightly higher than the others, just so he could see her and try to speak to her.

She had medium length blonde hair down to her shoulders but shaved on one side.

Abe had always thought she was incredibly pretty, and the moonlight on her face made it even more obvious. Abe was so nervous he couldn't speak. He opened his mouth but all that came out was a small squeak

Abbie smiled at him, 'It's definitely you,' she said remembering him doing that panicky thing before.

George looked at Abe with a frown, confused why he was acting that way and hadn't seen him do it before.

'Hi, I'm George,' he said as he walked up and tried to shake her hand.

Before George would have found it more difficult just to introduce himself to someone, especially someone as pretty as her, but now he had friends around him, he didn't find it so hard.

'I'm Abbie,' she said, smiling and shaking George's hand.

Frank, standing next to Abe, punched him in the arm, trying to make him act normally.

'Hi,' Abe said eventually. 'How did you get in there?'

Abbie looked at the back of the truck and then gave a quick scan of the others, '*Well,* it's a long story, but the short version is I did it to escape from the same place you did,' she said. 'When the alarm went off and things started to get bad, I tried to make a run for it and then I got trapped when everyone started to do the same thing and took the cars. I jumped in the back of the lorry hoping if someone took it, I would be able to jump out after a couple of blocks, but someone locked it.'

Frank was rubbing the back of his head as he realised, she was referring to him. 'Sorry,' he said with a nervous laugh.

Abe was happy he did though, thinking that she wouldn't have been there now with them if he hadn't.

George turned to Abe and asked him, 'Why are you smiling so much?' He had never seen him smile like that before.

They all looked at him, 'What? *I'm not,*' he said, stuttering. 'I'm just happy to be out of there.'

Abbie was looking at him and then started hugging herself with her arms, trying to warm up from the cold.

'Do you guys have somewhere we can be inside? I'm freezing,' she said.

'That's a good point,' said Frank, 'George, show Shaun and Abbie inside. Abe, help me with the gate so we can hide this thing round the back.

Abe wanted to be the one to show them upstairs because he wanted to see Abbie, but he decided it might seem strange if he argued and helped Frank with the gate.

Abe closed the gate after Frank had driven the lorry carefully around the back, next to a couple bins. It only just about fit between the two buildings.

Frank jumped out and walked over to Abe as he locked the gate back up with the chain that was on there before.

'Do you want to tell me who that lady was?' he asked.

Abe turned around and felt nervous, thinking he was talking about Abbie.

'Abbie? he said, and as he was about to explain, Frank corrected him.

'No,' he said. 'The one you and George were so afraid of back there.'

'Oh,' said Abe, realising he was talking about Anna.
He told Frank that she was the lady that worked for Decan and that she was his right-hand lady.

'Do you think she came here looking for you?' he asked.

'I don't know,' he said. 'I don't see how she would have been able to find us.'

Frank crossed his eyebrows as he thought about it, looking at the snow on the ground. 'Let's cross our fingers and hope not,' he said.

Abe and Frank went back upstairs to the apartment, and George let them in after looking through the peep hole to make sure it was them. It was so lovely and warm inside after being outside in the snow.

Abe followed George into the living room as Frank locked the door. He looked around and saw that Ethan was led out on one of the small sofas and Shaun was sitting on a wooden chair next to him.

'Where's Abbie?' he asked, noticing that she was the only one missing from the room.

'She's taking a bath,' he said, 'It seemed like she hadn't had one in a while.'

When Abe found out that Abbie was just next door taking a bath, he thought it was really weird. He had spent years trying to talk to her whenever he went into her shop, and only ever exchanged a few words. Now she was sharing an apartment with him, having a bath where he did and would probably be travelling with him from now on, at least he *hoped* that she would stick around. Thinking about it made him nervous though, and his chest became tight again and he became really hot and red-faced.

'What's wrong?' asked George.

Abe shook his head, fanning his t-shirt to cool himself down, before taking his jacket off.

'Nothing,' he said.

Frank had just stepped into the room after locking the door, 'He has a crush on her,' he said.

Abe turned his head fast towards Frank, 'No I don't,' he said in a panic. 'Shut up.'

Abe was already red from panic, but he was embarrassed now too.

Frank and the others thought it was funny though, and Frank was laughing in amusement.

Abe realised that if she was going to be sticking around, then he was going to have to get a lot better at talking to her without freaking out.

Then to make matters worse, the bathroom door opened, and Abbie came out just wearing a towel.

He told himself that he wasn't going to be a panicky mess next time he had the chance to talk to her, but it was like his body locked up into a tense statue.

'I don't suppose any of you have spare clothes lying around, do you?' she asked, only having the clothes she escaped in.

Unlucky for her, the people she had bumped into were all men.

Frank though stepped over from the kitchen and said, 'I still have all of my wife's old clothes, you can have a look through them if you like. They're in a box in my closet in the room on the left down the hall.'

When she said thanks and walked off down the hall, she smiled at Abe on the way out.

George turned towards Abe and said, 'You like her, don't you?'

Abe leant in towards George so he could talk to him quietly. 'Yes,' he said whispering, 'but keep it quiet.'

Shaun was sitting next to Ethan; he was not doing great.

Frank came over with a plastic bottle in his hand. 'Here,' he said, 'get him to take these, they should help in case he has an infection. You'll need to clean the wound as well and bandage it properly.'

'Do you have, any bandages?' Shaun asked, taking the bottle from Frank's hand.

'There are some in a first aid kit in the bathroom cupboard,' he said.

Just as Shaun left, Abbie came back into the room wearing a black lace type dress, that hugged her body.

Woah, thought Abe, as he saw her walk in. He had never seen her wear something like that before. He was used to seeing her in her work uniform and school clothes.

Abbie saw Abe look at her as he sat next to George. George was looking through his bird book again, using a little lantern to see by. She was about to go and sit beside him when Frank walked over.

'You found them' he said. 'It fits you well.'

Abbie turned and jumped very slightly. 'Yes, thank you for letting me use your wife's clothes.'

Frank smiled. 'No problem at all, she would have hated to see her clothes gathering dust in a box.'

Abbie looked down at the dress admiring it while smiling. 'It's a beautiful dress, she had very good taste.'

'Yes, she did,' he said after a short pause. 'What made you pick that one?'

'Black is my colour,' she said.

Frank smiled, not mentioning that the dress she had chosen was the one his wife kept for wearing to funerals.

Shaun walked in, slipping past her and sat back down next to Ethan to change the bandage on his hand.

Abbie went to go and sit down again but was interrupted for a second time.

'You must be hungry,' said Frank.

She hadn't thought about it until he asked, but she realised she *was,* she hadn't eaten anything in a while and the food she had managed to get was poor.

'Starving,' she replied.

Frank grabbed a pot off a hook on the wall and placed it down on the stove, 'I have some stew that I made,' he said, 'I hope you like it, Abe will tell you how good it is.'

Abbie turned and smiled, waiting for Abe to say something.

He suddenly felt put on the spot and didn't know what to say.

'Uh...yeah', he said. 'It's yummy.'

Abbie smirked.

Shaun looked up at Frank, smelling the food as it began to cook.

'Could I get some of that?' he asked.

'Me too,' said Abe, followed by George.

'Sure, I'll make some for everybody,' he said. 'But after we eat we should all get some shut eye, we need to get moving first thing in the morning.'

'Where are you going?' Abbie asked.

Frank looked at Abe, he was the one that had the maps and the plan.

'Well...seeing as you and Abe are friends, I'll let him go over it with you,' he said. 'That is if you're planning on sticking with us.'

Abe felt nervous again, worrying that she wouldn't want to.

'I don't really have anywhere else to go, so...if you'll have me, I'll come with you guys,' she said looking towards Abe.

Abe was looking right at her and when she looked back at him, he quickly shifted his gaze elsewhere, worrying that she would think he was weird or creepy.

Before Abe or Frank could say she was more than welcome, Shaun interrupted.

'And what about us?' he asked. 'Me and Ethan.'

Frank paused for a second. It was easier with Abbie, because Abe knew her, and she could be trusted, but they didn't know Shaun and Ethan yet, not that well.

Abbie was surprised, she thought they all knew one another already.

'Oh,' she said, 'do you guys not know each other?'

'They helped us escape,' said Abe.

'Yeah, they did,' said Frank, looking at Abe, not able to physically ask what he thought, but was hoping he would nod in his direction or something.

'We could definitely use the extra hands in a fight, if we get into one', said Abe.

'If it's fine with them, then it's fine with me,' said Frank.

Shaun smiled in relief. 'Thank you, guys,' he said.

'Food's ready,' said Frank, calling everybody up. Each of them went up and took a bowl, with only a small portion of stew now that it had to be shared around. The table was small, so it would only fit a few people. Abe, George, Frank and Abbie sat there as they ate together. It was quiet, making the eating noises very obvious.

Abbie had been stuck at that place for a little while, not as long as Shaun and Ethan, but longer than Abe and the others were there. It was long enough that the food she had just been given tasted like the best thing she had ever eaten, and it was taking every fibre in her body not to just pick up the bowl and eat it as fast as she could. She looked at Abe as he ate and said something to George that she didn't quite hear, and then he looked up but quickly his eyes darted away when he saw her looking in his direction.

Why won't he look at me? she thought.

'So, where is it we're headed?' Abbie asked him.

Abe took an anxious gulp and looked at her, for a moment only looking at her eyes and forgetting he was meant to be answering a question.

'There's a bunker not too far from here,' he said, 'we're trying to get there to wait until all the snow is gone so we can get to the one where my grandma is.'

Abbie started to look curious, 'How do you know where this one is?' she asked.

'I found a map,' he said.

He was expecting her to say something along the lines of - *How are you sure that it is there?* or *How are you going to get in?*

She just smiled and said, 'It's a good thing I found you then.'

Chapter 25

That night, George offered his room to Abbie, so that she would have a nice comfy bed to sleep in for the night instead of the floor or the sofa.

Abe was secretly disappointed and thought if she had slept on the sofa in living room, then it would be his chance to talk to her properly without anybody interrupting.

Everybody went to bed almost right away after they had finished their dinner. Abbie stayed in the spare room where George had slept, Frank in his room and the rest of them in the living room.

Ethan was still lying on the sofa, while Shaun slept on the floor next to him, and George slept on the floor next to the other sofa that Abe was on.

Abe spent hours unable to sleep, staring at the ceiling thinking about Abbie, what he could say to her when he finally got the courage to talk to her properly. He could hardly believe she was here, and he couldn't get her out of his head.

He fell asleep eventually, but he was woken suddenly in the middle of the night, only a couple of hours before sunrise.

There was the abrupt sound of screaming and a kind of waling noise. Abe was lying on his back still and when it woke him, his eyes shot open and he turned to his left.

There was someone on top of Shaun attacking him. Abe felt an immediate rush of panic and jumped up off the sofa.

George heard the noise too and woke the same time as Abe, shooting up.

Shaun was trying to hold the thing up in the air with his arms, but it was pushing down hard at him, snapping and trying to bite him while dribbling uncontrollably all over the floor.

How did it get in here? Abe thought, and then he realised that it hadn't gotten inside, it was already there. It was Ethan, Abe only realised when he got closer and saw him as he rushed forward to help.

Abe grabbed onto Ethan's clothes and pulled on him as hard as he could, throwing him off Shaun.
As he did, Frank, who had also heard the commotion, came running in, just behind Abbie.

Abe hadn't seen them standing there, while he was trying to save Shaun from the thing that was Ethan.

It stumbled backwards as Abe threw it towards the kitchen, but regained its balance quickly, looking Abe in the eye. It was hunched over as it made a chilling noise, readying itself to pounce back at Abe.

Abe could see people in the corner of his eye and noticed that Frank and Abbie were standing near in the doorway, but before either of them had the chance to jump in and help, this thing came flying forward through the air. Abe saw it coming and jumped forward, meeting it halfway so he could push it onto the ground and pin it down.

It looked up at him as Abe got the better of *it* snarling like an angry dog.

Frank rushed to the kitchen quickly grabbing a gun he had stashed in one of the drawers so he could kill it, before *it* killed or hurt somebody.

Something came crashing down into the centre of *its* head, quickly cutting out the snarling and groaning coming from its mouth.

Its head flopped back onto the ground, leaving its black eyes wide open.

Abe continued to hold it tight down on the ground, before he felt a light touch on his shoulder.

'It's dead,' someone said.

Abe looked to his right and saw a pair of legs standing close to him and then noticed that it was Abbie's hand that was on his shoulder. He stood up next to her from the floor and saw her wearing a shirt that was too big for her in place of pyjamas.

'Thank you,' he said.

Abbie smiled in response, and then Shaun came over squeezing passed the both of them to see Ethan lying still on the ground.

Shaun bent down beside Ethan's body and looked at him lying there for a couple of seconds before he shut his eyes with his hand.

Abe turned still standing close to Abbie, probably the closest he had ever stood to her.

'I'm sorry,' said Abe. 'I didn't know him, but I'm sure he was a good guy.'

There was a pause from Shaun as he stayed where he was, looking at the thing that had been his friend.

'No,' he said. 'He wasn't really. He was selfish, and a coward. He got me into trouble more times than I remember, and almost got me killed a few more. But he was the only thing that I had close to a friend while I was *there.*'

None of them knew how to respond, and instead remained quiet.

After a few moments, Frank stepped forward and placed his hand on Shaun's shoulder, in a consoling way and said, 'There's a shovel out the back, I can bury him for you if you don't want to.'

Shaun instead, stood up and picked Ethan up as he did. 'It's fine, I'll do it.'

He walked off out of the room with Ethan's body and went outside silently.

The room was left in a still and awkwardly quiet atmosphere. It was then that Abe could feel Abbie standing as close as she was and could just about feel her arm touching his, thinking how close her hand was to his own.

'Does anybody know what the time is?' she asked, 'I don't think I'm going to be able to get back to sleep now.'

Abe leaned to his left so he could see the clock on the stove as Frank turned to look himself.

'It's just after five,' said Frank, beating Abe to it.

'Maybe you could show me that map you told me about?' Abbie suggested.

Now that his body wasn't pumping with adrenaline from the fight, he felt a little less confident.

'Uh...yeah,' he said. 'Sure'

Abbie smiled and replied, 'Great.'

'Do you want me to show you now?' he asked.

Abbie looked down at what she was wearing and back at Abe after scanning the room quickly, 'Maybe I should get changed first.'

Abe smirked and said, 'Yeah,' followed by a nervous laugh.

'I'll make some tea,' said Frank.

Abbie came back and sat in the seat right next to Abe on the table in the centre of the kitchen.

George had started to try and read his book on the sofa but had been more tired than he thought and fell back to sleep.

Frank took him some tea, just in case he did wake up soon, and carefully took the book from under his face and closed it, putting it safely on the arm next to him.

Frank gave both Abbie and Abe some tea as well, and stood there for a second as Abe rolled out the map, before saying, 'I'll go check on Shaun and take him some tea.'

Now it was just Abe and Abbie in the room, except for George, but he was still asleep on the sofa.

Abe had the map spread out, showing all the different locations on the map where there were bunkers.

'What are all these?' she asked, leaning in and pointing at them.

'They're where people were supposed to go to keep safe from all of this,' he said. 'They're all bunkers, like the one we're going to.'

Abbie frowned slightly but a smile touched her lips. 'Where did you even get this?' she asked.

Abe suddenly feeling very proud said, 'I stole it from someone,' but then he thought if he didn't elaborate quickly, she might think that he was the bad guy.

'There was this guy that took me captive, he tried to get me to do stuff for him by lying to me and pretending he was my friend,' he explained, 'but I figured it out, stole his maps and broke me and George out.'

Abbie was taking a sip of her tea while she listened and smiled. 'Impressive,' she said.

Abe drank some of his tea, not knowing what else to say, but wanting to keep the conversation going.

'What happened to your family?' He asked.

Her face dampened like a candle starting to go out, and took a second before she answered, 'My Mom died, and I don't know *where* my dad is.'

Abe saw her smile fall and felt bad, thinking he shouldn't have asked.

'I'm sorry,' he said, 'I lost my grandpa recently. The guy who took us captive before I came here killed him.'

He missed him so much, and he felt so guilty for believing that he had run away and abandoned him.

Abbie put her hand on top of his, holding it gently. 'I know what you're going through,' she said, 'it was recent for me too.'

Her hand was cold, but *somehow* it made Abe feel warm.

The sun rose, and they all left, there was only enough space in the lorry really for three people, so Frank drove with Abe helping him navigate, and Abbie sitting beside him. Shaun and George took the truck that Abe and George got there in, and they used the lorry to tow it along behind them, with Shaun at the wheel.

They had been driving a couple of hours and George was sat up on his knees on the back seat looking through his binoculars for birds he saw in his book.

Abe had the map folded into a square on his lap of where they were, and where they were headed. It had been a little quiet most of the way, and when Abe thought of something to talk to Abbie about, he turned to talk to her, but she had her head leant against the window, taking a nap.

Abe hadn't noticed a little while later when she had woken up, until she asked how far they had to go.

Abe turned, shocked to hear her say something and then looked at the map.

'Not far now, we should only be another hour,' he said. 'It's mainly just a straight drive from here.'

Abbie looked at their surroundings, noticing that where they were was mainly open land. Not much grass or trees. There were none of *them,* out there either. Not as far as she could see.

'Do you know what we're going to find when we get there?' she asked.

Abe didn't really have any idea for sure what was going to be there, but he wasn't going to admit that with the risk of looking stupid.

'There should be a small base there protecting it. If there are people like there was supposed to be, then we should be able to get in pretty easily,' he said. 'But if it is empty, then we might have to try and find a way in by looking around the base ourselves.'

'What kind of thing would we need to find?' Abbie asked. 'Like a key?'

Again, Abe wasn't too sure, and had to take an educated guess. 'It will probably be more like a key card, or a computer.'

Abbie smiled, feeling slightly impressed with Abe for knowing all this.

Abe was just hoping that he hadn't just said a bunch of nonsense that was going to be proven wrong when they got there.

The hour passed quite quickly. There wasn't much to see on the way there, but they did see a broken-down car along the way with a body led beside it. Abe noticed that it made Abbie look sad when she saw it.

George then spoke to them over the radio and told them that he spotted a *Northern Flicker* through his binoculars, which seemed to brighten her mood.

Frank turned the lorry down a small road that led off towards the mountains, off the main road they had been driving down. There were no signs for this place, they only knew where they were going because of the map.

It better be right, thought Abe.

Abe was expecting maybe for some military vehicle to come speeding up the road after them asking who they were and telling them they were entering a restricted area. He had seen it happen so many times in the movies, but nobody came.

It made him feel nervous, it would have made things a hell of a lot easier if they had just been there and could let them in and maybe even show them how to get to the other base where his grandma was.

Frank stopped the lorry when they got to the end of the road, arriving at a big wire fence with a gate in the middle of it.

There was a barrier in front of them, with a little cubicle next to it where the soldier or security guard would have sat, but there was nobody there. They rolled down the windows on each side, listening out for signs of life, but there was none other than the sound of them breathing. They quickly rolled the windows back up, because it was getting cold.

'What shall we do?' Abe asked Frank.

Frank stared forward for a second, waiting. He thought maybe somebody might come out and greet them, but still no one came.

'I guess we have to try and open the gate.'

Abe took this as his chance to try and be brave in front of Abbie.

'I'll do it,' he said.

Abbie was on the seat nearest the passenger door, so she had to switch seats with him.

Abe's feet crunched down on the snow as he got out of the lorry. The cold wind was stinging his face, and he thought that the air even *smelled* cold.

He turned briefly and looked back at the truck where Abbie and Frank were watching him, before walking in the direction of the gate with a smile.

He approached the little security hut with caution. He couldn't see through the windows and wanted to be careful just in case there was one of *them* in there, but it felt even colder here than it did in the city, so he was hoping if there were, they would be frozen. He scraped the ice of the window off with his sleeve to look inside first, before opening the door.

It's empty, he said to himself. All that was in there was a little stool beside a very small desk.

Abe opened the door and stepped in; it was a lot quieter in there than outside because it was shielded from the wind. He looked around and saw a little flick switch on the wall beside the desk. He hoped that it opened the gate, so he flicked it, but all it did was raise the barrier.

Frank seeing the barrier open drove forward until they were right in front of the gate.

Abe was standing in front of the gate now, looking at it. It was one of the kinds that had wheels and rolled to one side to open.

He peered through the holes in the fence, thinking that he might see people or signs that there were people there at one time, but there wasn't much to see other than open land in the middle of some mountains that rose above them.

At least we'll have a little shelter, he thought.

Then out of nowhere a voice appeared through the air behind him, making him jump and make a squeaky *eek* noise.

He turned and saw that it was Abbie.

'Want some help?' she asked.

He smiled when he realised it was her and said, 'Sure, thanks.'

He walked over to the right-hand side of the gate looking for something that would have kept it locked, but he found it had been left open.

'That's weird', said Abe.

Abbie shrugged her shoulders, 'I guess there are normally guards here to stop people getting in if they're not meant to,' she said.

'Yeah, I guess,' said Abe.

He grabbed onto the edge of the gate, pulling to try and open it. It was a little stiff from the ice and from disuse and the cold metal on his hands made it even harder, so Abe used his sleeves as gloves to open it.

Abbie did the same and helped, opening the gate, making a loud screeching and clattering noise as it rolled open.

When they both walked back over to the truck, Frank was surprised that it was so easy to get in, but relieved.

'I thought we might have to force it open by driving through it,' he said.

'I know, we were really lucky,' said Abe, 'now we can lock it if we need to, to keep *them* or other people out.'

Frank drove forward, as Shaun asked what was going on over the radio. Abe answered him and told him that they got the gate open and now were headed inside.

After they passed the gate, they were able to see how quiet it was and because it was shielded by the mountains around it, they couldn't hear the wind as much.

They crept forward slowly, seeing that there were no buildings, and the path ahead lowered down on a small ramp into an opening in the mountain ahead.
All three of them were silently sitting on the edge of their seats, nervously looking around.

For some reason, Abe kept expecting something to jump out, and it occurred to him that if something did come at them now, they were going to be stuck.

He looked down the short tunnel, and at the end where there appeared to be a couple jeeps parked against the left wall, there was also a metal door. It reminded Abe of the kind you saw on submarines and big ships.

No one else had said anything, but Abe had quickly realised that because there were no buildings, or people, there was nowhere to look for any kind of key to get them in.

What do we do now? he thought, growing more and more anxious the closer they got. He was scared now that everyone was going to get angry with him, and especially worried about disappointing Abbie.

'Is this it?' Frank asked, driving the lorry up alongside the jeeps.

Abe was quiet and didn't know what to say.

'How do we get in?' Abbie asked.

Abe felt hot again. They were both looking at him, but he didn't have the answers.

Then Abbie pointed at something, 'What's that?' she asked.

Abe looked and saw a panel and computer on the wall next to the door. 'It must be how you get in,' he said.

This didn't make things much better, if it was a computer and they needed a password, then they were never going to be able to get in. There is no way that they would be able to guess it.

'Let's all take a look,' said Frank.

He called to Shaun and George on the radio, telling them to get out as well. Abbie was right, it was some kind of computer, but it was weird.

Abe walked up to it first and looked at it. It had a screen, and a little dip in the wall underneath, where there was what looked like a scanner in the shape of a square. Next to it was a glass tube that stuck out diagonally.

Shaun and George quickly caught up with them, looking around at the concrete tunnel they were all now standing in, waiting to get in this door.

'What's going on?' Shaun asked.

'Not sure yet,' said Frank.

Abe was looking at the computer screen, it was really dirty, and he had to wipe it clean with his hand. The screen was a dark green colour and was blank. He looked for a button, or even a keyboard, but there wasn't one.

'Try putting your hand on the scanner,' said George.

Abe was sweating, convinced that that wasn't going to work, placed his hand on the square glass panel. Nothing happened for a few seconds, but then a green line went across the panel covering his hand, going all the way down to the bottom and then to the top.

Abe's stomach suddenly knotted, and he felt the hairs stand up on the back of his neck. He heard everybody else gasp and looked back at them, seeing their eyes widen.

Suddenly, some dots appeared on the screen above, and it made a staticky computer noise.

Then to his surprise, his full name appeared on the screen followed by his date of birth.

Abe looked at the screen in shock. The others were shocked too, wondering what would happen when they did the same, and if that was what it took to get inside.

Was Abe on some sort of special list?

But that wasn't it, the plastic tube next to the scanner shot forward so it was further out of the wall, and some text blinked on the screen, *deposit sample.* Abe looked at it confused and then back at the others, not knowing what kind of sample it needed.

'I think you have to spit in it,' said Abbie.

Abe looked at it, seeing now that it was obvious.

But what do they want it for? he thought.

He also didn't really want Abbie seeing him spit into a tube, it was gross, and his grandma always told him that it was bad manners to spit.

However, he leant forward and spat into the tube, trying to cover it as best as possible so nobody could see it.

The others tried not to look at that part, because Abe was right, it was gross, but they were too curious about what was going to happen to turn away.

The tube disappeared, turning flat into the wall and then rising up.

It was a few seconds of waiting before anything happened, and Abe was staring at where the tube had been, waiting for it to come back, but then Abbie touched his arm and pointed at the screen.

Before he would have freaked out a little that Abbie was holding his arm, but he was too distracted by the tense situation that was happening.

He looked at the screen, and in big block capital letters it read, *ANALYSING,* with a little cog turning next to it.

It took almost a minute to finish, but it felt like several to Abe.

The screen went blank for a second, before it flicked a still image saying, *Analysis complete, result: Negative. Clear for entry.*

Then a second later, the metal door made a loud clunk noise and opened with a loud squeak, opening slowly to reveal a small opening. In there was a small glass cylinder, only big enough for one person.

Abe remained where he was, just staring at the open door, not being able to see past the cylinder, wondering what was inside. Everyone else was stood staring at him, waiting for him to walk forward.

'Go on,' said George, encouragingly.

Abe took a deep breath feeling anxious and stepped forward. He turned around just before the door, and he saw them all watching him with interest. In truth, he was scared of what might happen. The cylinder was small and made him feel claustrophobic. The idea of getting stuck in there almost made him tremble.

He looked at Abbie watching him, waiting for him to walk in, and it gave him the extra push he needed. He told himself to do it and look brave.

He went in. Looking down, he noticed the floor was made of metal that was covered in small holes. Nothing happened when he first stepped forward, but after a few seconds there was a loud noise as the cylinder suddenly shut fast, sealing him in.

There was another noise greater than the last as it locked, and then some kind of dull long beeping started. The only thing that he could see now, was the way he had come in, and everyone standing and watching. All of them looked concerned that now he had for some reason been shut in this thing.

There was a sudden loud burst from above him and he was surrounded by something white as it came hissing out from the ceiling. He cowered down to his knees letting out a panicked yell, expecting the worst, trying to cover his ears from the loud hissing sound.

After a few moments he found himself bent over with his eyes shut, crouched down. The hissing had stopped, but his body was tensed. He heard a dull tapping noise and opened one of his eyes to see Abbie standing next to the glass of the cylinder, knocking on it, looking at him.

'Are you okay?' she asked, her voice sounding muffled through the thick glass.

Abe looked at her and stood up, awkwardly smiling and uncovering his ears, trying not to look scared.

'Yeah,' he said. 'I'm good.'

She smiled at him and took a step back from the glass.

Abe looked down to his left and noticed that now there was a little screen with a button below it. The screen read, *Decontamination complete.*

Do I press it? he wondered.

He slowly reached for the button and pressed it down firmly. The screen changed saying, *Welcome.*

Then the door opened on the other side, revealing a metal staircase, leading far down with lights on the ceiling as it went down. Just before he stepped out, he looked at the screen, and noticed that at the bottom it read, *Current occupants:01*.

For a second, he became worried, before realising that it meant him.

At least we know for sure we're the only ones now, he thought.

He stepped out, looking behind him, hoping that now the others would get in too, nervous what might happen. The cylinder door that he had just walked through shut behind him.

Soon after Frank came through the door, and Abe sighed in relief. He wasn't able to see what was on his screen, but he assumed their result had been the same.

Chapter 25

One by one, the others got in just as Abe did. Each of them said they had the same result as the other, leaving them curious what other results there could be and what the repercussions would come of them.

Abbie came after Frank and Abe stood on the other side patiently waiting for her, and the others to get through.

Shaun was the last one in, and as he stepped out of the cylinder, he commented on how cramped it was, and what they were waiting for.

Abe was first down the metal stairs as he was the first one through. Even though he saw the computer tell him that the place was empty, he still had a spooky feeling that there could be something in there, ready to grab him when he turned a corner.

The stairs went down quite a way, but it was well lit. All he could see at the bottom was another hall that led off dead ahead.

It took a long time to search the place, a really long time, as well as a lot of walking.

It was easy for them to tell what room was on each level, because on the wall just outside of the stairs there was a sign, listing all the rooms on each level.

There was an elevator that could take you to any of the levels that were there, but Abe and the others thought that it might be a better idea to use the stairs, not knowing how reliable it was. If the elevator broke down with them inside, there would be no chance of someone just stumbling across them and helping.

The level they entered on only had a few different rooms, it was mainly a level for guards. It had a Guards office, a surveillance room and break area as well as showers.

The next level down had a few different areas, it had a canteen with a huge kitchen and serving station, a recreation room and even a gym next door. Below that for another five levels was just living quarters with bedrooms and a small bit of lounge space in the centre of each.

There was a medical wing and a surgery on the level below the living quarters and the one below that had a massive room for growing vegetables and fruits, all kitted out with special lights and units ready to grow everything. Next door was the food storage. It was full and untouched, but there was a section of the room with empty shelves, containers and refrigeration to store the food after it had been grown.

Abe thought that the one below that was one of the creepiest. It had a big room of cells, and it was chillingly quiet in there. Next to the holding area was the security office, a big armoury.

They weren't able to get inside to the armoury. There was a handprint scanner on the wall next to it, and a key card slot below, but it didn't allow them access. *That's not a surprise,* thought Abe.

They moved on to the bottom level and decided that they would figure out how to get into the armoury later, if they could.

The bottom level was really just for maintenance, it had a great big power room, with a caution sticker on the door. Opposite was the room with all the machinery that kept the place full of clean air, and the last two rooms comprised of a room with the equipment that kept the water running and clean, and then a place for general stores.

The stores room was filled high to the ceiling with boxes and boxes of stuff, all had labels and plastic around them.

Abe, looked at a couple of them, reading what was in them, and found there were batteries, bulbs, machine parts and lots of other things.

This place is huge, he thought.

'Can you believe how big this place is?' he said to Abbie. 'It's great, it has everything we need.'

Abbie was walking beside him as the others were walking back up the stairs to the top floor.

'It's pretty great, but there aren't that many rooms here for people to live in,' she said.

Abe turned and looked confused, 'What do you mean?' he asked. 'There are five levels just full of rooms.'

Abbie looked at him with a curious look on her face. 'Yeah, but...there's only roughly one hundred and twenty-five rooms in total, and they're only really big enough for one person or a couple.'

Abe looked ahead frowning as he thought about it, knotting his eyebrows together.

'Hmm,' he said. 'Maybe this was just built for a small town or something.'

Abbie kept walking with him, and then they both got back to the stairs beside the lift, and George was looking at the sign, detailing the different levels.

'We missed one,' he said.

Both Frank and Abe stepped up to where he was looking.

'What do you mean?' Abe asked. 'We stopped at every one on the way down.'

George shook his head and pointed at the little grey map on the wall.

'Yes, we did, but there is a level above the one we came in on.'

Frank and Abe looked closely, with the others now crowding behind.

'He's right,' said Frank.

They were all on the bottom level still, twelve levels down in total.

'Maybe we should just take the elevator,' said Abbie, looking at the others hopefully.

Abe in no way wanted to take the elevator, especially one that was underground and hadn't been tested in who knows how long.

He hardly ever took the elevator before all of this happened, when he was in shopping malls or if he went to a hotel.

Everybody else was shaking their heads and saying what Abe was thinking.

Abe hadn't answered yet, and watched Abbie walk over to the elevator and press the button, as the others headed for the stairs.

She turned and looked at him with a flirtatious smile. It was now just him left after George was the last to walk through the door to the stairwell.

Abe forced his face into a grin, feeling anxious but telling himself that he was going to take the elevator with her.

I can't let her go on her own, he thought.

If he was going to get stuck in an elevator with anyone, it was going to be Abbie.

The elevator came down, stopping with a heavy clunk when it hit the bottom, and the metal doors slid open allowing them both to step in. Abe walked in first and stood next to the left wall. Abbie followed him in and stood next to him.

Abe looked at her, noticing that it looked like she was chewing or pressing her lips together. He was nervous for two reasons. The long elevator ride, far underground, and because he was now in a small area alone with Abbie, and he didn't know what to talk about. He was hoping that she might start the conversation. Then he turned his eye, and quickly noticing that she was looking at him like she was waiting for him to say or do something.

Think of something to talk about, he told himself.

However, the elevator suddenly jolted, bouncing it slightly up and down, and making the lights flicker. Abe jumped out of panic, and without thinking, he grabbed Abbie's hand that was hanging beside his.

The elevator continued as normal, and as he quickly realised what he had done, butterflies filled his stomach. He became worried that she might think he was being weird or become annoyed at him for holding her hand without asking, but it had been a few seconds and she hadn't said anything or tried to pull her hand free.

Abe looked subtly to his right with his eye and saw Abbie smirking and he caught her eye when she quickly glanced towards him.

He felt like his hands were really warm against her nice cool skin. Their fingers were intertwined in a tight grip.

Soon the elevator came to a stop at the top level above the one they had come in on.

It took a few seconds for the doors to open, and Abe was trying to decide whether he should let go of her hand or remain holding it.

What do I do? he thought in a panic.

The doors opened and they both stepped forward at the same time. Abbie didn't let go of his hand, and he didn't let go of hers. She turned and looked at him.

Abe saw her, looking and as he met her gaze he couldn't help but notice how beautiful her eyes were. His heart was thumping heavy in his chest, and he could see that she still had a smirk on her face. It was dreadfully quiet where they were standing, and they hadn't yet taken notice of their surroundings. Then Abe heard footsteps hitting against the metal steps.

Abbie edged backwards, loosening her grip on his hand, 'I'll tell them we're here, already, shall I?' she said. 'And let them know the elevator is working okay.'

Abe was lost in a daze and had to shake himself out of it to answer, 'Yeah.'

When Frank, George and Shaun reached the top level where Abe and Abbie were, they looked around room by room together.

There was a short hall in front of them, this level was a bit smaller than the others. They started at the end of the hall working their way back. On their right was a radio room, but it was locked with the same security as on the lower level. To their surprise there was another armoury to their left. That too was locked, along with the next room on their right, which was the control room that stood next to the elevator and stairs.

The last room was unlocked though. Above it in block capital letters it read, *Commander's Office.*

Abe quickly realised that this was the level where everything was meant to be controlled from and was where the people in charge would have been.

But where are they? he thought.

The Commander's office was quite large, bigger than any of the bedrooms in the living quarters. There was a rectangular desk in the far end of the room away from the door they walked in and filing cabinets on each wall beside it, with a big map on the wall on the right.

Towards the end of the room there was another door leading somewhere, but as Abe and the others stepped closer, they saw there was a big brown envelope on the Commander's desk.

Abe picked it up, leaning over the desk and admiring its red wax seal on the back.

'Should I open it?' he asked, looking at the others standing behind him.

'Yeah,' said Frank. 'There might be something in there that will tell us who was meant to be here.'

'Or it could have something in there to tell us how to open the rooms that are locked,' Shaun added.

Abe broke the wax seal as he pulled on the fold of the envelope, making a satisfying cracking noise as it broke in half. The envelope felt quite heavy, there was clearly more than just paper in there. He emptied the contents of the letter out onto the desk, several sheets of paper fell out, and then a heavier object clunked as it hit the desk, landing on the paper.

It was a USB stick and a key-card; it was clear right away that the key card was to be used to open things.

Hopefully the rooms that were locked.

It wasn't clear what the USB stick was for though. It was black and in the shape of a key.

While Abe looked at the key card and USB, Frank picked up the sheets of paper on the desk, reading through the pages. The first one greeted the commander, but then went on to explain his orders and instructions. It became clear why the place was empty and why, like Abbie had mentioned, there were only a small number of bedrooms.

The documents said that this particular bunker was built specifically for a set group of soldiers. In the event of a disaster like a nuclear war or something else that made the surface uninhabitable, the soldiers were to take refuge in this bunker, analysing the situation and reporting to their chain of command.

It said that more specific orders would be passed down to the commander in time and said nothing more on what they were required to do, or who the people were.

The next few pages were instructions on what there was in the bunker, along with instructions on what to do when first arriving there.

Abe still had the key card and USB in his hand, so Frank passed him the instructions on what to do.

Abe switched on the Commander's computer and pushed the key card into a slot on the side of the keyboard. Then, after a few seconds of the computer loading, they were prompted to enter a key.

Abe inserted the USB key into the computer and waited. After a few more seconds the screen flashed, *Access Granted.* They noticed that to their left the map on the wall began to light up with green dots that were scattered across it. It took a few seconds for Abe to realise that those green dots coincided with the map that he had.

Everyone else looked at the map in amazement and walked over, admiring how many they were and pointing at where they were.

Then there was strange noise, like gears turning, and a small section on the panel of the desk next to Abe popped out like a CD tray, but with another hand scanner.

Abe was curious what it was for and without reading the screen or thinking about it, he placed his palm down, and it scanned his hand like the one had when he had entered the bunker.

There was a short tone that came out of the computer, followed by a female sounding computerised voice saying, 'Welcome Commander.'

Upon hearing this, the others turned around from the map to see Abe standing behind the desk holding his hand just above where the scanner had been, as it disappeared. His eyes were wide like he had been caught doing something he shouldn't have.

'What was that?' asked George, standing next to the others.

Abe looked at the screen, and where it had said, *Commander.* Now it typed out his name next to it, and then several pop ups appeared on the screen.

George walked around the desk to where Abe was standing, followed by the others, looking at the screen in front of him.

There were four different sections on the screen, one detailing the bunkers power, its water, another of the air filtration and then a summary of the bunker's surveillance and alarms.

They looked at the screen, amazed at what they were seeing and then saw that now in the top middle of the screen in big letters it said, *Commander Abe Stuart.* They all turned and looked at him, and Abe looked down sheepishly at the ground thinking, *Uh oh...*

Chapter 26

Once Abe had accidentally signed himself in as the commander of the bunker, it registered his handprint on the system, allowing him to open any of the doors that were locked.

It still didn't work for any of the others though. He imagined there was a way for him to delegate access to people maybe using the computer, but he didn't know how to navigate the system. It wasn't the easiest one to use, but he tried almost every day, sitting at the desk in the office.

He secretly really liked it, it made him feel important and like he was in charge. Just to be safe, he gave the commander's key card to Frank, in case he or someone else needed to get into the armoury at any point, until he figured out how to register everybody else's handprints on the system.

It took a couple of day's getting used to that place, especially with it having no windows and not being able to look outside.

He found out not long after getting to the commander's office, that it had its own living quarters, which was huge. It had a TV, a record player, a drinks cabinet and even its own bedroom. The bed in there was twice the size of any of the ones in the normal living quarters, though it was really far from where everyone else would have been sleeping, and it was too creepy to stay there alone.

There were enough levels full of bedrooms for them to have a level each, but they all quickly agreed that they should stick together and stay on the same level.

They could still have more than one room to themselves if they wanted to.

Abe wanted to be close to Abbie, so he picked a room in the middle of a row, near the lounge area. George put his stuff in the room next to his, and the others were spaced out close by.

They tried using the main cafeteria to eat in for the first day after they arrived, but it was too big and uncomfortable with so few of them there. Whenever somebody would speak, their voice would echo across the room and it felt empty, so they decided to use the guard's breakroom and kitchen instead on the entrance level. It was a lot smaller, nice and compact. They fitted in there perfectly, with a little extra space.

After searching around, they were even able to find some playing cards to keep themselves occupied. The lounge areas and the break room had small TVs of their own with DVD players, but no DVDs. When they first saw it, they were all excited, looking forward to seeing a movie again for the first time in ages, but then they realised that there was nothing to play.

When he first saw it, Abe had thought that he could ask Abbie to watch a movie with him one night, but now he couldn't.

Frank was interested in the radio room a lot, he thought that they might be able to use it to call out to see if there were any other survivors out there, or maybe even be able to contact the other bunkers somehow. He spent most of his time in there tinkering and calling out on the radio.

Abe decided to leave Frank to it, figuring once he had the hang of it, he can show the others how to use it.

If we can figure out a way to contact the other bunkers from here, then we will be able to tell for sure if my grandma is there, he thought, *and Ash.*

He had almost forgotten about Ash, he had been so caught up in everything, trying to escape from bases, running away from people and trying to figure out everything in the bunker, he had barely had any time to reflect.

I hope he's okay, he thought.

Abe started clicking around on the computer in the Commander's office and searching for anything else that might be useful. He hoped that there might be something on there that could tell them about the other bunkers, or who might be living in them.

George had been spending a lot of time in the gardening area. Frank had been helping him plant loads of different things, like tomatoes, potatoes, plums and other fruit and veg.

One day while they were down there, George asked Frank how long they would be staying.

Frank was watering some of the plants he had planted. 'A couple of months at least,' he said.

George carried on putting seeds in the soil with his hands and covering them up. 'What about this place?' he asked. 'It has everything, are we going to just leave it?'

Frank stood there quiet for a second as he carried on watering, looking up at the room. 'I don't know,' he said. 'We'll have to talk to Abe about it.'

George walked over to the counter where there were stacks of drawers and cabinets storing lots of different seeds.

'What are you looking for?' Frank asked.

George was searching through the draws and reading the labels on them. 'I'm looking for flower seeds,' he said.

Frank frowned curiously before asking, 'What do you want to grow flowers for?'

'I guess it would brighten the place up a bit.'

George carried on looking, 'So I can give them to Abe to give to Abbie,' said George.

Frank smiled, '*Here...*Let me help,' he said.

It took a little while of searching, but eventually they found where there were a range of different plants, including all kinds of flowers.

'These should do nicely,' said Frank, pulling out a pack of seeds, and suggesting that he plant those ones.

George looked at it, reading the label. 'Iris'?' he said.

There was no picture like there was normally on packs of seeds like you got in the supermarket, so George had no idea what they looked like.

'Yeah, they're very pretty,' said Frank.

'What colour are they?' George asked.

Frank took a second thinking and then said, 'Purple.'

George smiled and said, 'Cool.'

He walked over to one of the stations, looking for a place to plant them, thinking where he could put them out of plain sight so Abbie didn't see them if she came in, to make sure they could be a surprise.

Frank looked at the clock on the wall, noticing the time and then headed over to wash his hands, 'It's just about lunch time,' he said. 'You hungry?'

George was busy planting the flowers for Abe to give to Abbie, 'Nah I'm okay thanks, I want to finish planting these,' he said.

'Okay,' he said as he headed out the door. 'I'll see you later.'

Shaun had been spending all his time in the surveillance room on the entrance level, and walking around the bunker occasionally, keeping an eye on things. He was more or less the guard of things there now though nobody had appointed him. He just started doing it by himself, it kept him busy. He was headed to the guards break room to get something to eat and saw Frank in there.

'Hey Frank,' he said.

Frank was surprised to hear his voice, thinking he was the only one there.

'*Oh,* hey Shaun,' he said. 'How you doing?'

'Not bad I guess,' he replied, 'this place is sure a hell of a lot better than the last place I was in though.'

Frank was microwaving some soup. 'Yeah, it's pretty great here,' he said. 'It has everything we need.'

There was a bit of a silence while Frank waited for his food to be ready and Shaun looked through the cabinets, trying to decide what to have.

'Have you seen Abe or Abbie?' asked Frank.

Shaun kept looking through the food and shook his head as he answered, 'Not in person, but while I was looking at the cameras, I saw that Abbie was in the gym this morning and Abe was in the control room again.'

Frank frowned slightly and asked, 'Do you know what's going on between those two?'

Shaun pursed his lips and shrugged. 'No idea', he said. 'I've seen Abe looking at her a few times and the other way around.'

Abbie was in the gym, pedalling on the exercise bike. The bike had a screen in front of it with different things you could watch while exercising. You could make it so that you were cycling through a forest, across a snowy mountain or even the countryside. It was the closest thing they had to a working TV.

Watching a screen of cycling through the woods wasn't quite the same as the real thing though. She was starting to feel fed up with being stuck inside. She hadn't been outside since they got there.

Maybe Abe and I could go outside for a bit, she thought.

She carried on cycling until she finished her workout, planning on going to see Abe when she was done.

She saw George in the elevator on the way to go up to the upper level where she assumed Abe would be.

'Hey George,' she said.

'Hey,' he said.

Abbie frowned, squinting suspiciously. *He's quieter than usual,* she thought.

'You okay?' she asked. 'I'm going up to see Abe.'

For some reason George was holding the front of his coat together and it looked like there was something in there.

'I was going back down to the garden, but I'll get off here and take the stairs if you like,' he said. 'You can take the elevator.'

Abbie smiled and was about to say thanks and say she would just walk, but then she thought she saw his coat move.

'Is there something in your...?'

George suddenly panicked a little and walked off quickly towards the stairs. 'See you later,' he said.

Abbie frowned again and wondered what he might be hiding as she watched him run off down the stairs.

A few minutes later and she walked into the Commander's office, but Abe wasn't there. She looked in the control room and found him sitting and staring at the panel, resting his face on his hand.

The door had been left open and Abe didn't hear Abbie walk in, so he jumped when she said hello.

'Hey,' he said slightly startled.

Abbie was still wearing the clothes she had been wearing in the gym.

It was only one of a few times he had seen her wearing it. He had seen her while passing one day when she was on her way there, and she invited him to go with her, but he was worried he would embarrass himself and made an excuse that he couldn't go and would go another time. Thinking maybe he could sneak in there a few times by himself so he could practice.

'I was wondering if maybe you would want to go for a walk with me outside later,' she said looking at him with a smile.

Abe wasn't expecting her to ask and had been trying to think for days for something to do where he could invite Abbie and spend time with her.

'Yeah, that would be great,' he said with a big smile.

Abbie's smile widened. 'Great, do you wanna meet me at my room around six?'

Abe's stomach started to feel all funny again and his heart was beating fast, just like when he had held her hand on the first day there. That was the last time he had made any kind of progress.

'Yeah definitely, I'll meet you there,' he said.

Abbie just responded by continuing to smile and walked off to go shower and change.

Abe waited for her to disappear around the corner and almost jumped out of his chair into a dance to celebrate, but then quickly thought, *Is it a date, or is it just a walk?*

Now he was just anxious, having no idea which one of the two it was.

'She seemed happy when we held hands the other day,' he said to himself. 'Maybe I should get her something or take some dinner with us or something.'

It was 05:55pm, Abbie was in her room, and she had just slipped into a dress she had picked out from the clothes Frank had gifted to her. She was thinking how lucky it was she had these, because the only real clothes that was in the general store were scrubs, medical clothes and security uniforms.

The dress she had chosen had lots of flowers on it, and normally she wore makeup, but there was none of that to be found. A few moments later and there was a knock at the door, so Abbie checked herself one more time in the little mirror on the wall opposite the bed and answered it.

Abe was standing on the other side, looking as nervous as ever. He was trying not to make it look obvious and Abbie smiled when she saw him.

'Hey,' she said.

'Sorry I'm a bit early,' he said.

'That's okay, I'm ready anyway,' she said.

They walked off and Abbie closed the door behind her, and then followed Abe.

Frank and George were sitting on the couch together in the lounge area just outside. Abbie was standing close to Abe as they walked next to each other, and then she grabbed his hand with hers.

He hadn't been expecting her to take his hand and he had been working up the courage to do it himself. He hadn't noticed, but on their way-out George and Frank had turned their bodies around and were watching as they both headed for the elevator.

When they were in the elevator, Abbie went to press the button for the entrance level, but Abe stopped her.

'*Actually*...I have a surprise,' he said, and pressed the button for the bottom level.

Abbie had a curious look on her face as she wondered what it could be.

When they got to the bottom, Abe walked to the general stores with her and took her towards the back. There was a large metal door which she hadn't taken much notice of before because it was locked and had forgotten about it until now.

Abe walked up to the scanner next to the door and opened it. Inside was another elevator, much bigger than the other one there. It was big enough to fit a small truck.

Abbie was surprised to see it, 'Where does it go?' she asked.

Abe had a smug look and smile on his face. 'You'll see soon,' he said.

This elevator was way less smooth than the other one, but with Abbie there and holding her hand, Abe wasn't scared at all.

Within just a few minutes they came to the top and the doors opened wide, revealing a small tunnel like the one they arrived in. It was completely made of concrete. However, unlike the other one, this tunnel had a much bigger door on it.

Abe told Abbie that it was a cargo lift for bringing in supplies if they ever needed to bring in more, and that he found out about it on the Commander's computer.

It was a little chilly out, but thanks to them being in the tunnel, it was shielded from the snow. Then as they carried on walking, Abbie saw that there was something laid out on the ground towards the end.

Abe had set up a little tent at the entrance to the tunnel and next to it was a small camping stove with some food, and a pack of marshmallows.

Abbie's smile widened as she saw what Abe had prepared.

Abe was nervous that she might have questioned it and that he was wrong about it being a date after all.

'Where did you get all this?' she asked.

'I got it all from the storage room,' he said. 'It took a while, but I found some good stuff eventually.'

Abbie sat down in the opening of the tent in front of the stove, facing the clear night sky. There were stars scattered all across it and now there were no cars or planes going around, the sky was clearer than ever.

The moon was as big and bright as Abe had ever seen it, and it cast down a glow on Abbie's face.

The air was cool and crisp, and the heat from the camping stove helped to keep them warm as Abe heated up the food for them.

Then out of nowhere, as Abbie looked at the night sky, she thought she saw something in the distance and then tried looking harder to make out what it was.

'Abe, can you see that?'

Abe turned and looked. 'Yeah,' he said with surprise. 'It looks like lights.'

Both of them stared, forgetting about the food, and wondering what it could be.

Far in the distance there looked to be a tall building with lights on.

'Do you think there are people living there?' Abbie asked.

'I don't know,' said Abe. 'But we should tell the others.'

Abe and Abbie rushed back downstairs to find the others all sitting in the lounge area of the living quarters.

Abe was out of breath from hurrying, and started to tell them what they found, but he was panting, trying to catch his breath.

Abbie though, didn't seem to break a sweat and took over.

'We saw a building from outside in the distance with lights on,' she explained. 'We think there are people there, there could be a lot of them.'

As they all took in the information, their expressions ranged from shock to confusion.

'Where?' Frank asked.

Abbie wasn't sure if they knew about where Abe had taken them and waited for him to answer.

'Up the cargo lift,' he said.

Frank looked puzzled and repeated what Abe had said, 'Cargo lift?'

'Yeah, I found out about it on the commander's computer earlier and we went to check it out.'

Abe was a little worried that Frank and the others were going to be annoyed that he hadn't told them, but they seemed more interested in this building they might have seen.

'Are you sure?' Shaun probed.
Both Abe and Abbie nodded. They were all looking at one another, thinking what to do or waiting for someone to say something.

'Should we try and contact them?' Abe asked.

Frank and Shaun looked a bit dubious about the idea. 'I don't know,' said Frank. 'We don't know if they are friendly or not, they could just be like any of the other people we have come across.'

George interjected. 'Could we try reaching them on the radio?'

Frank had been trying to get the hang of the radio system there for days but hadn't had any responses from anybody.

'It's probably the only way we can be sure that we'll be safe if we try and meet them,' said Frank, scratching his chin.

'When was the last time you tried calling out on the radios?' Abe asked.

'This morning,' answered Frank.

'They might not always be monitoring the radio,' said Abe. 'Maybe we could take shifts and try calling out as much as we can and try to get a response.'

The group was quiet for a few seconds as they thought about what Abe had said.

'Yeah, and if we go meet them, me and Abe can go. We don't have to tell them about this place straight away, we can just pretend we're a couple trying to find somewhere safe to stay,' said Abbie. 'Once we're sure they're friendly, then we can tell them the truth.'
Frank was looking at them and then to the others, seeing if anyone had any other ideas.

'Hmm...we do really need more people that know more about looking after this place,' said Frank. 'There could be people there who know how to maintain the machines here and there may even be a doctor there.'

'So…what do you think?' asked Abe. 'Should we try it?'

They all looked around at each other in agreement, and then Abe said, '*Great*, I'll take the first shift.'

Chapter 27

The bunker was silent and there was a chill in the air. It was dark in the radio room, only a small lamp was lit on the desk and a glow from several dials illuminated the room.

Abe had found the perfect spot with his chair to sit, right under where the hot air from the vents was coming through, making him warm and cosy. He had been there for a couple hours now and everybody else had gone to bed while he took this shift. He had been calling out intermittently, giving the receivers a chance to respond.

His stomach growled, and it echoed through the room just as he went to click down the button on the mouthpiece. He placed his hand on his stomach holding it, it was starting to hurt a little, he was so hungry after he had to cut the evening short with Abbie.

He started to feel disappointed and a little sad, hoping that he hadn't missed his chance with her.

Then, came a tapping noise on the metal door before it opened and Abbie walked in. She had been tip-toeing the whole way there, trying not to wake anyone.

Abe saw her walk in, and his face broke into a huge smile. He hadn't even noticed what she had brought with her.

Abbie was holding a bag in her left hand. She pulled out a small burner, and some marshmallows.

'I thought I'd bring you something to eat and keep you company,' she said with a smile.

'I'd like that,' he said, looking back at her.

Abbie pulled the marshmallows out of their packaging, put a stack on a skewer for each of them and lit the burner.

Abe called out on the radio again before he started roasting his marshmallows. If he did one call out now, it would give him some time to roast them and talk to Abbie for a few minutes before having to call out again.

Before he had started broadcasting, him and Frank had agreed what they should be calling out. They decided that they would be acting as if they were sending out a call for help, looking for somewhere to stay. Once they got a response, they would tell them that they were using the radio that was in the truck, so they didn't have to tell them they were in a base or camp. Then, they would ask if they could come to the building, giving them the chance to see if they were friendly and if they were trustworthy enough to tell about the bunker.

The hope was that there would be people there that could be useful to them in the long run, like electricians, mechanics, engineers, doctors and nurses.

If they were lucky and the people were friendly then they could tell them about the bunker and offer them to stay there, and in return the people help keep the place running safely.

Abe really liked the plan, it gave him comfort knowing that if it worked, when he went to go find his grandma and Ash at the other bunker, then he would always have this place to fall back on. The one thing he had been worried about though and was throwing around in his head was, *who is going to go with me?*

Frank told him that he would go and help him in any way that he could. Abe knew that George would too. He wasn't sure about Shaun; they weren't exactly best friends like he was with George. *Not yet at least.*

The main person he was thinking about though was Abbie, would she stay, or would she go with him?

Do I ask her? he kept asking himself, but he was worried what she would say.

As he sat there after he finished calling out on the radio, roasting marshmallows with her and watching her smile, it gave him a little more confidence, thinking that if he did ask her to come, then she would say yes.

She is the one that offered to go and meet these people with me after all, he thought.

While they were eating, Abbie had asked him about his favourite movies, and told him to name his top three. Abe told her without having to think - all three were from the same series. Abe thought that she might think it was a rubbish choice, but he was surprised when she told him that they were her favourite too, only she put them in a different order.

Abe smiled and disagreed, playfully arguing that his choice was right, and she was wrong.

Abbie popped a few more marshmallows onto her skewer and then Abe's edging in closer to him.

Now Abbie was closer, he found himself unable to look away from her, and reached out to hold her hand. He didn't feel panicky anymore, just relaxed and warm.

They sat in comfortable silence now, the only sound was the marshmallows bubbling over the fire. Their fingers were intertwined, and Abbie looked up from the fire into Abe's eyes.

Abe found himself leaning in, forgetting about his marshmallows burning, and so did Abbie, getting closer to each other slowly.

All of a sudden there was a blast of noise that came from the radio calling out to them, startling them both.

They stopped what they were doing and turned to the radio, trying to listen to what it was saying and edging in closer, Abe turning up the volume knob.

There was a man on the other side. The quality of the sound wasn't great, and it was awfully tinny and staticky.

They were answering Abe's calls, telling him that they were nearby. He said they had a settlement that was safe, and people were welcome there, but he said that they would have to send someone out to meet them first and make sure they could trust them.

Abe answered as quick as he could, telling them that they would do anything they needed.

'Good,' said the man. 'How many are you?'

Abe looked at Abbie and then answered, 'Just two.'

The man took a few seconds to respond, making Abe a little worried, but then he came back.

'Okay, tomorrow morning at 9am, follow this road,' said the man, giving Abe co-ordinates for him to write down. 'You will see a burnt-out truck, put your weapons in the truck and then wait a few car lengths away in your vehicle and someone will come meet you and bring you back if they agree that it's okay.'

'Okay, we will,' said Abe. 'Thank you.'

'Good luck,' said the man and then signed off.

Abe and Abbie couldn't wait until morning to tell Frank and the others about what had happened. They had to leave early, and they had to be sure they knew where it was they were going and that they left early enough that these people didn't see them coming from anywhere near the bunker.

Abe woke Frank up first to tell him what had happened. He told him what they had talked about and what the plan was.

Frank said that Abe should go to bed and get some rest and leave as planned in the morning and that he would tell Shaun and George what was happening when they wake up.

Abe took his advice and walked back to his room with Abbie next to him. Halfway there he remembered how close he had been to kissing her, feeling annoyed that the message didn't come through a few seconds later.

Abbie went to her room and said goodnight, smiling as she looked at him, and he said goodnight back. The next morning, Abe spent a few hours just lying in his bed, waiting for the alarm to go off. He hadn't gotten that much sleep because he was too busy thinking about what he and Abbie were about to do.

Once the alarm did go off, he turned it off quickly so as not to wake the others, specifically George as he was only next door to his room.

He met Abbie in the break room on the entrance level. She was already there waiting for him to have breakfast before they went.

Abbie had a bowl of cereal and freeze-dried fruit mixed in, and Abe had the same. Breakfast was a little quiet and Abe was wondering if Abbie was thinking about the night before. He wondered if he should mention it but thought that it would make it awkward. He figured that his best bet was to try again, but he would have to wait until the time was right.

They left the bunker 08:00 sharp, to make sure that they were there in plenty of time. Frank helped them pinpoint the area on the map and told them roughly how to get there.

It was only a twenty-minute drive, and even with the little bit of snow and ice that was still out there, they managed to make it still in twenty minutes in the truck.

Both Abbie and Abe were keeping a lookout for the burned-out truck. Abe slowed down when they were close to the area they were meant to go to.

Abe had considered not taking any guns with them, but Abbie said that they might think it was suspicious and ask how they managed to survive just by themselves all that time without any weapons.

Abe spotted the truck first, seeing it just ahead, with its bonnet open and the sun glaring behind it, making it a little difficult to see.

It was still only 08:30 when they found it and thought that they would now have plenty of time to sit there and figure out what to say, but as they drove up to the truck and a cloud moved in front of the sun, they saw another vehicle just down the road from them. Sitting and waiting.

Neither Abe nor Abbie could see the driver or passenger, only that there were people in there.

'Is it them?' asked Abbie.

Abe looked trying to focus his eyes on them and thinking that they might signal them somehow.

'It must be,' he said. 'How else would they know that it is us?'

Then the car ahead flashed its lights slowly on and off twice.

Abe looked at Abbie, and then they got out together with their bags.

Abe stood beside their truck and looked ahead, expecting them to get out, and waiting, wondering why they weren't moving.

Abbie tapped Abe on the arm as she pointed to the burned-out truck.

'They're waiting for us to put our stuff in the truck,' she said.

Abe took the bags from Abbie, and then walked it all over to the rusty and ice-covered truck, placing all their bags and weapons inside.

Abe had his back to them now, and couldn't see them, but Abbie was keeping an eye out.

'They're getting out,' said Abbie.

Two people got out of the truck ahead, the driver and the passenger, but then something else came from the back seat.

Abbie looked at them, having to shield her eyes from the sun with her hand.

'*Abe!* Look out,' she yelled, as the thing that came from the back seat headed for Abe.

The wind was strong, and Abe only just heard what Abbie had said as his head had been buried in the truck as he put their stuff safely inside. He heard the sound of running, and as he turned around, he was hit in his chest hard, and knocked to the ground.

Abbie was standing next to him in a panic.
Abe was disorientated and it took a second to figure out what was going on when he looked up. His face had been splashed with something and making his top wet.

It was *Bud!*

Bud was on top of Abe, with all four paws on his body, drooling all over him and then started licking his face continuously with no intention of stopping. Abe couldn't believe it, he was over the moon and let out a childlike laugh of joy as he scratched Bud behind the ears and wrapped his arms around him, saying his name and calling him a good boy.

Abbie was relieved to see that Bud was friendly and he wasn't trying to attack him, but she was a little confused at how he knew him.

The other two people were now standing close to Abe, next to the burnt-out truck.

Abe looked up and saw them standing there, as he sat up. It was a middle-aged man, and a woman with red hair.

'Wait a minute,' said Abe. 'Zoe?'

Zoe was standing by Abe, smiling as she saw the two good friends reunite.

'Hello Abe,' she said. 'I told you I would find him.'

She put out her hand and helped Abe to his feet, and then introduced herself to Abbie.

'Hi, I'm Zoe,' she said. 'Me and Abe met some time ago when we helped him and his grandpa.'

Abbie shook her hand, 'Hi, I'm Abbie.'

'Lovely to meet you,' said Zoe. 'It is just the two of you then?'

Abe had a sad look on his face and nodded, thinking about his grandpa.

'Yeah, just us', he said.

Abbie saw Abe grow sad, and took his hand, while Bud sat next to him and nuzzled into his leg with his head. Abe was sticking to the plan, though, now he knew it was Zoe and her group, he was wondering if he should just tell her everything, *but* he hadn't seen the others yet and it wasn't just his decision to make. He had to be sure before he told her anything, even though thanks to her he had Bud back.

'I'm sorry, this is Paul,' she said, introducing the man that was with her.

Abe and Abbie shook his hand and said hello.

'I guess you better follow us then,' said Zoe. 'There's a lot that's happened since I last saw you. Stuff that you might not believe.'

Abe looked at her with an intrigued frown as she started to back towards her truck.

'What kind of stuff?' he asked.

'I'll tell you when we get back to our base, you're going to want to sit down for this, it's gonna take a lot of explaining for you to understand.'

Meanwhile, in a small bedroom, there was a middle-aged man with medium length wavy hair and white teeth. He was talking to a man with a white beard who sat on a chair next to a small single bed where there was an old man lying down.

'Do anything you can to make sure he makes it,' said the middle-aged man to the one in the chair.

The man in the chair was a doctor and had a small bag by his feet full of medicine. He pulled several things out and handed them to the man standing in the room.

'He'll be okay,' he said. 'Really what he needs is rest, water and some food.'

The middle-aged man placed the medicine on the cabinet next to the bed, and then poured a glass of water using the jug next to it.

'Shall I call you when he wakes?' asked the doctor.

The middle-aged man stood up and then there was a knock at the door.

'*Yeah,* thanks doc,' he said. 'That would be great.'

He walked towards the door as it opened, and a woman was there with green eyes, brown hair and jeans.

'Sam, it's your brother. He's moving soon,' she said.

Sam became anxious as he heard the news and pried for more info, 'Already? How?' he asked.

'I don't know,' said the lady. 'You better come quickly.'

'Okay,' said Sam, as he followed her out of the room, closing the door behind him.

Chapter 28

Abe and Abbie were in their own truck with Bud on the back seat wagging his tail staring at them both and panting excitedly. They were following Zoe from behind. Soon they came into a very small town, and not long after they saw what looked like the building they had seen the night before with all the lights on.

'Look, there it is,' said Abbie.

Abe turned and said, 'Oh yeah,' as he frowned and pointed something out. 'It's a hotel.'

They had to drive up a short series of ramps to get up to the elevated bit of ground that the hotel was sitting on. The area around was quite empty and quiet, nothing but open concrete floor, except for where there were cars and a few trucks parked outside, though only a few of them looked driveable. Some of them had broken windows, doors and bonnets missing. One of them was just an empty shell and looked like it had been completely scrapped for parts.

When they reached the outside of the hotel, Zoe was already out of the truck and she was signalling for them to park in an empty space, next to a string of cars.

Abe gave Abbie a quick glance as he stopped the truck, smiled and then they both got out together, including Bud who jumped out after Abe.

Zoe walked up to them and said, 'your truck should be safe here, I'll make sure that nobody tries to use it or think they can take anything off it for parts.'

'Is that why so many of these cars are missing doors and stuff?' Abe asked. 'Do you pull things off them and use the parts?'

Zoe nodded. 'Yeah, if you jump in our truck, we'll drive in through the garage and I'll show you.'

Abe and Abbie walked behind her towards the truck, with Bud by Abe's side.

Just as they were getting in, Abbie had a quick glance at the surrounding area, and noticed just how small the town was. There were only a few shops around and this was the only hotel. There weren't even really any high rises, except for the hotel itself. She did see, a short distance away, that there was a doctor's surgery, and she was wondering if Zoe and her people would have thought to go there and take what medical supplies they had.

She was thinking by how prepared they looked - there was a slim chance that they hadn't been round almost every building and taken everything they needed. As Abe hopped into the back, calling Bud up first onto the seat, he saw a blue glint in the corner of his eye. Suddenly, recognition sparked in him, and he looked over to see if it was what he thought it could be.

It's a video rental, he thought to himself.

He was so disappointed when he found out there were no DVDs in the bunker, and now he knew what Abbie's favourite movies were, he thought, *Maybe I could get over there and get us some movies?*

Paul drove them around to the back of the hotel where there was a steep but short ramp that led down to a huge metal garage door. When he got to the bottom of it, Zoe passed him what looked like a little white plastic card with a maroon pattern on it, and then he swiped it on a metal thing on the wall, followed by two long distinct blasts from the horn.

327

Abe figured it was to let whoever was inside know that it was them coming in and nobody else.

Bud had moved so that basically half of his body was on Abe's lap, and he was licking his face again.

Zoe saw how happy Bud was to be with him and smiled, letting out a quiet laugh, 'I can't tell you how many times he saved my life,' she said. 'He's a good dog to have around.'

Abe smiled back in agreement, 'I can't thank you enough for looking after him for me,' he said.

'Don't mention it,' Zoe responded.

The garage door folded open slowly with a thud and a metal creak and revealed just how big it was under there. Both Abe and Abbie were surprised to see it, there were cars and jeeps all throughout, with people walking around.

As Abe looked closer, he could see car parts on the ground next to some of the cars. There were people working on them, fixing or maybe modifying them.

On their way through to park, Zoe called over what looked like one of the mechanics by whistling and shouting at him.

A mechanic in oily blue scrubs ran over wiping his hands with a rag. 'What's up boss?' he said.

Zoe pointed back the way they came with her head and said, 'there's a truck just out there that's not on the list, make sure nobody messes with it.'

The man smiled as he nodded and said, 'Will do.'

'This place is amazing,' said Abe.

'Wait till you see the rest of it,' said Zoe.

Abe and Abbie were both looking around at all the people there, specifically the people working on the cars. They were thinking the same thing. Mechanics were just what they needed, they already had one thing they could cross off their list.

Then Abe remembered what the mechanic had said to Zoe. *He called her boss. Does that mean she's running this place?*

'How many people are there here in total?' Abe asked, looking at Zoe.

'Well at first there weren't that many at all, just a few of us from the original group that you met before. We came into some trouble and unfortunately, we lost a few along the way,' she said, 'but when we came here, we ran into a few of the folk who used to live in the town, still here and surviving together. Some of the people that were left here used to work in the town and looked after it, they knew exactly what needed to be done to keep most things running, like the water and power.'

'Once we found this place, we figured that it would be the best for us because there would be enough rooms for people to have one to themselves and they would even get their own toilet and shower. With it being a hotel, it gave us the added benefit of being able to give people key cards for the rooms so people could have some privacy. That even helped with the rest of the place, keeping people out of important rooms they weren't meant to go in, like where we have been storing the food and the guns. After a little while, I guess people saw the lights on in the building like you did and came here looking for somewhere safe to stay, and now there are around a hundred of us.'

Abe was impressed by everything Zoe had said and what they had set up here, it was almost as perfect as what they had back at the bunker, but there was a question that still remained.

'And who's in charge?' Abe asked.

Zoe looked at Abe in the review mirror as the truck came to a stop and smiled as she said, 'I am.'

In a room higher up in the hotel, there was a radio on a wooden desk letting out a crackling noise, as someone on the other end was waiting for a response.

The woman that had been to fetch Sam from the room with the doctor came in and picked up the receiver as Sam came, in behind her.

'He's here,' she said. 'Are you still there?'

Sam sat down on a wooden chair next to the desk and the radio. There was a long wait, and nobody came back.

'Do you think he got him?' said Sam. 'Maybe he found out someone else was helping us.'

But then there was a loud scratch like noise that buzzed through, followed by a voice.

'*Anna,*' he said frantically. 'Thank goodness you came back, I had to go away for a bit. Someone came down the hall and saw that I was in here and was questioning what I was doing. They've been keeping this room locked up to almost everybody since you know who swiped the keys from in here.'

Anna looked to Sam with a small smile and passed him the mouthpiece.

'What's going on there?' asked Sam.

There was a brief pause from the man and then he came back, 'He's planning to move. And soon.'

Sam became worried and he leant forward closer to the radio.

'How soon,' he asked.

'Within the next week,' the man replied.

Sam leant back in the chair with both frustration and confusion, as he rubbed his face with his hand.

'It doesn't make any sense why he is going now,' said Sam. 'How is he planning on getting in there?'

'I don't know,' said the man. 'But he has something planned, he's moving every single one of his men out with him.'

Sam rested his face in his hand as he thought for a few seconds before he came back up.

'Okay, try and find out what you can, but if he gets suspicious, just get yourself out of there and get here as fast as you can,' said Sam.

'I'll try my best,' he said and then signed off.

After they were parked downstairs, Zoe and Paul signed the truck in that they had been driving, along with all the guns they had to a man behind a caged room. They handed Abe and Abbie's weapons in too, but told them that they could keep their bags.

Zoe took them to the reception, walking them up the stairs at the back of the room. The reception area was oddly dark though, except for the few lights that were on, lighting the room. The windows and glass doors had been completely boarded up, stopping any kind of natural light from getting inside.

It proved that this place wasn't as perfect as Abe first thought. The boarded-up windows and doors would probably hold out against *them,* but if any real people came to try and get in without permission, then it probably wouldn't take them very long.

The man behind the reception desk was dressed in thick clothing and had a handgun clipped to his belt, as he sat behind the computer tapping away on the keyboard.

Zoe walked round to the side of the desk and leaned on it with both her arms and looked at the man.

'Can you allocate these two a room please?' she asked.

The man looked at them both quickly and then said, 'sure,' as he pulled out what looked to be a weird small little printer from out of a drawer under the reception desk.

He typed away and clicked some things on the computer, before the little printer started to make a buzzing noise and then spat out a little plastic card. The man took the card, wrote down a number on the back of it with a pen and then passed it to Zoe.

'Mike is still taking care of that guy in the room next to this one,' said the man. 'Just a heads up.'

Then Abe saw Zoe lean in closer to ask the man something a little quieter.

'Is it *just* Mike in there?' she asked.

The man responded by nodding and said, 'Yeah, I think so.'

Zoe turned and looked at Paul for a few seconds before she looked back to Abe and Abbie.

'I'm sorry you two, but there is something I need to go do quickly,' she said. 'Paul will show you to your room.'

Abe started to feel a little suspicious and like there was something she wasn't telling him, something that she was trying to hide.

'I thought there was something that you needed to tell me.'

'There is,' she said. 'But don't worry, I'll tell you soon, I just have to make sure of something first and then I'll send someone down to get you. Here's your key.'

She held the key card out towards both Abe and Abbie. They both paused for a second, waiting for the other to take it.

Abe realised at that moment that there was just the one card, and that him and Abbie were going to be sharing a room together, because they thought they were *together*.

Abbie reached out and took the card from Zoe and said, 'Thanks.'

Zoe walked off and then Paul turned to the two of them and said, 'Follow me.'

Chapter 29

Back in the small bedroom, Mike was sat on the wooden chair at the end of the bed where the old man was still laying.

Mike was holding a tobacco pipe in his hand, which he was attempting to clean.

Then the old man on the bed started to make stirring noises, turning Mike's attention to him.
He slowly started to wake up, but was disorientated, not really having much of an idea where he was.

Mike stood over him, holding his pipe on his lip.

'*John...*can you hear me?' said Mike, clicking his fingers.

John opened his eyes slowly as he turned to lean on one side so he could pull himself up to sit up in the bed.

'Mike?' said John, sounding confused.

Mike smiled and moved back to his seat, puffing on his empty pipe to make sure it was clean.

'Finally. Happy to see you awake.' he said.

John pulled himself up further, so he was leaning with his back against the headboard.

'What happened?' he asked.

'Took a nasty bump to the head apparently,' said Mike. 'You had a big gash on your head too. If Anna and Sam hadn't had brought you in when they did then we might have lost you.'

John touched his face, as he rubbed the sleep out of his eyes, and felt that his hair was missing when he moved his hand up to the top of his head. There was a big cut there with stitching in it now.

'Where are they now?' John asked.

Mike bent down pulling a round tin out of his bag and opened it, pulling out tobacco to put into his pipe.

'They're here, but Anna came and got Sam. Sounded like something urgent.'

'Have they found Abe?' John asked.

Mike shook his head. 'No, not yet', he said. 'But I better go get Sam. I said I'd call him when you woke up.'

'Thanks Mike,' said John. 'Wait...How long was I out?'

Mike paused as he got up out of his chair, and said, 'A few days.'

Damn it, thought John, before saying, 'I need to see Zoe and find out what's been going on.'

Mike walked over to the table next to the bed before he left and passed the water to John, followed by some medicine, telling him to take it.

'Don't go running anywhere, not yet,' he said. 'Wait until Sam gets down here, he'll be able to fill you in.'

Just outside in the hall, Paul was walking ahead of Abe and Abbie, showing them to their room.

'Here it is,' he said.

Abbie smiled at him and they both said thank you as they opened the door and went into their room.

Just as Paul was leaving, he looked back as he remembered something.

'If you need tokens for the shower, just go back down to the reception and ask,' he said and then leaving them to settle in.

Abe looked at the room as he walked up to the bed, seeing that it was quite nice. There was a little

335

shower room just beside the door that you came in through and then it opened up into a cosy square bedroom with a double bed in the middle of it. There was a very small sofa, just big enough for two people to sit on and watch the TV.

Abbie came in behind him after she closed the door and looked around admiring the room as well.

Abe was wondering what they were going to do about sleeping. There was just the one bed.

Should I offer to sleep on the sofa? he thought.

Abbie didn't seem to be bothered by it.

'I can sleep on the sofa if you want, and you can have the bed?' Abe offered.

But then Abbie stepped in close, 'It's fine, we can share the bed,' she said.

Abe gulped, unsure how to respond.

Abbie took a step back and said, 'I'll go get us some shower tokens, shall I?'

Abe was still a little frozen from feeling anxious, and nodded before he said, 'Yeah, that'd be great.'

Abbie walked out of the room and closed the door behind her, and as she did an old man was coming out of the room opposite her as well.

'Good morning, Miss,' he said as he slightly tipped his head.

'Morning,' she replied with a smile.

'My name is Mike, what's yours,' he asked.

'Abbie', she said happily as she shook his hand, thinking how friendly he seemed.

Abbie came back to the room only ten minutes after she had left. She brought back two shower tokens, one for the each of them. The man in reception told them that each token would give them three minutes each.

While she was gone, Abe had been pacing around the room thinking about what he could talk to Abbie about and wondering how long they were going to be there sharing a room together and what might happen.

It didn't take long for them both to shower and get changed again, because the showers were so short. Abe let Abbie go first though and when she was done, she came out of the shower, fresh and clean wearing just one of the towels around her body.

She gave him his token as she came out, walking passed him in her towel, still wet from the shower as she went to the bed to get dry and change, allowing Abe to shower himself. When he was done, he chose to change back into his clothes in the bathroom, feeling too nervous to do it in the room where Abbie was sitting.

Now that they were both showered and dressed, all they had to do was wait for Zoe to call them to go talk to her.

Abe was starting to feel impatient and was really curious what she had to tell him.

'I'm going to see if I can find Zoe,' he said to Abbie.

'Shall I come with you?' she asked.

Abe shook his head as he walked towards the door saying, 'No it's okay, I'll only be two minutes.'

Sam was in the elevator with Anna, going back down to see John after Mike had given him the news that he was awake.

'Are you going to tell him?' asked Anna. 'About your brother?'

Sam took a second as he looked at Anna and walked out of the elevator.

'I have to,' he said. 'But he's still going to want to find Abe.'

Then someone who was walking through the hall noticed Sam and stopped where they were going to talk to him.

'Hey Sam,' he said. 'I think Zoe is looking for you.'

Sam stopped and turned to the man, 'Did she say what it was for?' he asked.

The man shook his head and said, 'No, but she seemed to really need to see you, like it was something important.'

Sam looked down at the floor as he wondered if he should go see her first, but instead said, 'tell her if you see her, I'll be right up, I just need to see John first. He's only just woken up.'

'Okay,' the man replied.

Abe had left his and Abbie's room and was now walking down the hall, looking left and right, at the few people that were walking around. He thought it was odd that it was crowded.

Maybe if I look for that Paul guy, he can help me, he thought.

But then he saw the last person that he expected to see, and he froze staring at the man walking towards him.

Decan!

It took a while when he first caught a glance to realise it was him. He questioned himself for a second but then he saw that the woman that was with him was Anna and his face became hot and twisted in anger, his fists clenching.

Sam looked up as Anna stopped in her path grabbing him on the arm and pointing. She looked shocked, like she had seen a ghost.

'Abe?' said Sam, both confused and surprised to see him.

Abe looked to his left and then to his right for something to grab and use as a weapon, but all there was that was around him was a few plants, cream wallpaper and the red carpet on the floor.

He ran straight at Sam, not even trying to get to Anna.

Sam took a step back holding out his hands saying, 'No, stop. *Abe.'*

But Abe didn't listen and jumped towards him. Anna tried to intervene and stop Abe from getting to Sam and was able to grab him and hold him back.

Abe fought with her, and was trying desperately to pull out of her grip so he could get to Sam.

Sam stepped over to him and grabbed him by the arms, trying to calm him down.

'*Abe,'* he said. 'Abe...listen to me.'

Abe was still clouded by rage and wanted only to get back at him for killing his grandpa and lying to him.

'You killed my grandpa,' he spat.

Sam shook his head and said, 'No Abe, he's here.'

Abe stopped fighting. He looked at Sam, trying to take in his words.

'What?'

'Your grandpa is here, he's alive,' said Sam. 'We've been trying to help him find you.'

Abe looked between Anna and Sam with a confused frown.

'Where is he?' he asked.

Sam let go of him and stood back up straight alongside Anna.

'Come with me,' said Sam.

Abe watched them walk back the way he came, looking suspiciously at the them both the whole time.

This has to be some sort of trick, he thought.

He stayed where he was standing and let them walk down the hall towards his room, and then saw Sam walk up to the door opposite his and then knocked.

There was a short silence before Abe saw the door open and Sam look at someone.

John was stood in the doorway and said, '*Sam.*'

Abe saw his grandpa and his eyes widened in pure shock. He couldn't believe what he was seeing and immediately froze and as he did, Sam pointed in his direction.

John looked down the hall and saw Abe standing there, still and motionless. He stepped out into the hall looking as shocked as Abe felt.

'*Abe?*' John said, as Abe stepped forward and rushed towards his grandpa.

Chapter 30

Once Abe had caught Abbie up with everything and explained that his grandpa was still alive, he found that he had a million questions to ask.

What happened? Why is Decan going by a different name, and why is he helping my grandpa?

Not long after Abe saw his grandpa and he had spoken with Abbie, Zoe had caught up with them too.

She told Abe that she was sorry. She had hoped to avoid the conflict between him and Sam happening by telling him the whole story first and then taking him to his grandpa, but the plan had gone sideways.

Abe, Abbie, John, Anna and Sam, were now all in Zoe's office on the top floor.

The room was huge, and you had to enter a set of double doors to get into it. It was once the penthouse suite but now it was where Zoe ran the base from.
It had a huge round table in the middle of the room with a map spread across it and there were a few people that were dotted around the room

Abe only noticed one of them, it was Paul who he and Abbie had met earlier, and he was on the upper floor looking over the balcony into the sitting area, where Zoe took them to sit down so they could tell Abe everything. When they sat down, Zoe, John and Sam were talking to each other, trying to decide who was best to tell him, and it ended up being John.

'Abe,' he said, 'Sam is the one who saved me. He's Decan's brother, and Decan is the one who tried to have me killed by sending me away with one of his thugs. Decan lied to you when he said I had run away, so he could try and turn you against me, by pretending that *I* was lying to *you*. Sam didn't know that his brother was sending me away to be killed, and when he found out he came after me and killed Decan's man.'

'You see, Abe,' said Sam. 'I used to work in that building that we had been using as a base, and I had access to the maps and contingency plans in case anything like this ever happened.'

'When the outbreak started I and a few others set up camp there, and then went to get Decan. He was in prison at the time, but he's my brother and I couldn't just leave him to die. Only...when we went to get him, he insisted on bringing other inmates back too, and there were too many for me to stop.'

'When we got back to the base it got harder and harder to control him. That place wasn't equipped for us to stay in long term, and he became obsessed with getting into one of the bunkers. That's where you and your grandpa came in. He wanted to use you to get access to it. He knew that it was unlikely that known criminals would be allowed in but two vulnerable people...that would be a different story.'

'All that makes sense I guess,' said Abe. 'But where do you come into all of this? Why did you pretend to be Decan?'

Abe was finding it hard to take it all in and believe it. Part of him still thought it was one of Decan's tricks, but his grandpa was alive, and he was here vouching for the man that was sitting beside him; a man that looked so much like the one that Abe wanted revenge against for playing with him and lying to him. Sam took a second before answering, looking down at his hands as he tried to find the right words to make Abe understand.

'Well,' he said finally. 'When it became clear that John wouldn't co-operate with my brother's plan, Decan decided that he would need to turn you against him, to get you on side. To make it look like he was a liar I was supposed to meet with you at the same time as Decan was meeting with your grandpa. That way when John told you he had spoken to Decan, you would lose trust in him.

Anger started to boil up in Abe's chest. He had been a part of it the whole time, and it had nearly gotten his grandpa killed. Before he could say anything, though, John put a hand on Abe's shoulder.

'I know what you're thinking Abe,' he said. 'But just hear him out. I've had a lot of time to think about it and I really believe that by playing along, it was the only way that Sam could try and keep us both alive.'

Abe looked at his grandpa and then back at Sam, allowing him to continue.

'I'm really sorry for my part in it Abe, please believe me, but I thought that by going along with it that I could take care of you, and also make sure that things didn't get out of hand with your grandpa. If I had said no, I'm certain that Decan would have locked me up as well and then I wouldn't have been any use to anyone.'

'But it didn't work though, did it?' said Abe. 'He still tried to have my grandpa killed.'

He was looking at Sam in an accusing way. He was still finding it hard to look at him without feeling angry or seeing his brother.

'No, you're right,' replied Sam, meeting Abe's eyes. 'I realised then that my brother was completely beyond all reason. He would do anything to get what he wanted, even killing innocent people, and I just couldn't stand by and do nothing.'

'It's like I said Abe,' said John. 'Sam saved me, and he's been helping me ever since.'

Abe put his head in his hands. It was a lot to process, and it was all happening so fast. He realised there was still one important question unanswered.

'So, what *is* your brother's plan?' asked Abe.

Sam looked at the others and then leant forward.

'The same basic plan remains as he had before. He still wants to get into that bunker and take it for himself,' Sam explained. 'How he plans to get in there now I don't know. My brother hasn't ever really been one for rational thought.'

'However, I still have contact with someone there at the base and he has told me that he has some kind of plan and that he is moving every single one of his men out within the next week.'

Abe became worried at the thought of that. 'So what do we do?' he asked. 'Are you trying to stop him?'

Sam looked at Anna and then back at Abe. 'We were going to be, but first we were trying to help your grandpa find you, and then this morning me and Anna found out that he was planning on moving out soon, and then we bumped into you, and here we are,' said Sam.

Then Abe stopped and remembered something.

'Wait...I have another question,' he said, turning to Anna. 'If that's all true, then when me and George were trying to escape, why did you come after us?'

Anna took a few seconds to answer. 'I *was* trying to help you Abe, when I took you to that radio room, it was Sam you were talking to. We weren't meant to be there and that's why I stayed outside to guard and make sure that one of Decan's men or he himself didn't come along.'

Abe turned to Sam, 'so why didn't you just tell me this then?' Abe asked. 'If it *was* you I was talking to, then you could have just told me.'

'I wanted to,' he said. 'But I couldn't, my brother could have been listening, and I knew it was going to be hard for me to convince you of all this in person, let alone over the radio.'

'Sam was on his way back like he said, when he got back, he was going to get you and George out of there and take you to your grandpa,' said Anna.

Abe stopped again for a second as he looked at Anna, remembering that he shot her.

'Okay,' he said. 'Then I guess I'm sorry...for shooting at you.'

Anna smirked unexpectedly. 'If you didn't and you had just escaped then Decan would have killed me. He was already suspicious that I was helping Sam do things behind his back.'

Abe thought that what she said was kind of funny, thinking that it was odd that shooting someone could actually be helpful and that they would thank him for it.

'Where is George?' asked Anna, as Abe had been lost in thought.

Abe froze and turned to Abbie with just his eye, feeling like he had been caught out in a lie.

He never thought that he would be in a room with these people and be the one being questioned about lying.

'He's not that far away,' said Abe in a strange tone as he was thinking hard how to explain it.

Zoe leant forward slightly squinting her eyes, 'I thought you said that it was just you two?'

Until that moment, Abe hadn't realised that Abbie had leaned in closer, taking his hand and then whispered to him, 'Just tell them the truth.'

Abe took a breath. 'George is my friend,' he said looking at Zoe, and then glancing at the others.

'George is in a *small* bunker nearby that I was able to find using the maps I stole from Decan when I escaped.'

Zoe sat back in her seat, and Abe thought that she was going to be annoyed most of all people because he had actively lied to her and told her that it was just him and Abbie.

'I'm sorry I didn't tell you Zoe,' he said apologetically. 'I had to be sure I could trust you first. We have had problems trusting the wrong people in the past.'

Zoe looked at him and had her arms crossed.

'It's okay Abe,' she said. 'If anything, I should be apologising to you for not telling you about your grandpa sooner.'

Sam was sitting in the chair sat back as well with a smirk on his face, amused at the thought of how angry Decan would have been after Abe outsmarted him the way he did.

'Are there other people there as well?' Zoe asked him, intrigued.

'That's actually one of the reasons Abbie and I came here,' he said. 'There are a few of us, but really, we need more people to help keep the place running, like mechanics, doctors and electricians.'

Zoe's face filled up with excitement. 'We have all those,' she said. 'And people who can help defend the place.'

Sam butted in and said, 'That's all great, but it's going to be no good if we don't stop Decan. He doesn't just want the one he's heading for now, he wants all of them, and if he finds out we're at this one, then he'll come at us first and do whatever it takes to take it from us.'

Then it was if a light had snapped on in Abe's head as an idea sparked.

'Then let him,' he said.
Sam and the others turned with a confused look.

'What?' they said in confusion.

Abe sat forward to the edge of his seat, 'If we let him come to us, then we can drive him away from the other place, keeping whoever is in there safe, and giving us a better chance at beating him,' Abe explained.

Sam and Anna looked at each other and then Sam looked at the ground, thinking it through.

'No,' he said. 'If we just told him that we were here, he would know we were up to something and he may not come, at least not when we wanted him to.'

'But you're his brother,' said Abe. 'Surely he'll listen to you.'

Sam shook his head, 'No, like your grandpa said, he stopped listening to me a long time ago, I've not been able to control anything he does in a long time.'

'Abe is right though,' Zoe interjected. 'If we can get Decan out here, we might actually have a chance. All our people are here, and we probably know this area better than he does.'

'That's all well and good, but it's useless if we can't get him out here,' said Anna.

Abe was watching Anna as she spoke and then had another idea. 'Wait, you said that you still have someone in there you can trust right?' Abe asked, looking at both Sam and Anna.

They both nodded, looking at each other, and Sam said, 'Yeah.'

Abe started to get a little excited as the plan was forming in his head and he explained it to the others.

'Well, can't you somehow get him to get Decan out here,' said Abe.

Sam moved his hand to his chin as he frowned and thought about it, 'No I don't think he would go for it,' said Sam. 'He already said that my brother is suspicious'.

They all sat back in their seats, just as it seemed like they were getting somewhere.

'What if he tells him as if he is betraying you?' said Abe. 'Like when I shot Anna and he thought that she was still on his side.'

Sam and Anna looked at each other with much more lighter expressions.

'It could work,' said Anna.

'It worked with you,' said Sam.

Zoe was almost standing up now and John was on the edge of his seat too.

'Then how do we do this?' Zoe asked. 'We'll have to be careful how we pass the message on the radio, just in case Decan is listening.'

Sam shook his head. 'He won't be, not now, not when he is planning something like this. Not unless he already knows something.'

'How soon can you get in contact with him?' Abe asked.

Sam turned to him and said, 'I should be able to talk to him tonight.'

They all looked at each other waiting for agreement and then Abe said, 'I guess that settles it then. Once we do this, then we need to prepare to fight Decan.'

John turned to Zoe, 'Do we have enough guns?' he asked.

Zoe took a second before replying. 'Maybe, but not sure if there will be enough for everybody.'

Abe and Abbie looked at each other, knowingly.

'Together we do,' he said. 'Just get Decan and everyone else to the bunker, *we* can make sure there are enough guns.'

Chapter 31

Abe and Abbie went back to the bunker together, taking John and Bud with them. They had to tell the others what was going on and convince them of the plan.

Other than Abe the only person there who had really had a run in with Decan was George.

When Abe got to the bunker and explained to him, with his grandpa, what had happened, he was suspicious at first, and if anybody else had told him that story then he wouldn't have believed them so easily, but he trusted Abe with his life.

John hadn't met George yet, but when he did, he was pleased to meet him. The first glance was a bit of a shock for John because of his different looks, and Abe hadn't told him about it. Abe didn't really notice it anymore and had basically forgotten about it.

Abe gathered Frank, Shaun, and George into the guard's breakroom. He was there with Abbie, Bud and his grandpa.

Bud was sitting by Abe's side at first, but then it was only a few seconds until he snuck over to George and started playing with him, licking his face and then rolling onto his back so George could rub his tummy.

Now that Abe knew how many there were of Zoe's people, he actually thought that the guards break room might not be big enough for all of them.

The introductions between Frank, Shaun and John were short, although John was delighted to see the little set of friends that Abe had acquired along the way. He was even more happy and surprised to see the way he was now standing in front of them all telling them what was about to happen. John thought that somehow over the time they had been apart Abe looked much older and maybe even taller.

Frank and Shaun were just expecting them to come back and report what or who they found there in the building. They figured that they might come back and say they have a mechanic and maybe a nurse or a doctor, but they weren't in any way expecting them to come back and tell them that there were over a hundred people there and they would have all the guards, electricians and mechanics that they would need. They certainly weren't expecting to be told that they would have a doctor as well as all of those.

However, that wasn't the most shocking part - Abe went on to explain that they had to now go into a huge fight with Decan, and Zoe and her people along with Decan's brother Sam and Anna, were going to be coming to the bunker to fight them together.

'I'm sorry that I didn't consult you first, but it's something that needs to be done,' said Abe, worried that none of them would want to be getting into a fight that they didn't really have a stake in. 'If we don't stop him and draw him here, then he might get into the bunker where my grandma is and my friend Ash. Not to mention that it could be filled with hundreds or maybe even thousands of more innocent people.'

Frank and Shaun sat there quiet for a few seconds until George put his hand in and said, 'I'll do whatever you need.'

Frank turned and looked at Shaun and then at George with Bud on the floor. He remembered how alone he had been for a while before this had happened and afterwards, it had been even worse. He couldn't even go to the shop anymore and have a conversation with anyone behind the counter or go to the café and read a book and talk to someone there about it.

Now he saw the room with Abe, Abbie, Shaun, Bud and John, he liked that he kind of had a family and people to be around.

The last few days he had spent working in the garden with George had been some of the best in a while.

'I'm in,' he said. 'Anything to keep this place safe.'

Shaun didn't say much, and when they all looked to him waiting for an answer, he only nodded. Abe suddenly felt a wave of relief and felt like he could breathe again. He had thought that they might all say that they didn't want to be a part of it and leave him there.

'What happens now?' asked Shaun.

'Well, tonight Sam will be calling out to his guy on the inside and pass the message across. Hopefully Decan will take the bait and head straight out here,' said Abe.

'How can you be so sure he will?' Frank asked.

Abe chuckled slightly. 'Once he knows that me, George, Grandpa and his brother along with Anna are out here in a bunker, he won't be able to resist,' he said. 'He'll think that there are only a few of us and this place will be easy to take from us.'

It was a couple of hours later and Sam had already sent out the message. He, Anna, Zoe and her people were all running around, packing and grabbing everything that they needed. Mainly they were taking the essentials and the guns with them.

They decided to escort the more vulnerable people first and get them into the bunker, making sure they were all safe first, just in case Decan somehow got there quicker than they expected.

Once they had everybody ready in the cars and trucks in the parking lot beneath the hotel, they headed out slowly, keeping an eye out for unwanted visitors.

Sam was at the front of the convoy, along with Zoe, and then Anna was at the back in a car with Paul. There wasn't as much snow now, making it much easier to navigate and drive. But it also meant that the creatures that were once frozen by the ice like dead statues, were now thawing out.

Soon they would have an answer to if *they* could survive the ice or not. A lot of the people that followed Zoe had bets on it, but Zoe didn't want to be a part of it, fearing that they could be a ticking time-bomb just waiting for the sun to come out so that they could jump out on them.

Mike always tried to reassure her, telling her that it was just impossible that a human, no matter what infection they had, could never survive being frozen like that.

George was in the gardening area, tending to the plants while the others in the bunker were getting ready for everybody else to arrive.

Abe came in quietly, not alerting George to his arrival until he spoke.

'Hey George,' he said.

George was startled and jumped slightly, and then tried to hide the plants he was tending to behind his back. Abe was curious and knotted his eyebrows as he tried to look around him.

'What's that?' Abe asked.

George let out a sigh, he wanted to keep them a surprise, but it was too late and so he stepped out of the way.

'They're flowers,' he said. 'I've been growing them for you to give them to Abbie.'

Abe smiled, surprised at how thoughtful George was, and so he gave him a hug.

'Thank you,' he said.

He looked at the flowers properly, and thought how pretty they were, noticing the nice purple colour they had. He wondered when the best time would be to give them to her.

'I need to ask you a favour,' Abe said to George.

George looked at him, 'Sure, anything,' he said.

'When me, Abbie, and the others are out there fighting Decan, can you look after Bud for me?' he said.

George paused for a second wanting to say both yes and no. He would do almost any favour Abe asked him, but he also wanted to help and be part of the fight.

'Okay,' said George.

He smiled gratefully and thanked George again.

'What's happening now?' George asked Abe.

'Well, Sam has sent the message to the guy in Decan's base, and now he, Zoe and the rest of them are on the way here,' said Abe. 'All we have to do now is wait for him to arrive.'

'Do you think that he'll come right away?' George asked.

Abe nodded. 'Yeah, I think he will.'

Frank and John were in one of the trucks, waiting just down the road from the bunker ready to meet Zoe and the rest of them and guide them to the Bunkers gates.
They hadn't really had that much time to talk, but after a little while of silence John eventually broke the ice.

'Thank you for helping Abe and looking after him.'

'No problem at all,' Frank said turning to John. 'If it wasn't for him and George, I wouldn't be here.'

John smiled to hear Frank speak highly of Abe, and he realised that he didn't have to worry about being there for him all the time anymore to hide him under his wing from everything and everyone.

Just a few seconds later, there was a sand cloud in the distance as the convoy with Zoe, Sam and Anna came up the road. Frank switched on the engine to the truck and did a U-turn, ready to drive off and have them follow them to the bunker.

Shaun was sitting in the guard's office, ready and waiting for them all to arrive. All he wanted now was for them to get there, brief them on where everything was and get the fight over and done with, and then finally maybe he could relax.

Abbie was sitting in the commanders living room where Abe had taken Bud to wait while he went to see George.

Bud was more than happy where he was, chilling on the comfortable rug that laid in the middle of the room, while Abbie gave him all the attention that he wanted.

Abe came walking in through the metal door, saying hello as he came in.

'They're on their way,' he said.

'Did you talk to George?' Abbie asked.

Abe nodded as he walked over and leant down to greet Bud.

'Yeah,' he said. 'He agreed to what I asked him to do, although he seemed a little reluctant at first. I think he wanted to help us fight.'

Abbie carried on paying attention to Bud as she listened to him.

'Are you sure you don't want to stay in here too?' he asked her, wanting to keep her out of the way of danger.

Then she looked at him with a face that was obviously about to say *No*.

'Not if you're going,' she said.

Abe smiled and then he quickly realised that he was trying to do the same exact thing that his grandpa had been trying to do to him almost his entire life.

As he watched Abbie there with Bud sitting next to him, he felt that warm feeling in his chest come back. He was thinking just how much he cared about her now and wanted to tell her there and then, before anything bad could happen that would stop him.

All of a sudden, Shaun came in. 'They're here,' he said. 'They're coming in now.'

Abe and Abbie turned at the same time.

'Great,' said Abe, 'I'll be right down.'

Chapter 32

Later that night, Abe was in the Commander's office, with everyone else, Abbie, George, Frank, John, Shaun, Zoe, Sam and Anna.

It was time to make a plan of action for when Decan arrived. It was likely that he would be there soon. For almost an hour they had been all looking at a map of the area that was spread out on a wooden table.

They had thrown about a few ideas, but there was one major worry.

They weren't one hundred percent sure exactly how many people Decan would bring and what sort of weapons he had available. He could out man them, and if they came out of the bunker gates, ready to fight, they could get trapped in the tunnel and they would have no chance of winning.

Abbie however had an idea that was better than anyone had come up with so far.

'What if we can back them into the tunnel?' she said. 'If we wanted to, we could even close the main gates on the tunnel, sealing them in there a bunch at a time, leaving us with only a small amount of people to fight.'

Everyone looked at her as she suggested it and thought about it.

'But we would have to come out of the bunker into that tunnel, we'd be trapping ourselves in there with them?' asked Sam.

Abe looked back at Abbie after what Sam had said and noticed that she didn't seem disheartened at all by what he had said.

'There's a cargo lift that goes up to the top of one of the mountains,' she said.

Everyone, including Sam, became wide eyed with surprise.

'Where is the cargo lift?' Zoe asked, leaning forward. 'How do we get to it?' she realised instantly that the idea could work.

Abe turned to Zoe to answer this one. 'It's on the bottom level in the storeroom,' he said.

While the others stood around the table at the map, Abe was looking at Abbie with a smile, impressed and happy that she was the one to come up with the idea.

'There,' said Frank, pointing at a very small line on the map.

'What about the cargo lift?' Zoe asked. 'How big is it? We don't want to have to take loads of trips up in it.'

Abe took a second to think as he tried to picture it in his head.

'It shouldn't take any more than two trips, it's quite big,' he said.

For the next hour, they all looked at the map together, studying it and deciding exactly how many people they were going to send up there, how many they were going to keep behind as a reserve, and how they were going to get down the mountain to surprise Decan from behind.

Once they had all agreed on the plan, all they had to do now was wait for Decan to arrive.

While they waited, people didn't know what to do with themselves. It was quite late after they had finished planning, and people were thinking, *Do we just go to sleep?*

Soon enough, people went to their rooms to get some rest, while some people stayed up keeping guard, in case Decan arrived in the night.

Abe was struggling to sleep. He was too anxious to even try close his eyes and think about sleeping. He was terrified that everything he had now was going to be lost and taken from him. He was praying that there weren't going to be any problems with their plan, and most of all, he was wishing that Abbie would be safe and that she might not even have to fight.

While he was busy wondering and worrying about everyone and the plan, his eyes grew heavier and heavier, before he eventually slipped into a sleep.

Suddenly, there was a blast in the air of the bunker, screeching throughout every room, with lights flashing all around.

Abe was forced awake in an instant, as he heard the loud alarm blaring.

Frank came to the door of his room and knocked before he let himself in quickly.

'He came,' said Frank frantically.

For some reason Abe was shocked, and he froze for a second as the fear became more real. He knew that Decan would come, but now that he was there, he couldn't believe it.

It only took a few minutes for Abe and the rest of the people from the planning meeting earlier to rush to the commander's office.

Almost everybody looked as panicked as Abe felt. He was the last one to arrive, and the rest of them were standing around the same table, except for George who was sitting in the corner now with Bud, waiting for him to arrive.

'Can we see how many people he has?' Abe asked, as he looked at the time in the clock that was above the map on the wall, seeing that it was six in the morning.

Shaun was standing at the table, dressed in security uniform that he had gotten from the bunker.

'I was in the surveillance room when he arrived,' said Shaun. 'There's a lot of them and there's no easy way to tell, but there looks like there are well over a hundred of them.'

Everyone else was looking down at the table, with worried looks.

'So, he does outnumber us,' said Zoe.

'Yes,' said Abe. 'But he doesn't have our plan.' Then he turned to Shaun on his right and said, 'Do you know how we can get the surveillance on the commanders computer?'

Shaun walked round to the computer without hesitation, and it only took a few clicks before he had it up and ready.

Abe walked round and looked, seeing the wave of people that were waiting outside with what looked like trucks and lights all around them.

'And we can control the doors from here too and close them in the tunnel?' said Abe.

Shaun nodded and said, 'Yeah,' as he showed him how to work it.

'Great,' he said. 'Now we just need someone to control it from here while we're out there.'

He looked around the room at each of them, thinking that he could ask Abbie to do it, giving him the perfect excuse to get her to stay behind, but he knew she would argue and instead turned to his grandpa.

'Grandpa, can *you* do it?'

John paused for a second and was about to say no so he could be out there with him to make sure he could keep an eye on him and watch his back to make sure he didn't get hurt, but then as he was looking at him, he realised that he didn't need him to.

'Yes, no problem,' he said.

Abe turned back to the others and said, '*Great, now...*'

Just as he was about to say something else, they heard a distorted loud noise, and then Shaun looked to be in shock as he stared at the screen, watching the people outside.

'Guys...there's more,' said Shaun, as he called them over with his hand.

Abe and everyone else walked over to the computer, huddling around the screen and looking at it carefully to see what Shaun was talking about.

As they all looked at the screen, they saw that at the back of the flood of people that were outside with Decan, there were big trucks pulling up behind them, forming a kind of half circle and blocking the people in.

On the back of the trucks, it looked like there were shipment containers.

Meanwhile outside Decan's force of men was marching towards the tunnel of the bunker, ready to try and force their way in.

There was the sound of loud music roaring from behind them, along with the sound of engines. At the back of the crowd, there were trucks blocking them in between the mountains and the tunnel, with nowhere to go. A few men appeared on top of the trucks, and walked into the centre of the shipment containers, where there appeared to be what looked like makeshift doors.

There was a man crossing his tattooed covered arms as he stared down at the sea of people in front of him. Then, all the other men on top of the containers bent down and let the doors on the sides of them fly open, allowing heaps of bodies to fall out.

Back in the Commander's office, Abe and the others were staring as hard as they could at the screen, trying to make out what was going on.

'Is that?' said Abe.

Shaun had a look of pure hatred on his face. 'Yep, it's Janus.'

There were piles and piles of *them*, falling out of the containers that Janus had brought with him.
Once they had fallen out, each and every single one of them clambered to their feet and raced towards Decan's men.

Abe couldn't believe that he was there, it didn't make any sense.

'How did *he*, find out where we were?' he asked.

Then Sam hung his head slightly as he closed his eyes and let out a breath of frustration.

'He must have been listening when I sent the message about where we were,' said Sam.

Anna looked at Sam and the rest of them, 'He must have been trying to figure out where we were to get revenge after we took down his base.'

Abe then realised that he hadn't asked why Anna had been there in the first place. He wanted to question her, but there was a more important issue at hand.

'What do we do now?' said John.

Abe, though, wasn't worried in fact he even looked relived.

'This is a good thing,' he said, making everybody look at him strangely.

'What do you mean?' Shaun said.

Abe turned their attention back to the screen. Those *things* were still running at Decan and his men. There were bullets flying at them, knocking them down to the ground as they came running. It looked as if some of Decans men were even running and trying to get away, but they had nowhere to run with all the trucks in the way.

'They can't hold them back,' said Zoe. 'They're killing Decan's men.'

Abe grabbed the mouse for the computer, and quickly navigated to the controls for the door to the tunnel.

'Is the door closed?' he said to Shaun.

Shaun took a second, feeling panicked, and tried to remember.

'Yeah I think so,' he said.
'Open it,' said Abe.

Outside, Decan was at the front of the crowd closest to the bunker's big metal door, that closed them off from the tunnel.

He was yelling at the men he had with him to get him inside. Someone ran for one of the trucks to try and ram it open, while the others with him were firing at *them,* trying to keep them away from him, while another was grabbing an RPG from another truck nearby.

Then, as the one in the truck started towards the door and the other came running over with the RPG, the doors let out a loud clunk noise and began to open.

Decan looked up in shock and anger, wondering how it was opening, but too distracted to think that it might be a trap, and soon as there was a crack big enough for him to slip through, he did.

Just as a bunch of his men tried to come through the door, they began to close again and Decan looked up at the tunnel with an angry growl as he grabbed a machine gun from one of his men. He aimed it at the men trying to follow him in.

'Get out there and fight those things,' he yelled.

He also saw the man with the RPG freeze in front of him and he pushed him out of the door, just as the doors were closing.

'Blow up those trucks as soon as you get the chance,' he said.

Meanwhile back in the office, Abe and the others were watching on the computer as Decan retreated into the tunnel as Abbie planned, trapping himself in.

'What about the door?' George asked, looking worried.

Abe looked at him without a worry, 'It's locked completely, nobody can get in unless it is opened from here,' he said. He looked back at the screen and saw that almost three quarters of Decan's men had now been ripped apart by those things outside.

Then there was an eye stinging glow on the screen as something raced towards the trucks where Janus was. As soon as it met with the truck, there was a huge explosion, which rattled the walls of the bunker, sending strings of dust and dirt tumbling down from the ceiling.

Abe heard a whine come from Bud and George hugged his arms around him to comfort him in the corner.

They all looked at the screen and saw that there was a break in the line of trucks, but now there was a great big fire there instead, burning away.

'We should go now while we can,' said Abe. 'Come in from behind like we planned and finish them off.'

Everyone agreed as they grabbed what they needed and rushed off. John went to go with them, but Abe still needed him to control the gate.

'I need you to open it when we're ready and we have killed *them* and Decan's men,' said Abe. 'There are only a few of them with Decan now in the tunnel, we'll be able to get him no problem. Just open it when I give you the signal on the radio.'

John was short of words and just nodded as he saw Abe and the others leave through the door, rushing out together.

Now it was just him, Bud and George there, waiting together until it was all over.

Chapter 33

They drove down the mountain as fast as they could with almost all of the people they had that could fight. The fire that was burning in between the trucks was starting to die, and some of the surviving men had started to run, trying to dodge the infected that were left, were still tearing at people's flesh.

Abe and the rest of them came flying through the fire in their trucks, knocking over both the men that were trying to run away and the things that were chasing them.

The convoy stopped at the furthest point away from the tunnel and everybody jumped down, guns at the ready, and moved like a slow wave taking out each of *them* and the remainder or Decan's men.

It didn't take long for them to reach the top and get close to the tunnel's gate. There were now around twenty of Decan's men, laying down their weapons and attempting to surrender.

Abe was with Zoe at the front, and Zoe was yelling at the men by the tunnel to get on their knees. They closed in on them like the pincer of a crab, covering them from all sides so they couldn't escape. As they got close, one of the men dived for his gun and aimed from the ground up at them and fired, causing Abe and the rest to open fire on all of them, knocking them to the ground in seconds.

It wasn't clear right away if Zoe, Sam or anyone else had been shot, but then they heard someone call out to Abe, to *come quick.*

Abe turned to the sound and rushed over, to see Frank lying in Shaun's arms with blood coming from somewhere around his torso. His shirt was covered in so much blood that it was hard to tell just from looking where he had been shot.

Frank looked pale as he clutched his side and let out a groan in pain.

Abe jumped down beside him onto his knees.

'*Frank,*' Abe exclaimed. He looked over to Zoe calling her over.

Zoe rushed and saw Frank lying there and immediately called her people over telling them to run for one of the trucks and rush him back up the mountain and get him inside to Mike.

'You're going to be okay Frank, just hang on. Zoe's going to take you inside and get you patched up.'

Abe moved close as his eyes filled with tears and pleaded for him to try and hold on while they took him inside. Frank looked tired now and he was taking deep, and slow breaths.

'Just a few more minutes,' said Abe as the truck was hurtling towards them.

Frank grunted and cleared his throat and said, 'Make sure you go to my room and look on the shelf next to my bed. There's another book there for George...give it to him for me, will you?'

Before Abe could answer his eyes closed, just as the truck stopped beside them and the people rushed over to pick him up and take him away.

Abe's face was now flowing with tears, but it wasn't over yet. Everyone was standing around him, and he stood up wiping the tears from his eyes with his sleeve.

Abe looked at the metal gate on the tunnel, still closed waiting to be opened so they could finish the plan. He took the radio from his side and called up to his grandpa as everyone stood ready, aiming their guns.

'Open it,' said Abe, calling up to his grandpa.

Then the same clunk as before let out as the doors opened, followed by the sound of bullets.

Abe and the others hid from them, using the opening doors as a shield, and slowly they moved their guns around the corners of the doors and opened fire.

It was only a few seconds until there were no more bullets coming from inside of the tunnel.

They all went rushing in, still aiming their guns, looking around for Decan and his men.

'Where is he?' said Abe, as he saw that Sam too was looking for him.

All of Decan's men were now lying dead on the floor, with their guns scattered all around. There was an arrogant and evil laugh that echoed from the back of the tunnel

'Come out,' yelled Sam, just as they saw him walk through the middle of the tunnel from behind a truck. Abe turned as he heard the footsteps and saw him walking out. He pulled his gun back up, aiming straight at him and softly placing his finger on the trigger.

Decan was smirking and stared Abe in the eyes and said, 'Do it.'

Abe could feel the camera in the tunnel watching him and he glanced up quickly, knowing that George and grandpa were looking at the screen as this happened. He could hear George in his head, telling him not to do it, and knew that his grandpa would be saying the same thing. He continued to stare at Decan with anger and hate, and then lowered his gun.

Decan laughed as he looked at Abe and the rest of them. Anna and some of Zoe's people walked over, keeping their aim on him as they grabbed him by his arms to stop him from being able to move or make a run for it.

Zoe lowered her gun now too and watched as they dragged him towards her and Abe.

'What shall we do with him?' Anna asked, looking at Sam, Abe and the others.

Abe looked at Sam, expecting him to say something, but he was waiting for Abe.

He looked back at Decan's, arrogant face and said, 'Take him inside and lock him in one of the cells.'

Chapter 34

Sometime later, Abe found himself lying in his bed, in a deep sleep. He awoke slowly unsure of how long he had been sleeping. He sat up, seeing someone sitting in the middle of his room. His thought was that he didn't recall there being a chair there before.

Then the person came forward into the light.

Frank was sitting in a wheelchair, with a smirk on his face as he looked at Abe.

'Frank?' said Abe, surprised but also incredibly happy to see him.

Frank rolled to the side of his bed 'Afternoon Abe,' he said.

Abe frowned and said, 'Afternoon?'

Frank let out a chuckle. 'Yes, it's 2pm,' he said, 'After the fight was over, you were so exhausted that when you tried to give Abbie a hug you nearly collapsed, so she helped you inside and put you to bed.'

'She, George and everyone else were worried at first, but Mike checked you out and said that you just needed rest. Abbie almost had to drag George from your side to leave you to sleep.'

Abe pushed himself so he was leaning against the wall. 'Where is he? he asked. 'Is everyone else okay?'

Frank nodded. 'Yeah, they're all fine,' he said. 'Zoe has been taking care of things while you rested and told everyone where they're needed and assigned them jobs.'

Abe had a still look on his face as he heard that Zoe had started to run things, 'I guess she's in charge now then,' he said.

Then Frank shook his head. 'No not at all, she made it very clear she would only take charge if you wanted her to. She just wanted to make sure everything was in place as soon as you woke up.'

Abe was looking at Frank and noticed that there were the flowers that George had been growing sitting on the shelf behind Frank.

'Did George bring those?' he asked, pointing at them with his head.

Frank turned in his chair to look at them and flinched as his wound hurt him.

'Yeah,' he said, holding his hand on his middle. 'He brought them here ready for when you wake up to give to Abbie, so you can ask her to the party.'

Abe was concerned that Frank looked to be in pain, and also confused when he mentioned the party.

'Are you okay?' he asked. 'And what party?'

Frank nodded and then moved his hand back to his lap. 'Yeah I'm okay, just a little sore', he said. 'While you were resting, a bunch of the others thought it would be a good idea if we had a party, to celebrate everything that we've achieved.'

Abe smiled as he thought of an idea and glanced at the flowers.

'We could have a dance,' he said. 'There's a record player in the commanders living space, I bet I could hook it up to the PA system and play some music in the rec room.'

Frank smiled at the idea. 'That's a great idea,' he said. 'I bet Zoe even has some records that she brought from the hotel.'

Then he leaned in a little closer. 'She even said that they got all the movies from the video store nearby,' said Frank.

Abe's smile widened. He had planned on going there himself to get a few for him to watch with Abbie, but now he didn't have to.

Once Abe was dressed, he headed from his room over to see Abbie, to ask her to be his date to the party. Her room was only a short distance away from his, and he had already started to feel hot and flustered from the nerves. He knocked on her door and as she opened it and saw it was him, she smiled and jumped forward to give him a hug.

'How are you feeling?' she asked, standing close in front of him.

He smiled looking at her and said, 'A lot better now thanks.'

'Have you seen anyone else?' she asked.

Abe nodded, 'only Frank,' he said.

Abbie brushed his arm and said, 'You should go see the others, they'll want to know you're awake now, especially George and your grandpa.'

'I will,' said Abe. 'I was just about to go see them, but I wanted to ask you something first.'

His stomach knotted with nerves as he tried to work up the courage to ask. Abbie stood there waiting patiently for him to speak.

'Do you want to go to the party with me?' He asked with a slight stammer. 'As my date.'

Abbie smiled and only took a second to answer, 'Of course,' she said happily. 'I'd love to.'

Abe felt a burst of relief and he let out a breath he didn't realise he'd been holding.

'Great', he said smiling widely, showing his teeth. 'I'll go say hi to George and the others then.'

Abbie smiled as she stood in the doorway and Abe started to back away.

'Okay, great,' she said. 'See you later.'

'See you later,' said Abe as he walked away with an excited skip in his step.

George and John were in the Commander's office, talking with Zoe. They had been discussing some sort of plan.

'Are you sure it's a good idea to go so soon?' Zoe asked John.

John nodded. 'I think now will be a time as good as any, now that we have Decan locked up and that other guy is dead,' he said.

Zoe was standing next to him with her hands crossed, while George was playing with Bud on the floor.

'At least wait a few days, or even a week,' she said.

'Don't worry,' he said. 'I won't be going anywhere until I have talked to Abe anyway.'

George looked up and asked, 'do you think he'll want to go with you?'

Then just as John was about to answer, Abe walked in.

'Who?' Abe asked. 'And go where?'

John stood up from the seat and walked towards Abe, with a happy surprised look.

'*Abe,*' he said. 'You're awake.'

George and Zoe followed John over, taking it in turns to greet him and give him a hug.

George held his hug for the longest and looked at him asking, 'Are you okay?'

Abe nodded and said, 'I'm fine.'

Then Abe looked back to his grandpa, wondering what he was talking about, worried that he was planning on going somewhere.

'Where are you going?'

Zoe looked at John and started to walk out slowly. 'I'll leave you guys to it,' she said.

Now it was just Abe, George, John and Bud who was jumping on Abe as he said hello too.

'We were talking about making a move soon to go to the other bunker in search of your grandma,' he said.

Abe had a slight frown and looked a little disappointed. He wasn't ready to leave yet. He was finally starting to feel happy and settled.

'How soon?'

John had an awkward smile as he looked at Abe. 'It's up to you,' he said, 'Sam and Anna are going to come with us to help. Zoe said she would come too, but someone needs to stay behind and look after this place. She has family there too, so she said really she wants to go.'

George looked to Abe and said, 'Can't you stay while they go and run it?'

Abe looked back at George with a half-smile, as he tried to think over his options. On the one hand, he wanted to stay in the bunker, but he wanted to find his grandma as well. He certainly didn't want his grandpa going anywhere without him.

'Can I have a few days to think about it?' He asked.

John nodded, 'of course,' he said. 'The party is tomorrow anyway, we can talk about it after that.'

George stepped forward in excitement as he remembered the party. 'Did you speak to Abbie?' he asked Abe.

Abe's smile returned and he nodded. 'Yeah', he said, 'she said she wanted to go with me.'

Both his grandpa and George smiled and said how happy they were for him.

Abe told them that he was planning on using the record player to play music so they could have a dance.

John thought it was a great idea and said that he would happily sit in the office changing the records as the night went on.

On the night of the party, Abe was in his room getting dressed ready to go pick up Abbie. She said to be there by six, just in time to arrive at the party in the recreation room upstairs.

Luckily, he was able to get some slightly smarter clothes from someone who came from the hotel. They had brought all kinds of things with them that they had added to the store of the bunker. Day by day, the place was becoming more and more like a home.

He checked himself in the mirror, admiring his clothes and tie, ready to go pick her up and trying to tell himself not to be nervous while repeatedly having to dry his sweaty palms.

He walked from his room over to Abbie's door, holding his hand in the air as he took a breath before knocking.

Abbie was in her room, and it was only a few minutes to six. She had just slipped into a dress from the box of clothes that Frank had gifted to her.
It had lots of flowers on it and went down to just below her knees. She could already hear that the music had started as it echoed down through the levels.

There was a firm knock at the door, and she checked herself in the little mirror on the wall one more time before she went to answer it. She opened the door and saw Abe standing there dressed in some smart clothes she hadn't seen him wear before.

'Hi,' she said, with a happy smile.

Abe looked at her as she stood in the door smiling and was admiring her dress. It was incredibly pretty and thought it made her look beautiful.
He told her how amazing she looked and then handed her the flowers that George had grown.

Somehow, her smile widened as she took the flowers from him. She sniffed them before she put them safely in her room, and then they headed off to the party, holding each other's hand.

Shaun was in the guard's office checking on the people that were now the guards sitting in there, and then walked to the surveillance room, checking that everything was okay, and that people were doing their jobs.

He really liked his new job; it gave him a sense of purpose and like he was finally doing something worthwhile and that he was protecting people.

George and Frank were in the gardening area together with Bud sitting by their feet.

'I have a gift for you,' said Frank.

George was in the back, and he was holding a box that he brought from somewhere where he had kept it hidden.

'What is it?' he asked.

Frank picked up a small book that was sat between his right leg and his chair and passed it to George.

George took it and opened the dark brown cover, seeing that it was another book about birds. He smiled and gave Frank a hug to say thank you.

'What's in the box?' Frank asked.

He brought it over and placed it on Frank's lap. 'I found it a little while ago and I've been keeping it a secret,' he said as he opened the box.

Inside was a small bird, tweeting and jumping as he saw George and then Frank.

'I found it outside and it was injured, so I saved it and brought it inside,' said George.

George took some food from the table and passed some to Frank so they could feed him. Bud was now standing next to them, looking at the little bird and wagging his tail.

George petted Bud on the head and said, 'Look Bud, this is Jeremy, you two can be friends.'

Abe and Abbie walked into the recreation room, to see that everyone was having a good time. They could even see Sam and Anna dancing in the corner of the room.

Abe was nervous as he had never really danced before, especially with a girl, but as he and Abbie walked into the middle of the room and started dancing to a slow song, and the low light of the room brushed their faces. He saw her smile and he felt her hold him close to her, it made him more confident and happier than he had ever been.

Epilogue

After the party, it was decided that Abe would stay behind at the bunker and run it while Zoe, John, Sam, and Anna went to the other bunker in search for their families.

Abe missed his grandma deeply, and Zoe said she would stay behind and look after things while he went with his grandpa to find his grandma and Ash, but then Abe pointed out that there wouldn't be anyone to meet her family when they eventually got there. Zoe was grateful and knew that everyone and the bunker itself would be in good hands while they were gone.

Her kind words gave Abe a great deal of confidence. Abe also knew that he wouldn't be doing it alone, and that he had some of the best people possible to help him.

Frank, Abbie, Shaun and George would be there with him by his side. All he had to do now was live up to the expectation and make sure that everything ran smoothly while they were gone.

Abe was in the surveillance room on the entrance level, standing there with Shaun watching his grandpa and the rest of them leave on the screens.

'You'll be happy to hear that we found Janus' body when we were clearing up outside,' said Shaun.

Abe waited a second before he responded as he saw the trucks disappear off the screen and out of view.

'Good,' he said, turning to Shaun. 'I bet you were happy more than anyone, you were really the only one here who knew him.'

Shaun smiled slightly and said, 'Yeah, it's just a shame that Ethan didn't get to see it. Janus is the reason he's dead.'

Abe thought for a second that in a way, if it wasn't for Janus, then they may not have won the fight, or if they did then not all of them might have survived. He decided to keep that thought to himself.

When Abe got back to the commander's office and walked into the empty room, he saw that there was an object on the table.

When he got closer, he noticed that it was a present that someone had wrapped and put it on his desk. He picked up the rectangle thing wrapped in colourful paper and looked at the note stuck to it with a small bit of tape.

Dear Abe, I brought this with me, thinking I could give it to you to show that I'm not my brother and that I care about you. I hope that we can put all this behind us and one day be good friends. I'm sorry I couldn't bring more, it's all that I could fit in my pocket.

Regards, Sam.

Abe smiled at the note wondering why he didn't give it to him before he left, and carefully pulled the wrapping paper off.

It was his Gameboy, that he had given to George. He remembered how upset George was when he had to leave it behind when they escaped together. George even apologised to him, feeling bad after he had given it to him.

He walked down to the gardening level where George was as always, tending to the plants with Frank on the other side of the room.

'Hi Abe,' said George, happy to see him.

Abe walked over with Bud following by his side. 'Hey George,' he said.

George said hello to Bud as well and kneeled to give him a fuss.

'I got something for you,' said Abe.

He held out the Gameboy and handed it to him and seeing George's face light up with surprise and a happy smile.

'How did you get it?' he asked Abe.

Abe shook his head softly and said, 'I didn't, Sam did. He brought it with him, it was the only thing that he could bring, but it belongs to you.'

George held it in his hand and tried turning it on, surprised that the batteries still had a little bit of life left in them.

'It's yours,' said George. 'He brought it for you, you should keep it.'

Abe refused, 'No, you keep it. It was a birthday present.'

George smiled and said thank you.

'You wanna go for a walk?' asked Abe, 'I was about to take Bud for his run around outside.'

'Sure,' said George.

Then, Abe and George headed outside together and took Bud for a nice long walk.

ABOUT THE AUTHOR

Growing up in rural Wales, C.E. Williams spent much of his childhood using his wild imagination to make up stories. Nowadays, he lives with his wife and their dog in England, and he can often be found drinking tea and scribbling ideas for novels and characters...making his list of future writing projects longer and longer.

The Remnants is his first novel.

To get in touch with the author and stay up to date with new releases, go to his website at www.cewilliamsbooks.com

Printed in Great Britain
by Amazon

18949316R00222